Secret of Were

By the same author

The Devil's Protection

Secret of Were

Susan Clitheroe

ROBERT HALE · LONDON

First published in Great Britain 1998

ISBN 0 7090 6159 5

Robert Hale Limited
Clerkenwell House
Clerkenwell Green
London EC1R 0HT

2 4 6 8 10 9 7 5 3 1

Photoset in North Wales by
Derek Doyle & Associates, Mold, Flintshire.
Printed in Great Britain by
St Edmundsbury Press, Bury St Edmunds, Suffolk.
Bound by
WBC Book Manufacturers Limited, Bridgend.

One

Miss Sylvestra Harvey paced back and forth across her uncle's study with the restless energy of a caged tigress. William Harvey watched his niece's impatient movements with mingled apprehension and resentment. Really, he would have to have a word with that new butler. Damn it, a man's study was his sanctuary! The one place he could relax with a glass of port and the sporting journals, perhaps even blow a cloud, without being plagued by the females of the house.

Mr Harvey was not particularly noted for his powers of perception, but it was apparent even to him that Sylvestra was in the grip of some violent emotion. With a sinking heart he took in the tightly clenched fists, the mulish cast of her exquisite profile, the stormy lights in those slanting green eyes. For all his genuine fondness for his niece, William Harvey could not help wishing on occasions such as this that she was cast more in the mould of his daughter Emily. Emily was a timid mouse of a girl who would never dream of challenging the authority of her parents. A vain wish. It would hardly have been accurate to describe Sylvestra as timid. She held her tall, slender figure with unconscious poise, and there was nothing mouse-like about the flaming copper curls that framed her porcelain features. William Harvey sighed inwardly, poured himself a generous measure of brandy and waited for his niece to master her emotion.

The pacing stopped abruptly and Sylvestra swung round to face her uncle, exclaiming as she did, 'But there is not the slightest need for me to go to London, Uncle William. I am going to marry Perry.'

This was pronounced with an air of irrefutable logic, and indeed, to William Harvey it did make very good sense. His indolent nature was ideally suited to a bucolic existence and even in his youth he had never craved the heady delights of the Metropolis. To him, there seemed little point in going to the trouble and expense of rigging out a girl in the highest kick of fashion, and on top of that wearing oneself to a thread dragging her to endless parties, when there was a perfectly unexceptional young man quite willing to get himself legshackled.

But Mr Harvey knew full well that his wife did not share this privately held opinion, and so the best he could manage in reply was, 'No reason why you shouldn't. Marry young Maynard, that is. Thing is, no reason not to go to London. What I mean is, can do both.'

This feeble response was rewarded with a look of burning reproach. 'How can you say that, Uncle? You know what Aunt Julia is.'

William Harvey certainly knew. He had been securely tied by bonds of matrimony to Julia Harvey for more years than he cared to number. In fact, he was confident that no one *knew* quite as well as he. But if those years had taught him anything it was that on occasion it is best to know nothing whatsoever. And so he duly replied with well-feigned ignorance, 'Your Aunt Julia only wants you to have a season in London, nothing wrong with that, get some town bronze. Thought that was all you gals thought about, you know, Almack's and whatnot.'

This sounded weak even to his own ears. No one who had spent more than five minutes in Sylvestra Harvey's company could possibly have bracketed her with her frivolous and pleasure-seeking peers. The sole offspring of indulgent parents, Sylvestra had spent more of her formative years in the stables than in the schoolroom. In her home county, she had the reputation of a first-class horsewoman, but that cut little ice with her aunt, who found it inconceivable that the daughter of Sir James and Lady Anne Harvey (herself the daughter of an earl, no less) could be so woefully lacking in feminine accomplishments. Her etiquette on the hunting field was irreproachable; the drawing-room was another matter entirely.

That aside, the death of Sylvestra's mother when she was only fourteen had left her effectively the mistress of her father's mansion house and estate, Earlam Park. When, two years later, Sir James had fallen prey to a wasting disease, it was Sylvestra who had nursed him, as well as taking on the running of the estate. A year later, her father had passed away. The estate was entailed to his nephew Geoffrey Harvey and Sylvestra was consigned to the guardianship of his only surviving brother. Her own mistress for so many years, it was hardly surprising that Sylvestra had not slipped easily into the role of schoolroom miss.

Her uncle's inappropriate remark, not unexpectedly then, provoked only a gurgle of laughter. William Harvey attempted to compose his plump features into a disapproving frown. The effect he achieved put Sylvestra forcibly in mind of a disgruntled bloodhound and, try as she might, she could not contain her amusement.

'Oh, Uncle, do not talk such fustian! You know how little I care for such so-called pleasures. Come, sir! It is you who are my guardian when all is said. You have only to tell Aunt Julia that you do not wish me to go to London and that will be an end to it.'

'I have only to . . .' repeated her uncle faintly, literally dumbstruck at the thought of this unlikely scenario. And she accused him of talking fustian!

Perceiving she had knocked her opponent off balance, Sylvestra pressed her point home hard. 'I can see perhaps that Aunt Julia might not quite like it, but, after all, she will have quite enough on her hands launching Emily without having to worry about me.' And as her uncle seemed to have momentarily lost his powers of speech, she added with more optimism than accuracy, 'I am sure you can bring her round.'

In the entire course of his married life, William Harvey had never once succeeded in bringing Mrs Harvey round. In fact, he could not even remember ever having attempted anything so foolhardy. Clearly this conversation was getting out of hand. It was time he put a stop to it before it journeyed any further into the realms of the fantastic.

'Now, Sylvestra, my dear, everything has already been set in motion for this trip. I would not dream of disrupting your aunt's plans.'

'But, Uncle—'

'Enough. That is all I have to say on the subject.'

Sylvestra was forced to admit defeat. It did not in the least surprise her that her Uncle William should side with his wife. Set against the indomitable will of Julia Harvey, the most convincing argument lost all its force. Sylvestra was not so easily cowed as her uncle and Cousin Emily, but even she was inclined to think there was more chance of stopping the mail coach with a feather than swaying Aunt Julia from her chosen course.

'Very well, Uncle,' sighed Sylvestra resignedly, lowering her eyes to hide the irrepressible mischief lurking in their emerald depths.

William Harvey felt a twinge of guilt when he saw his niece's woebegone face. He made it a policy never to involve himself in his wife's schemes if he could at all help it, but one thing he knew for sure was that Mrs Harvey's plans for Sylvestra did not include marriage to Captain Peregrine Maynard. But it was the briefest of pangs for he very quickly remembered the two blissful months of peace he would enjoy when his wife and her charges left for the capital.

So he ushered Sylvestra to the door, saying with false heartiness, 'Well, now, who is to say that you won't enjoy it? Ten to one you won't want to come home.'

This was so ridiculous that Sylvestra could maintain her

pretence of acquiescence no longer. She darted an impish look over her shoulder at her beleaguered guardian.

'On the contrary, Uncle, I think you will find I am back before you know it, and with my aunt's blessing!' A remark which left Mr Harvey doubly thankful that he would be separated by a day and a half's ride from his warring womenfolk.

Sylvestra, meanwhile, made her way purposefully to the little parlour she shared with her cousin, scampering up the stairs with an unladylike haste that would certainly have earned her a sharp reproof from her aunt.

This room was Sylvestra's favourite in the house. It was set aside exclusively for the use of the young ladies and was rarely entered by anyone else. For that reason Mrs Harvey did not deem it worthy of her attention. Despite being the youngest of three sons, William Harvey enjoyed a comfortable income that had enabled him to buy a substantial property in the small Berkshire village of Brimpton Mewsey and his wife to indulge in her passion for interior design.

Mrs Harvey prided herself on being à la mode and, as she ranked herself amongst the principal ladies of the district, she considered it her peculiar duty to introduce London fashions to her provincial neighbours. Since Mrs Harvey's enthusiasm was tempered by neither moderation nor good taste, every extreme and abomination of every transient fad was guaranteed a home within the walls of Mewsey Grange, and the citizens of Brimpton Mewsey were left with a very odd impression of the ways of city folk.

The private parlour which the young cousins shared was pleasantly cluttered with furniture that had over the years been usurped by more modish rivals. When Sylvestra entered, Emily was comfortably ensconced in a faded red damask armchair before a cheery fire, very properly engaged with her embroidery. This was immediately set aside upon Sylvestra's appearance.

'Well?' Emily asked breathlessly, her soft brown eyes anxiously scanning her cousin's face.

Sylvestra cast herself down with a gloomy sigh on to a footstool before the fire. 'Much as you would expect. Uncle William cannot be persuaded to intervene. It looks as though I have no option but to accompany you to London.'

'Oh, I am sorry. I know how much you hate the idea, but perhaps it may not be so bad as you think.' She paused, blushing faintly. 'I must own I am a little relieved. The thought of meeting all those strange people without you to bear me company quite sinks my spirits. Do you think me dreadfully selfish?'

Sylvestra was immediately contrite. 'Good Lord, Em, why did you not say so? It is I who have been selfish. I don't suppose you are looking forward to this confounded expedition any more than I. Of course I will come. After all, we are not in the Dark Ages, Aunt Julia cannot force me into an arranged marriage.'

'Do you think that is really Mother's intention?' asked Emily apprehensively.

'I can think of no other reason why she should be so insistent that I go,' reasoned Sylvestra. Adding with rueful irony, 'If she has told me once then she has told me a thousand times I am not fit for polite company. Why would she risk the mortification of my hoydenish ways had she no ulterior motive?'

'Oh, Sylvie, I am sure Mother does not think you would disgrace her! Why, I know you will take far better than I. You are far prettier, and you are not afflicted with my stupid shyness.'

Sylvestra laughed aside this praise. 'You are very sweet to try to save my feelings, but I hope you are wrong! I fully intend to live up to my aunt's poor opinion of me. Believe me, before too long Aunt Julia will be positively delighted to see me married to Perry and off her hands.'

At the mention of Perry, Emily jumped to her feet scattering her embroidery silks to the floor. 'Why, I nearly forgot! A letter came for you.' She hunted feverishly through her work bag before triumphantly drawing forth a single sheet of sealed paper. She handed it to her cousin, saying blushingly, 'Was it very wicked of me? I knew how angry Mother would be if she thought you were receiving correspondence from Captain Maynard, so I concealed it from her.'

Sylvestra accepted the missive, exclaiming with mock horror, 'Why, Emily Harvey, I never knew you were such a schemer!'

Emily immediately looked dismayed. 'Oh, pray do not say such things! You know how much I hate deception.'

Sylvestra caught her hand saying laughingly, 'Pea-goose! You have done nothing but save me from a tremendous scold. Besides, what Aunt Julia could find in one of Perry's dreadful scrawls to offend her sense of propriety I cannot imagine.'

Emily looked a little askance at this derogatory reference to the precious love letter, for beneath her placid exterior beat the heart of a true romantic. To Emily, an avid reader of the novels of the Minerva Press, her beautiful cousin was the epitome of the romantic heroine. Not only had she been orphaned and cast from the home of her birth, now, through the ravages of war and the disapprobation of her legal guardians, she was forced to endure painful separation from her childhood sweetheart. It wanted only a wicked rake bent on seduction to complete the picture. Regrettably for Emily's unalloyed enjoyment of this real-life romance, Sylvestra had a deplorable tendency to disobey the conventions which generally dictate the behaviour of the lovelorn maiden desperate for news of her absent lover. In her cousin's situation, Emily felt sure she would have quite pined away. Sylvestra could not even boast an interesting pallor.

Emily's expression of mild reproach was not lost on Sylvestra, who correctly divined its cause, and said mournfully, 'I can see you think me a heartless jade. Alas for the poor captain, I am not blessed with your tender sensibility.'

Emily might not share her cousin's sharpness of wit, but she was well aware when Sylvestra was roasting her and she said with some asperity, 'You know I think no such thing! But I must own that if it were *my* betrothed all those miles away fighting that monster

Napoleon, I would not be able to bear it with your equanimity. And when I received a letter from him—'

'You would shed so many tears upon it, the thing would become illegible before you could compose yourself well enough to read it,' interposed Sylvestra naughtily.

'Sylvestra Harvey, you are a wicked tease! Now open that letter or I swear I will open it myself!'

Sylvestra looked in amused surprise at this unwonted vehemence, but did as she was told and broke the seal of the letter. She spread out the sheet on her lap and read quickly through the brief contents, occasionally chuckling at some comment or other.

'You will be relieved to know, Em, that Captain Maynard is enjoying excellent health. He tells me he has found very snug lodgings with a Spanish family and that not only is the lady of the house a first-rate cook, she is possessed of two very beautiful daughters inclined to view an English captain in the light of a demi-god!'

'Oh Sylvie!' exclaimed Emily, shocked to the core of her romantic soul. 'Surely he does not describe them as beautiful?'

'No, you are right, those are not his exact words. Let me find the passage. . . .' Sylvestra scanned the sheet, the twinkle in her eyes belying her serious tone. 'Here we are. . . . "Two of the most exquisite pieces of Nature I have ever clapped eyes on!" On second thoughts, perhaps it is as well Aunt Julia has not seen this.'

'Oh my poor Sylvie!' Emily's brown eyes filled with tears of sympathy, but Sylvestra was apparently far from mortified by this evidence of her beloved's roving eye.

'Poor Sylvie? You had better say poor Perry! You may be sure the lady of the house will give him short shrift if he attempts to start a flirtation with one of her daughters. I believe Spanish girls are allowed far less licence than we are.'

'Sylvestra! You cannot think Captain Maynard would *flirt* with one of these girls.'

Perceiving that Emily was genuinely upset, Sylvestra hastily changed the subject. 'Of course not. Only listen to this! Perry says his father has written that our Cousin Geoffrey is setting the whole neighbourhood by the ears! Apparently he is set on turning Earlam into a replica of an Indian palace. To quote Sir Ralph Maynard, "It is more like the harem of some heathen potentate than a gentleman's residence". Good Lord, I wish I might see it!'

'You must dearly miss Earlam, Sylvie,' said Emily sympathetically. 'It must have come as a dreadful shock being forced to relinquish it to a cousin you had never even met.'

'Well, yes, I do miss it, but it would be wrong to say it came as a shock,' said Sylvestra fairly. 'Very soon after Mama died, my father explained about the entail so I had plenty of time to accustom myself to the idea. Indeed, that was what gave me the idea to marry Perry. Sir Ralph's estate marches with Earlam Park, you see, so I will be able to settle close to my old home.'

'That was what gave you the idea to marry Captain Maynard?' Emily could hardly believe the evidence of her own ears.

Sylvestra grinned ruefully. 'Now I have let the cat out of the bag. It was I who suggested marriage to Perry, not that he didn't think it a capital idea, but I suppose you will think it unforgivably forward of me.'

'No, no, of course not,' replied Emily faintly. She was not sure what she thought. 'But surely, I mean, that cannot have been the only reason you wished to marry Captain Maynard?'

'Oh no,' replied Sylvestra cheerfully. 'Perry has always been my best friend – when I think of the scrapes we used to get into! And, of course, I am sincerely fond of him.'

'Fond?' queried Emily gently.

Sylvestra coloured slightly. 'Oh, I do not pretend to feel anything stronger than that, but to be sure it is more than many marriages are based on. Besides, Perry accepts me for what I am. He will not expect me to be forever playing propriety and minding my wretched tongue.'

Emily would have liked to say more, but it was not in her nature to question the behaviour or opinions of others, especially not her beloved cousin whom she admired more than anyone else in the world.

Sylvestra, knowing how much her admission must have shocked Emily, said by way of consolation, 'You must not think that because ours is not a *grande passion* that I, *we* are not determined to marry.'

'But if Mama is against it.'

Sylvestra frowned in acknowledgement of this formidable barrier to her future plans, but before she could respond, the impediment herself entered the room.

Short in stature, Julia Harvey made up for her lack of inches with an air of bustling self-importance and an overly loud, querulous voice. In her youth she had been accounted a well-looking girl, and indeed Emily was much in the same style. But while Emily's plump prettiness was accentuated by her sweet disposition and the gentle expression in her large brown eyes, the passing of the years and an increasingly shrewish temper had eradicated all trace of former comeliness in Mrs Harvey.

The daughter of a moderately wealthy man of business, she was fortunate in having an ambitious and tenacious mother. When this enterprising lady succeeded in snaring for her daughter the youngest son of a minor baronet, it was commonly thought Julia had done better than could be expected for the daughter of a cit without the benefit of a large dowry. Julia Harvey had accepted the offer with alacrity, fondly imagining herself established amongst the leaders of the ton. When she realized that her husband had neither the desire nor ability to cut a dash in London society, she was inclined to think she had struck a very poor bargain, a circumstance William Harvey had never been allowed to forget. But while those aspirations may have been forced to lie dormant for many years, they had not subsided. All Mrs Harvey's ambitions now rested on her only daughter, and they far outstripped those of her own mother. There would be no younger son for Emily, she was destined to make a brilliant match. This had been Mrs Harvey's aim since the birth of her daughter, and every moment after had been devoted to that end. Emily had been sent to a very select seminary for young ladies and had returned with all the gentility and decorum her mother could have wished for. The only fault Mrs Harvey could detect was a lack of ambition. But then, she reasoned, a malleable girl was perhaps a more attractive marriage prospect to a young lord used to going his own way.

It might be thought from this that Mrs Harvey was a heartless mother, but in common with many people of strong opinion, it never occurred to her that others did not share her point of view. Mrs Harvey genuinely believed she was doing the best for her daughter and for that, if nothing else, she must be given credit.

The news that she was expected to house an orphaned niece hardly came as a welcome surprise, but Mrs Harvey was prepared to accept the destitute waif with suitably condescending charity. The arrival of Sylvestra, who even to a parent's eye clearly outshone Emily in beauty and whose handsome fortune succeeded in making her daughter's portion look paltry by comparison, had not formed part of Mrs Harvey's plans. In the circumstances, it was to be expected that she should view her new charge with some hostility and this was further fuelled by Sylvestra's refusal to be daunted by her aunt's constant criticism. In a moment of rage, Julia Harvey had informed her niece that she would never find herself a husband unless she mended her hurly-burly ways. The impudent girl had replied with shocking pertness that her aunt need not worry on *that* score since she was already engaged and the seal was set on Mrs Harvey's resentment. If she had been asked before this unfortunate incident her plans for her niece's future, Mrs Harvey would probably have responded with some feeling that she would welcome with open arms any man willing to rid her of the ungrateful baggage. But in her anger she had promptly vetoed the match and Julia Harvey was not a woman to go back on her word.

Since that day she had succeeded in coming up with a far more rational reason for her disapproval: why should the unknown Captain Maynard benefit at the expense of her own family? Mrs Harvey had a younger widowed sister, Mrs Clive. There was no great bond of sisterly affection between the two, but Julia Harvey believed very strongly in the principle of blood being thicker than water, and she would have done anything reasonably in her power to improve her sister's position. Mr Clive had not been so great a catch as William Harvey, being only a clergyman of modest income. He had died leaving his widow and son far from comfortably positioned, and while Mrs Harvey would not have gone so far as to dip into her own purse to alleviate their need, if she could promote a match between her undeserving niece and her nephew, Mr Frederick Clive, then she felt she would have done her sister a very great service.

So as Sylvestra had correctly surmised, her aunt would have been more than happy to leave her at home. Besides the fact that her presence would undoubtedly eclipse Emily's lesser claims, it did not suit her at all for her wealthy niece to come to the attention of the numerous fortune hunters that doubtless littered London society. Had it not been for one crucial circumstance, Sylvestra would have been granted at least one of her wishes and been allowed to remain in Brimpton Mewsey.

Mrs Harvey was not averse to spending her husband's money in the cause of her social advancement, but Mr Harvey's means did not stretch to the hire of a town house in the heart of fashionable London and Mrs Harvey had resigned herself to a less exalted address. But then it had occurred to her that if her niece to was to make her debut also, then the trustees of her fortune might reasonably be expected to contribute to the venture. This had proved a correct assumption. The modest inheritance Sylvestra had received from her father was under her uncle's care, but the substantial fortune, (positively indecent in her aunt's view) that had come to her from her mother was in the care of Messrs Grindrod and

Cavendish. These legal gentlemen greeted Mrs Harvey's plan with approval and undertook to establish the visiting party in fine style.

It was the news that a charming residence in Green Street had been bespoken on their behalf that brought Mrs Harvey, feeling justifiably triumphant at this smart address, into the private parlour. Unfortunately, since it was her aunt's habit to erupt into rather than merely enter a room, Sylvestra had no opportunity to conceal her billet-doux. With a swiftness and agility surprising in one of such solid build, Mrs Harvey crossed the room and twitched the offending sheet of paper from her niece's grasp before the two young cousins had time to gather their scattered wits.

'And what is this?' Since her aunt's sharp eyes had already fastened on the untidy signature of Captain Maynard, Sylvestra judged this to be a rhetorical question and so offered no reply. Instead she waited in stoical silence for the inevitable retributions to rain down upon her head.

Reading through the illicit correspondence, Mrs Harvey was a little galled to find it contained nothing more shocking than soldier's cant. And, indeed, if her judgement had not been clouded by her anger at her niece's defiance, she might have found the letter encouraging in its lack of ardour. But the mere fact that Sylvestra had once more shown herself impervious to the acerbic rebukes with which Mrs Harvey was used to keep her entire household, from husband to pantry boy, in check, was enough to fan the flames of her smouldering resentment.

'You shameless hussy! I take you into my home and what do I receive in return? Nothing but ingratitude and deceit. Well, you may be sure I will not stand for it any further. Consorting with soldiers, indeed! A fine way for the granddaughter of an earl to behave, I must say.'

Sylvestra was moved to protest at this rather jaundiced description of her behaviour. 'Aunt Julia, I hardly think receiving a letter from a childhood friend' – with admirable tact she forbore to refer to the captain as her betrothed – 'who had the approval of both my parents, could in all fairness be described as "consorting with soldiers"!'

'You may let me be the judge of that, miss! I think I am in a better position to say what is right or wrong than a chit who has not the slightest notion of how to comport herself with even the semblance of modesty or propriety.'

Emily, who felt that for all her dread of her mother's anger she was honour bound to reveal her own part in the deception, intervened timidly at this point, exclaiming in quavering accents, 'Oh, indeed Mama, you must not blame Sylvestra, it was I who concealed Captain Maynard's letter from you.'

Mrs Harvey's face turned as red as her daughter's had paled. Nothing was more likely to enrage her than the information that Emily, usually the most compliant of daughters, had deceived her mother for the sake of her wayward cousin.

'I had thought better of you, Emily. I had hoped that you may have provided an influence to the good on your cousin, but I see that in fact the reverse is true. You have allowed yourself to be corrupted by her artfulness. When I think of the sacrifices I have made to have you educated in a proper manner! Is this how I am to be repaid? With treachery?'

Emily shrank from her mother's wrath, tears of distress filling her eyes. Sylvestra had become inured to her aunt's vitriolic outbursts, but she knew how easily Emily's sensitive spirit was crushed by her mother's fury.

'You are wrong, Aunt Julia, it is not artfulness that led Emily to conceal the letter from you but rather her tender heart. Surely you cannot rail at her for that?'

'Hmph!' snorted Mrs Harvey, by now thoroughly incensed. 'Tender heart indeed! Nothing more than romantic nonsense picked up from all those foolish novels no doubt. Well, the sooner you realize that it is nothing more than flummery the better it will be for you, Emily Harvey! Do you think I sent you to Miss Pinner's establishment so that you may marry a . . . a half pay officer? Next you will be telling me you have developed a *tendre* for the dancing master!'

Emily shook her head vigorously. 'Indeed no, Mama! I never thought of such a thing!' Which was no more than the truth since Emily had not to her knowledge ever encountered so dangerous a character as a half pay officer, and the dancing master, being portly to the point of rotundity and with an addiction for the extreme fashions of the dandy, was more likely to be the object of ridicule than romance in the eyes of his young pupils.

Apparently satisfied that she had quelled any lingering vestiges of rebellion, Mrs Harvey at last chose to divulge her news. 'We go to London next week, girls; Green Street, no less. I hope you will both bear in mind that Mr Harvey and I have gone to a great deal of trouble and expense to give you this opportunity – an opportunity, I might add, that I would have given my eye teeth for when I was your age. I would not have wasted such good fortune and neither I am determined shall you. You had better realize that I intend you both to have made respectable alliances before the season is out. Emily, I am persuaded you at least will realize your duty to your parents. As for you, Sylvestra, you may think yourself very lucky if any man of taste can be induced to make you an offer!'

And on this climactic note, Mrs Harvey swept from the room, leaving the young ladies to ponder their fate and to view with even greater foreboding their impending trip to the capital.

Two

The driver of the sporting curricle deftly guided his team of perfectly matched bays along the broad gravel driveway that led in a graceful sweep to the imposing frontage of Were Court. The equipage would certainly have won the admiration of any gentleman of sporting proclivities, and the most critical judge of horse flesh would have been hard pressed to find fault with the high-stepping Welsh breds.

But a solitary vehicle, devoid of outriders or postillions to lend its occupant consequence, and without a noble crest to adorn it's doors, would hardly have been expected to cause too great a stir at the residence of His Grace, the Duke of Were. Nonetheless, the curricle had scarcely come to a halt before the ancient oak doors were thrown wide and two nimble footmen attired in the distinctive black and silver Carston livery scampered down the stone steps to attend the lone traveller. They were followed with less alacrity but equal enthusiasm by an elderly butler, his faded grey eyes alive with eager anticipation.

The driver threw the reins to his diminutive tiger and swung down from his carriage with lithe grace. He stood and surveyed the red brick façade with its countless mullioned windows, a commanding figure in his many-caped greatcoat and gleaming top boots.

'Master Evelyn! Master Evelyn, welcome home!'

The unfeigned delight of the butler's breathless welcome brought an amused smile to Evelyn Carston's face, replacing the rather brooding expression that had preceded it and magically transforming his strong stern features.

'Lambert, you old devil. And as sprightly as ever! No doubt my father's best brandy has something to do with that.'

The butler straightened his bony shoulders indignantly. 'My Lord Marquis, you know I have never touched strong spirits in all my years' service.'

Evelyn threw back his handsome dark head and laughed out loud at this. 'I know no such thing, you old fraud. But what is this? *My Lord Marquis?*' Twas Master Evelyn a moment ago.'

Lambert, still very much on his dignity, inclined his head in a gesture of apology and replied pompously, 'A momentary lapse, My Lord, which I beg My Lord will be so generous as to overlook.'

Evelyn laughed again, his brilliant blue eyes sparkling with wicked mirth. 'Come down off your high ropes, man. I have not forgotten who plucked me out of the ornamental lake by the ankles, even if you have!'

Lambert was not proof against his favourite's cajoling, and a reluctant smile creased his lined face at the memory; one among many incidents of similar ilk which had littered the misspent youth of Evelyn Carston. But, at the same time, he shook his head, obstinately standing his ground.

'No, My Lord, it would not be right. You are now the Marquis of Derwent and I hope I know what is due to your station.'

A shadow crossed Evelyn's bronzed face and he said in a low voice filled with bitterness, 'Believe me, Lambert, I would as lief forget that title.'

The butler took his sudden change of mood to be grief for the dead brother whose title he had inherited.

'It was a terrible tragedy, My Lord. The master took Lord Vincent's death very badly. And that poor young bride, her with child as well.'

Evelyn, lost in his own far from happy thoughts, looked up sharply at this last piece of information. 'Lady Elizabeth was with child?' Lambert nodded an affirmative and Evelyn passed a hand across his face. 'Good God, Vincent, how did we come to such a pass?'

The butler was at a loss to understand this cryptic utterance. After all, no one could be held responsible for the sudden squall that had taken down the *Genevieve* and with her the Marquis and Marchioness of Derwent. But the anguish in those blue eyes touched the butler's old heart and he said gruffly, 'It is good to see you back where you belong, Master Evelyn.'

Evelyn managed a lopsided grin at this. 'If that is your opinion then you are undoubtedly in the minority, Lambert, my old friend.'

There was a moment of silence as the thoughts of old man and young lord were drawn irresistibly into the past. Then Evelyn straightened his athletic frame and gave himself a mental shake. The time had come to set matters right, and that would not be done by wasting his time in maudlin regrets.

'Come, Lambert. It will not do to keep His Grace waiting.'

'No indeed, My Lord!'

The patent horror in the butler's voice did much to restore Evelyn's good humour, and after delivering brief but precise instructions as to the care of his cattle, Evelyn Carston stepped across the threshold of Were Court for the first time in five years.

'I see you have not lost your bourgeois habit of hobnobbing with the servants.'

As the greeting of a father to his long estranged son this did not bode well for future relations, but it provoked a profound relief in Evelyn Carston. He had expected his father to have aged – five years is a long time to a man in his sixties – but the change he found had shocked him deeply. Neither his brother Vincent's erratic correspondence nor his mother's more regular letters had prepared him for this frail old man. But then, he reasoned,

Vincent's letters had characteristically been filled with his own problems to the exclusion of all else, and the duchess had undoubtedly wanted to protect her son from further worry.

Five years ago, Gerard Carston had been a vigorous, upright man in the same mould as his youngest son. Now crippled with gout and arthritis, he seemed to have shrunk to a pitiful caricature of his former self. The ebony cane with its elaborate silver embellishments had always been there; once a mere affectation left over from a more elegant era, now a vital crutch for the duke's bent and wasted form.

Thankfully though, if His Grace's caustic opener was anything to go by, the disintegration of his body had not extended to his mind. For that reason, Evelyn was able to ignore a remark which was surely designed to antagonize him, and reply in the blandest of tones, 'Good morning, sir. I trust I find you in good health.'

An incoherent snort was the only response to this polite enquiry. The duke had chosen to be standing when his son entered the room, despite the obvious pain it caused him. Having made the point that he was no helpless invalid, he crossed the room by means of slow tortuous steps and seated himself in a winged armchair before the fire. Watching his father's painful progress across that few feet of carpet, Evelyn longed to go to his aid, but he knew the duke's pride could support no man's pity, least of all that of his despised younger son. And so he stayed resolutely still, his face a mask of indifference.

'Well, you may start by fetching me a brandy, Derwent.' There was the slightest of hesitations before the duke pronounced Evelyn's title, and Evelyn knew how much it must cost him to call anyone but Vincent by that name. Evelyn made no move to obey his father, however.

'I feel sure your doctor has forbidden brandy, sir.'

'Forbidden? Hah! I would like to see him try! Fetch me the brandy and be quick about it.'

'Nevertheless, he has doubtless advised against it.'

Two spots of hectic colour burned in the pale parchment of the duke's cheeks. 'Damn you, sir, I said brandy!' he roared.

Evelyn remained unmoved and the duke was forced to fume in impotent rage before saying, a distinct note of challenge in his voice, 'Vincent would not have disobeyed me so.'

This obvious ploy provoked only a wry, humourless smile. For years, Evelyn had striven to equal Vincent in his father's eyes. No longer.

'No doubt you are right, sir,' was his noncommittal reply.

The duke gave a bark of harsh laughter, acknowledging defeat with a dismissive wave of his hand. 'I'll say this for you, Derwent, I've never been able to bullock you, not even when you were a boy.'

Even such slight and grudging praise warmed Evelyn's heart, and impulsively he stepped towards his father, his hand extended. 'Come, Father. Can we not shake hands and be reconciled?'

Dark gimlet eyes met eager blue and slid away. The duke seemed to wrestle with some inner demon before placing his pale and twisted hand into his son's strong grasp, saying with obvious reluctance, 'As little as I may like it you are my heir, and I suppose it will not do for us to be at odds. But you have brought shame upon the name of Carston once, and I'll not stand for it again.'

Evelyn pulled back his hand as if it had been burned, a look of cold fury replacing the almost boyish eagerness.

'Damn it, sir. When will you admit the truth? It is time the record was set straight. Vincent is dead—'

'How dare you, sir! How dare you!' The duke's face turned from deathly white to dark red as he struggled to his feet, violent rage lending strength to his enfeebled body. 'Vincent is dead and every day I wish it had been you on that blasted vessel, *your* body rotting at the bottom of the sea. Vincent was a gentleman, not a damned whining hypocrite and philanderer. You are not fit to follow in his footsteps. Well, I may have to accept you as my heir, but by God, you ceased to be my son the day you brought disgrace on this family.' Breathing hard, the duke sank back into his chair like some grotesque rag doll, the torrent of rage leaving his body spent and lifeless.

Only the slight pallor in his cheeks and a tightening about the lips betrayed Evelyn's deep anger and hurt at his father's bitter onslaught. His voice was icy cold and expressionless.

'There is clearly nothing to say then, sir. But I should warn you that if the truth is not told the name of Carston will be tainted beyond repair, and I for one will not allow that to happen.'

'Get out, damn you.' It was barely more than a whisper but it was redolent with hatred. With a curt nod, Evelyn turned on his heel and exited the library, his long strides taking him across the entrance hall and out into the spring sunshine. The duke's terrible malevolence was so tangible that it seemed to pollute the very atmosphere of the house and Evelyn drank in the crisp clean air thirstily, his fists clenched at his sides as he fought to contain the floodtide of emotions which threatened to engulf him.

Evelyn did not know how long he stood there, filling his lungs again and again with the sweet floral scented air, as if to rid himself of some poisonous contamination. It was the gentle swish of skirts on the parquet floor behind him that finally recalled him to his surroundings.

'Eve? Eve, can it be you?'

At the sound of that beloved voice, Evelyn swung around, warmth instantly banishing the desolation from his eyes. 'Mama!' In a moment he had gathered the little duchess to his chest, hugging her so fiercely that half laughing, half crying she protested he would crush her to death.

Immediately he released her and held her at arm's length, his eyes fearfully scanning her face for any of the appalling signs of deterioration he had seen so recently in his father. Apparently he was satisfied, for after kissing her soundly on one smooth cheek he exclaimed, 'Why you are as beautiful as ever, Mama!'

'And you are a bigger flatterer than ever you were, Evelyn Carston!'

But even allowing for filial bias, Helen, Duchess of Were was still a remarkably pretty woman. Petite in stature, her waist was as slender as the day she married, her dark hair, if streaked with silver, was as thick and luxurious as ever, and her blue eyes, as brilliant as her son's.

'Oh, Eve, Eve. How good it is to see you. If only the circumstances could have been different.'

The duchess could not go on, her voice suspended by tears and, giving her hand a comforting squeeze, Evelyn led her to a nearby couch. After a few moments, the duchess composed herself.

'All those letters, Eve. Why did you not tell me?'

'What would you have had me tell you, Mama?' His tone was light, but his expression had become watchful. Surely she could have no inkling of the truth, he had taken such pains to protect her from it.

The duchess shook her head sadly. 'Oh, Eve. Did you think you could hide it from me? Remember, I reared you, you and Vincent.'

Evelyn continued to watch her intently, but volunteered no response. The duchess sighed and raised a fond hand to his cheek. 'Of course, I could not know the whole. If I had, do you think I could have let things continue for so long? But Vincent, I think, knew I must suspect. He told me all not a week before . . . before the accident. Poor Eizabeth, she did not deserve— Oh, good heavens!'

The sudden noise of breaking glass caused the duchess to start to her feet and hurry towards its source, the library. But Evelyn, his heart filled with sudden dread, was there before her and the sight that greeted his eyes caused him to instruct Lambert, who was crossing the hall with all the speed his aged body could muster, to call for His Grace's doctor. The duke lay slumped in a pathetic heap before the fire, splinters of a brandy glass littering the stone hearth. Evelyn was at his side in a moment, his fingers seeking and thankfully finding a pulse, albeit weak and erratic. Grim-faced, he swiftly loosened the elaborately laced cravat and gently lifted the frail body into the armchair. The duchess, pale but composed, appeared at his elbow with a glass of dark liquid.

'Here, Eve, he must take this. It is his heart you know, it is not strong. He has had these turns before, but if we can but get him to swallow Dr Hornbill's mixture then he will recover quite quickly.'

Evelyn accepted the glass and lifted it to his father's blue lips. At first, it seemed that the medicine was having no effect but then a tinge of colour began to appear on the livid features, and in a moment the duke was struggling to free himself from his son's firm grasp.

'Gently, sir. Lie still a moment and get your breath.'

But the sound of Evelyn's voice had a far from soothing effect. Rather it made him struggle all the more, and Evelyn was forced to release his father.

'You still here! I thought I told you! I want you out! Out, do you hear! Out!' The duke's voice rose in hysterical rage, but his body had not the strength of his fury and he collapsed in a paroxysm of coughing. The duchess sank to her knees before her husband.

'Hush, Gerard! Do not try to speak. We have sent for Dr Hornbill, he will be here any time now.'

'I don't need that quack. I will be well enough once I know *he* is no longer under this roof,' muttered the duke peevishly, gesturing in Evelyn's direction. But the sound of his wife's voice seemed to have a calming effect, and the hacking cough ceased to rack his frame.

The duchess, satisfied that the worst at least was over, turned to her son, saying simply, 'Eve.'

Lord Carston was not immune to the unspoken plea contained in that single word and his stern features softened. 'I will be in the drawing-room,' he said in a low voice only she could hear.

It was some time before the duchess joined her son, and when she did she looked pale and worried. Evelyn helped her to a chair and fetched her a glass of wine. 'Is Father worse?' he asked anxiously.

The duchess shook her head. 'No, my dear, but the attack was severe and it has sapped his strength. It will take time for him to recover.'

Evelyn ran his hands through his dark hair. 'I should never have come here. This is my doing.'

'No, you must not say that. Your presence may have thrown him into one of his tempers, but the doctor has warned him time and again how it would be if he continued to drink as he does.'

Evelyn did not look convinced. 'Well, I shall not stay and make matters worse. I will return to Derwent House, for if I know Father he will fret and fume until he knows I am off the premises.'

The duchess sighed sadly, but could not deny the truth of what he said; even Dr Hornbill had tactfully implied as much.

'When he knows the truth, Eve, things will be different.'

'The truth would kill him!'

'No, but he must not be told until he is stronger. Will you trust me to speak to him, Eve? It will come better from me.'

'I have sworn all along that you would not be dragged into this damnable business, Mama—'

'This is as much my problem as anyone's,' cut in the duchess firmly. Adding softly, 'Please Eve, after all these years a few more weeks cannot hurt, and then I will try to make your father listen to reason.'

'Very well.' Evelyn gave in reluctantly. 'It is perhaps as well that I return to London. I have left Marianne alone, and heaven knows what mad schemes she will devise without me there to restrain her.'

'Marianne is in England!' exclaimed the duchess in consternation.

'Of course! I could hardly abandon her in Europe with Napoleon on the rampage.'

'But London! You are surely risking discovery; you know how servants gossip. Would it not be better to stay out of town? The hunting lodge in Leicestershire perhaps.'

'You need not worry. My servants are paid well to keep their tongues between their teeth. I own I had thought of taking Marianne and Edward into Leicestershire, but you may depend upon it she would be making mischief as soon as my back was turned, for she is as wilful as ever.'

'I wish I might see the boy,' said the duchess wistfully.

'You will,' Evelyn assured her. 'And, please God, before so very long.'

The duchess put her hand to her cheek distractedly. 'What a dreadful mess it all is! Will we never see an end to it?'

Evelyn took her hand comfortingly, saying with a confidence he was far from feeling, 'Of course we will, Mama. It will soon be in the past, I promise you.' He rose to his feet. 'And now I must go if I am to reach London before nightfall. I have an appointment with Vincent's man of business early in the morning. I did not mean to tell you Mama but Vincent left his affairs in a sorry state. It will take all my time to untangle them.'

The duchess smiled sorrowfully. 'My poor Eve. It seems you must shoulder all our burdens.'

Evelyn laughed and shook his head. 'You must not imagine me chained to my desk day and night. I intend to go into society. I think it is time I came out of the shadows. After five years of cloistered living I believe I am long overdue a little dissipation!'

'But Eve, society can be so cruel. Would it not be better to wait a little?' asked his mother anxiously.

Evelyn shrugged carelessly. 'I must face the gossips sooner or later. Besides,' he added a touch grimly, 'it will be interesting to discover who my true friends are.'

'Do you attend the Leimsters' ball, Miss Harvey?'

'I believe—'

'Of course, we would not miss it for the world!' interposed Mrs Harvey swiftly before Sylvestra had a chance to frame a reply to

Lady Wynchip's polite enquiry. 'It will be my dear Emily's first ball, though I fancy no one would suspect, for a better behaved girl one could not hope to find. My niece, unfortunately,' she added, in the tones of one severely tested, 'had not the benefits of an education at Miss Pinner's seminary.'

It was hard to say who was least gratified by this speech. More embarrassed to be the recipient of praise than of censure when it was at the expense of her cousin, Emily could only blush miserably and hang her head. Sylvestra, too, coloured up, but in her case, anger rather than shame was the cause.

'Indeed?' was Lady Wynchip's stiff response, the lift of one delicately arched eyebrow expressing her view of such a vulgar statement.

If it had not been for the fact of a younger son of expensive tastes and only moderate income, Lady Wynchip would most certainly never have made the effort to become acquainted with Mrs Julia Harvey. An earl's granddaughter with thirty thousand a year, however, was enough to guarantee the house in Green Street the honour of a call from Her Ladyship. And if it was not for the fact that the said son had failed in his promise to arrive some five and twenty minutes earlier on the pretext of escorting his mother home and thereby affording Lady Wynchip with an excellent opportunity to steal a march on all the other female relatives of improvident young men, Her Ladyship would not have spent above ten minutes in the company of Mrs Harvey.

Mr Aubrey Wynchip was late, a circumstance that irritated Lady Wynchip greatly, but surprised her not in the least. She therefore gritted her teeth, turned her shoulder upon Mrs Harvey and once more addressed Sylvestra, saying graciously, 'You will doubtless feel a little nervous, my dear. It is not easy I know, for a young girl with no one to show her how to go on. I should be only too happy to offer you the benefit of my experience.'

Sylvestra thanked her for this kind offer with proper gratitude and fought to control her twitching lips. She was beginning to enjoy the conflict of wills that was steadily developing between her aunt and their visitor.

Mrs Harvey pursed her lips and sat very upright in her chair; she might be in high alt at having attracted one of the acknowledged leaders of the ton into her drawing-room within a mere week of their arrival in the capital, but the inference that she was unable to give correct guidance to her young charges could not be allowed to pass unchallenged.

'Oh, you need not fear, my dear Lady Wynchip. If Sylvestra will but follow her cousin's example, she will not go far wrong. You may be sure that no daughter of mine will be found wanting.'

'Mr Aubrey Wynchip,' intoned the butler; a timely intervention perhaps since the atmosphere between the two ladies was becoming more charged by the second.

Mr Wynchip sauntered into the room with the careless sangfroid indispensable to any young man with pretensions to fashion. This façade of studied ennui was shattered however when Mr Wynchip was confronted by the spectacle of Mrs Harvey's drawing-room and its occupants. His casual progress came to an abrupt halt, the nonchalant greeting to his hostess dying unspoken upon his lips. This was an understandable if slightly exaggerated reaction to the splendour of the scene before him.

It had not taken Mrs Harvey long to stamp her personality upon the decor of the house in Green Street. She had branded its muted elegance as positively shabby, and had set about transforming the reception rooms into what she considered a suitable setting for entertaining the cream of London society.

The drawing-room, or Nile Room as it was now styled by the mistress of the house, was regarded by Mrs Harvey as a personal triumph. And indeed she had surpassed herself. The current Egyptian craze had been embraced wholeheartedly and unrestrainedly. The delicate eggshell-blue walls had been repapered in a wide stripe of vivid blue and white, and against this startling background the effect of gold brocade backless sofas, their gilt legs carved into crocodiles, sphinxes and countless more improbable creatures of the Nile, was quite literally blinding.

But while it was a sight to stop any person of taste dead in their tracks, Aubrey Wynchip's dramatic response cannot be thus excused. Mr Wynchip was possessed of an impressionable and imaginative disposition which manifested itself in a leaning towards the poetic. By chance, Mr Wynchip had on the previous evening attended a performance of *Antony and Cleopatra*. So much affected was he by this powerful tragedy that the hours since had been devoted to composing a epic poem dedicated to the unmatched beauty and spirit of that most famous of Egyptian queens. Unfortunately, part way through the second stanza his muse had deserted him, leaving to struggle in vain to do justice to his subject. This was the reason for Mr Wynchip's belated arrival at Green Street, for though he might adopt the demeanour of the angry young man, he was by nature polite and obliging besides having a lively dread of his mother's sharp tongue.

It was blinding inspiration rather than the effects of Mrs Harvey's penchant for interior design that rooted Mr Wynchip to the spot. The exotic setting certainly played its part, but the vision of a Titian-haired goddess with slanting emerald eyes was the overriding factor. Mr Wynchip had found a living and breathing muse.

The poet himself presented no everyday picture. To do him justice, of those young men who had chosen to ape the picturesque dress and manner of my Lord Byron, Aubrey Wynchip was more suited than most to the style. With his blond hair falling in artistic disorder over his pale brow, and brooding classical features above a carelessly knotted cravat, he was undeniably an exceedingly romantic figure.

Not one, however, that either of the senior occupants of the drawing-room were disposed to admire. Seldom had Lady Wynchip endured a more testing half-hour and she was inclined to view her dilatory son as being solely responsible. Mrs Harvey had done her homework and knew to the last guinea what every sprig of the nobility was worth. There is no greater enemy to the ambitious mother of a marriageable daughter than a personable young man without a feather to fly with. Aubrey Wynchip fell squarely into that category and could, therefore, not expect any extraordinary civility from Julia Harvey.

The coolness of her greeting went unremarked. Mr Wynchip was wholly absorbed by Miss Sylvestra Harvey. Lady Wynchip watched indulgently as her son bowed reverently over the heiress's hand before seating himself at her side, a piece of good sense which went a good way towards soothing the lacerated feelings of his mother and enabling her to bear with admirable fortitude a further fifteen minutes of Mrs Harvey's conversation.

It was a conversation Sylvestra would certainly have enjoyed, containing as it did several glaring hints from her aunt regarding her ambitions for her daughter and some hardly more subtle remarks from Lady Wynchip condemning the folly of those members of the gentility who aim above their touch. Sylvestra, however, was obliged to give her attention to Mr Wynchip, who wasted no time in making his admiration for her clear.

An earnest frown creasing his pale brow, he said in a low throbbing tone, 'Miss Harvey, I must tell you that when I walked into this room I experienced nothing less than a . . . revelation!'

Sylvestra raised her eyebrows, laughter dancing in her green eyes. 'How very extraordinary, Mr Wynchip. My aunt will be most flattered, it is all her own design.'

'Ah, you choose to deliberately misunderstand me, Miss Harvey! You are her equal in both wit and beauty!'

'My aunt?' queried Sylvestra, unable to keep a note of comic incredulity from creeping into her reply at this unlikely description of Mrs Harvey.

'Your aunt?' said Mr Wynchip blankly, oblivious to the mischief dancing in those emerald orbs. 'No, I refer to that most fêted beauty of ancient times, Cleopatra!'

'Cleopatra! Forgive me, sir, but that seems a strange comparison.' Sylvestra's knowledge of history was by no means comprehensive, but she was fairly sure that the Egyptian queen had not been blessed with a head of copper curls.

'To the literal mind, perhaps, Miss Harvey. But in the eyes of a poet, an artist, the resemblance is immediately striking.'

'You are a poet, Mr Wynchip?' asked Sylvestra politely, hoping to divert him from his bizarre compliments.

'A poet? To call myself thus would be to bracket myself with the genius of my Lord Byron, which I think you will agree, would be an act of presumption on my part.'

'I was not aware Lord Byron had a monopoly on the title of poet, Mr Wynchip. I think you might safely presume to call yourself whatever you like,' responded Sylvestra a little tartly. She could find nothing in Byron's work to warrant the absurd adulation showered upon him by the ton, most of whom she doubted had even read his verse. Sylvestra simply saw this ridiculous hero worship as further evidence that in London society no opinion was so strongly held that the fickle wind of fashion could not change it.

Mr Wynchip was briefly taken aback by this seeming lack of appreciation for the brilliance of his mentor, but then realized, of course, that Miss Harvey was trying to be kind.

'You are too good, Miss Harvey, but I know my limitations. My work has always fallen short, has always lacked that indefinable essence that separates the commonplace from the true work of art.' He leaned towards her, his eyes burning with enthusiasm. 'But now that essence, always so tantalizingly out of reach, is there for me to grasp!' And he reached out as if to pluck some invisible force from the air, gazing into space, a rapt expression on his beautiful features.

'How – er, how very fortunate for you!' said Sylvestra, unable to do justice to this momentous turn of events, but feeling it clearly behoved her to make some response if only to jolt her companion back from whatever plane he was currently occupying.

The dreamy eyes gradually refocused upon Sylvestra's face. 'Passion! Fire!' exclaimed Mr Wynchip, pounding his fist into his palm to emphasize his point and causing all the ladies to jump. 'With you, Miss Harvey, to inspire me, these qualities surely cannot continue to elude me!' continued the poet, oblivious to the looks of astonishment and disapproval his extraordinary outburst had generated.

'You flatter me, Mr Wynchip, but really, I am not worthy of such an honour,' protested Sylvestra, by no means taken by the prospect of forming the subject for one of Mr Wynchip's works; especially if his poetry was as lurid as his conversation.

Lady Wynchip chose this point to intervene, saying indulgently, 'You must forgive dear Aubrey, Miss Harvey; his enthusiasm when it comes to his precious verse has a tendency to overcome his manners.' She then addressed herself to Mr Wynchip with a playful admonishment that concealed more than a hint of steel. 'Really, Aubrey, whatever will Miss Harvey think of you? If you had thought to enquire you would have learned that the Harveys attend the Leimsters' ball this evening. I am sure you will wish to secure a dance with Miss Harvey now, for it is a certainty that such a charming addition to society will not have an empty card for long!'

Mr Wynchip gladly took the hint and Sylvestra graciously promised to save him one of the country dances, kindly forbearing to express her surprise that he did actually dance rather than stand and brood darkly in a corner as was reputedly Lord Byron's habit.

Having achieved her object, Lady Wynchip rose to leave, summoning her son peremptorily to her side. Mrs Harvey, smiling through gritted teeth bade her guests goodbye, expressing the conventional hope that they would call again soon. But the smile quickly disappeared when the drawing-room door was finally shut behind her visitors. Julia Harvey's first encounter with London aristocracy had not gone at all to plan. She might be blind to the personal attractions of her niece but she recognized the lure of money. Sylvestra's wealth was a constant thorn in her side and it rankled deeply that she must thank her undeserving niece's presence in her household for Lady Wynchip's visit. The sooner Sylvestra was married to her cousin Frederick and returned to obscurity the better!

Three

'I think it is very mean of you to leave me here, Carston. Why, it is an absolute age since I have been in civilized company! I can't understand why you bothered to bring me back to England if you did not intend to let me stir beyond the door. I may as well have stayed in Florence.' Lord Carston's beautiful companion, charmingly attired in a chemise dress of palest pink crêped muslin, pouted prettily and threw herself down disconsolately upon a day bed. Golden curls framed a china-doll complexion from which wide blue eyes sparkled with frustrated tears. A bewitching sight, but not one Evelyn Carston was disposed to admire. He showed no sign of hearing her complaint, but continued to make adjustments to his cravat, even a number of exaggerated sighs failing to distract him from this task. In the end, to get his attention, the lady was forced to stamp her feet crossly and cry, 'Oh! You are perfectly detestable, Carston! Why won't you answer me?'

'Marianne, we have discussed this countless times. I see little point in repeating myself,' said Evelyn wearily, without bothering to look round.

'No, we have not discussed it. *You* have decided I must moulder away in this beastly house whilst you are out enjoying yourself. I never agreed to it.'

Evelyn gritted his teeth but replied calmly, 'I hardly think the Leimsters' ball will afford me much pleasure. But don't you see,

Marianne? It will only make matters worse if I fail to appear in public. Society will see it as an admission of guilt and that will make our task all the harder.'

But Marianne was in no mood to listen to reason, exclaiming angrily, 'Why should I suffer? I have nothing to be ashamed of.' She added spitefully, 'Besides, what is the use of ingratiating yourself with the match-making mamas? When they discover you are not the eligible bachelor they suppose, you will quickly fall from favour.'

'I have no intention of encouraging any hopeful mamas or their daughters for that matter. I wish you would rid yourself of the notion that I am keeping you concealed here to further some dastardly ends of my own. It is for your sake and Edward's. Until my father has accepted you both you can be sure the ton will not.'

'And when will that be? You promised you would speak to the duke and yet you are back from Were and nothing has changed!'

'Believe me, I am as impatient as you are to see this matter settled, but my father is a sick man. We must both be patient until he is well enough to face the truth.'

'Oh, that is easy for you to say!' exclaimed Marianne pettishly, her cheeks flushing angrily. 'Whatever you say, you cannot deny that it would suit you very well if Edward and I did not exist. Well, I am sick to death of being patient! I listened to your advice five years ago and I am still no better off. If you tell me once more that I must be patient, I will scream!'

Evelyn knew it was pointless to try and reason with Marianne in this frame of mind and so he abandoned his attempts at conciliation, simply shrugging infuriatingly and saying, 'Then by all means scream the house down, Marianne. I, unfortunately, must excuse myself, but I am sure the servants will find it most edifying. Good evening, madam.' And with a mocking bow he swiftly exited the room, knowing full well what her likely response to his lack of sympathy would be. In the event, the figurine that was flung at his retreating head was done so with more force than accuracy and smashed harmlessly against the wall. Barely flinching at the sound of breaking china, Evelyn merely remarked to his astonished butler that the lady of the house had apparently taken a dislike, as unaccountable as it was violent, to the Dresden shepherdess, and would doubtless appreciate the removal of its remains from her sight. Then, with a murmured word of thanks, he accepted his evening cloak and cane from a studiously wooden-faced footman, and sauntered out into the night.

Sylvestra regarded her reflection in the mirror and scowled awfully. If the romantic fiction Emily so delighted in was to be believed, this was an important milestone in the life of any heroine worth her salt. The night of her debut, and the young maiden's heart flutters with nervous anticipation. She dons her gown and behold! The unremarkable schoolroom miss is transformed by the seamstress's magic into a beautiful young lady whose fair countenance would stir tender passions in the breast of the most stony-hearted of heroes. Well, Sylvestra had never rated her looks so very highly and indeed, had never paid more attention to her appearance than was necessary to avoid her aunt's disapproval. A wet winter's afternoon was more likely to find her reading her uncle's sporting journals than leafing through the pages of *La Belle Assemblée*. Despite herself, however, Sylvestra had been infected by the bustle and excitement of her first shopping expedition in London. She was not indifferent to beautiful things and it was impossible to see all those rich fabrics and exquisite gowns without wondering how such finery might look on her.

Sadly, in Sylvestra's case, the modiste's spell had gone awry. Not that the blame should be laid wholly at that woman's door. Mrs Julia Harvey's opinions on female apparel were as strongly held as her views on interior design and the results were equally startling. Her notion of the kind of toilette suitable for a young debutante had nearly reduced the poor dressmaker to hysterics. The style must be pretty and feminine, dictated Mrs Harvey. Unfortunately for Sylvestra, her aunt's concept of pretty and feminine involved covering every inch of gown indiscriminately and lavishly with a quantity of frills, flounces, ribbon and lace.

'Oh, Duffey, I look like a a badly iced wedding cake!' exclaimed Sylvestra in comic dismay. The maid primmed her lips, but restricted her response to an eloquent sniff. To say that her young mistress had taken the words out of her mouth would have been a lie; Duffey would never have so far forgotten her position as to express herself with such freedom. That is not to say she did not hold an opinion, and in the case of Mrs Harvey's taste it was an exceedingly poor one. But she could not believe that someone with even Mrs Harvey's dearth of aesthetic judgement could, in all honesty, imagine that rose pink would do anything to enhance the appearance of a damsel with Sylvestra's flaming locks. *That*, Duffey shrewdly put down to spite. She may only have been in the Harvey household for a week, but she had quickly learned how bitterly Mrs Harvey resented her niece's wealth and noble connections.

No such suspicion crossed Sylvestra's mind. Not because her own opinion of Mrs Harvey was any higher than that of her maid, but if her aunt's intention really was to marry her off to an eligible young man, then the rose-pink ball gown would do little to further her cause. Sylvestra could only conclude that she had neither the build nor the colouring to carry off current fashions, and since she had not the slightest desire to inflame the passions of even the most handsome of heroes she was able to bear this with cheerful stoicism.

Sylvestra's critical self-study was interrupted by the entrance of her cousin. Winking mischievously at her disapproving maid, Sylvestra executed a jaunty pirouette, exclaiming merrily as she did so, 'Well, Emily, am I not the most elegant creature you ever set eyes on?'

Emily's eyes widened at the blinding effect of Titian curls and rose-pink muslin. 'I–I'm sure it is the height of fashion, Sylvie,' she responded lamely.

Sylvestra shook her head and chuckled, 'What a rapper! Say it! I look an absolute fright. If this is the way Aunt Julia means to snare me a husband then I fear she will catch cold! Indeed if it were not so mortifying I swear t'would be amusing to see her try!'

'Oh, Sylvie, if only there was something I could do. Perhaps if you were to wear my dress.' Emily plucked at the skirts of her lavender-blue silk distractedly. This generous offer was laughingly turned down. While the shade would have been a great improvement, Sylvestra hardly thought appearing in a gown designed for a young lady at least six inches shorter than herself would do anything to render her appearance less hideous.

'You must not worry on my account, Em. I have no ambition to take the town by storm. I will leave that to you. Why, you look as fine as fivepence!'

Indeed, the fussy style Mrs Harvey favoured suited the soft prettiness of her daughter surprisingly well, lending her a kind of kittenish charm. Emily blushed and disclaimed before anxiously reminding her cousin that Mrs Harvey awaited them below ready to escort them to Lady Leimster's ball, their first London party. Sylvestra needed no second prompting, and her eyes alight with unholy glee, she fairly skipped down the stairs. It would almost be worth the embarrassment of appearing in public thus arrayed to witness Aunt Julia's reaction to her appearance.

Sylvestra was destined to disappointment. Mrs Harvey's strongest emotion on seeing her niece in all the glory of her new ball gown was malicious satisfaction that her daughter would not be outshone on her debut by her hoydenish cousin. Consequently, she stunned Sylvestra by greeting her entrance into the drawing-room with an approving smile and saying with rare amiability, 'Very respectable, Niece. I swear I have never seen you so presentable.'

That was the beginning and end to her aunt's praise. The journey to the ball, mercifully short in Sylvestra's opinion, was entirely taken up with Mrs Harvey's inexhaustible list of strictures on the appropriate behaviour for a debutante entering the *haut monde*. By the time the carriage drew to a halt at the door of the Leimsters' house in Berkeley Square, poor Emily had resolved to find a corner to hide in as soon as possible, as this seemed to be the only way to avoid the numerous pitfalls awaiting her. Sylvestra was more amused than daunted, this plethora of trivial rules just serving to increase her contempt for London society.

Although the season had barely got under way, Lady Leimster had succeeded in attracting enough guests to her soirée for it to be declared a sad crush and hence something of a triumph. Unlike her two charges, Mrs Harvey had no intention of remaining quietly on the periphery. Julia Harvey had waited many years for this moment and she was determined to be at the hub of the night's proceedings. Her beady eyes quickly fastened on their hostess and she surged through the crowd, her affected tones resonating through the scented air.

'My dear Lady Leimster, you are to be congratulated! The whole of London is here!'

Sylvestra and Emily, trailing meekly in her wake, could only cringe at this singularly inappropriate greeting and wait for the inevitable crushing snub.

Lady Leimster had never seen Mrs Harvey in her life and the invitation had been extended somewhat half-heartedly on the premise that it did no harm to have the latest heiress at one's party if only for the purpose of attracting the single gentlemen. Fortunately Lady Leimster, besides being very good-natured, had an appalling memory, and hearing herself thus hailed, understandably presumed that the rather odd-looking woman in the purple bloom satin bearing down so relentlessly upon her must be an acquaintance.

'Why, Mrs . . . er, why what a pleasure it is to see you, and your beautiful, er, daughters, too. I am so glad you could come,' hazarded Lady Leimster, smiling helplessly at Sylvestra and Emily, her rather protruding, faded-blue eyes taking on an even more anxious expression than usual. She was a birdlike female with a head of improbable gold curls and a bony angular figure, which a taste for low-cut clinging gowns did nothing to enhance. Her voice was breathless and childlike, and that together with her air of fragile femininity might once have held a certain appeal. In a lady of her mature years the effect was, unfortunately, rather ridiculous and she was clearly no match for a woman of Mrs Harvey's forceful personality.

Mrs Harvey smiled broadly, the way a crocodile might do before it proceeded to devour its prey thought Sylvestra idly.

'Julia Harvey? Lady Buckminster's breakfast? I am sure I do not wonder at you not remembering me, such a crush as it was! Dear Lady Buckminster, her parties are always such a success, I declare I quite envy her!'

Sylvestra and Emily could only look on in wide-eyed wonder at this piece of outrageous audacity. To their certain knowledge, Mrs Harvey had never even met Lady Buckminster let alone attended one of her entertainments. It was a calculated risk on Mrs Harvey's part, and it paid dividends. Lady Leimster had been thinking of how to politely extricate herself from the clutches of Mrs Harvey, whom she had privately stigmatized as a vulgar, pushing woman, but the mention of Lady Buckminster's name put an entirely different complexion on matters. Lady Buckminster was one of the most influential matrons of the ton and an invitation to one of her very select gatherings immediately conferred social acceptability upon the recipient.

Magically, Lady Leimster's smile became warmer, and she said with a good deal more sincerity, 'Why, of course, Mrs Harvey, what a pleasure!' and then to the Sylvestra and Emily, 'We must find you young ladies partners, though I can see that will not be a problem, for you are both such pretty girls!'

Lady Leimster's prediction proved correct, although Sylvestra shrewdly suspected that her popularity had a great deal more to do with her wealth than any particular admiration for her person.

However, she had come to the conclusion that until Mrs Harvey's plans for her became clear, she might just as well try and make the best of it. And so she graciously accepted the invitations to dance and curbed the acidic retorts that sprang to her lips at the fulsome compliments showered upon her by her partners, all of which she considered to be as ridiculous as they were insincere. Mr Wynchip was the exception to this, as not even Sylvestra could doubt that the admiration he professed was genuine. His hopes would have received a severe set-back had he known that the object of his worship viewed his attempts to captivate her with considerable amusement.

Few ladies could remain impervious to a handsome young man, especially if he has a tendency to gaze ardently into their eyes whilst reciting a sonnet dedicated to those 'twin orbs of emerald light'. Sylvestra Harvey was one of those few. Perhaps Mr Wynchip would have been more successful had he not attempted to declaim this ode to his partner's beauty during the course of a country dance. When the movement of the dance separated them the poet's whispered words must perforce be broken off, and Mr Wynchip had to content himself with sending smouldering looks across the floor, surely designed to set Sylvestra's knees trembling. It was her lips rather than her limbs these antics set aquiver, but Aubrey Wynchip was moderately satisfied with the effect of his art, wrongly taking the bright eyes and flushed countenance to be a sign of enchantment, rather than barely controlled mirth. With a last burning look that threatened to completely overset her, Mr Wynchip reluctantly relinquished Sylvestra to her next partner, Sir Horace Royston.

There could be no greater contrast between two men. Sir Horace was a big, bluff man, clearly uncomfortable in his fashionable evening wear. But he shared one similarity with Aubrey Wynchip, and that was the need to marry money. Only the threat of losing his precious hunters had persuaded Sir Horace to give in to his sisters' entreaties and come to London in search of a wealthy wife. If they expected him to go to any extraordinary lengths to woo the fortunate lady he set his sights on then they were to be disappointed. 'I'm no great hand at this dancing game, but if you want to take a turn with me then I'd be obliged to you, Miss Harvey,' was the charming way in which he had solicited Sylvestra's hand for the cotillion.

Now, as he led her on to the floor, Sylvestra could not resist asking him in sweetly innocent tones if he had any aptitude for poetry. He threw her a frightened look, before saying bluntly, 'You'll not get any fancy words out of me!'

Apparently she would not get words of any description out of him, since Sir Horace needed to focus all his concentration on the execution of the dance steps. This he did with a good deal more enthusiasm than grace, and it was lucky for Sylvestra that her own movements were more deft or her feet would quickly have become black and blue. The hated gown was not so fortunate. The dance was barely half over when an audible rip brought welcome escape for Sylvestra, whose fear for her own feet was secondary to that for her partner's health. The stifling heat of the ballroom and his own energetic antics had turned Sir Horace an alarming shade of puce.

'Oh, my dress!' she exclaimed, adding with more relief than regret, 'I am afraid you must excuse me, Sir Horace, I will have to mend this tear.' And before her breathless partner had chance to offer to escort her, Sylvestra was threading her way through the crowded ballroom. Leaving the heat and clamour thankfully behind, Sylvestra set off in search of the ladies' retiring room. Mrs Harvey had been at pains to point out its location, for not even the fairest complexion can retain its perfection in such adverse conditions, and Emily and Sylvestra were under strict instructions to attend to their appearance at least twice during the course of the evening. Wandering in vain from room to room, Sylvestra wished she had paid closer attention to her aunt. Lady Leimster's town-house was an old building and therefore not blessed with the spacious apartments of its more modern counterparts. Consequently, Sylvestra was soon lost amongst the labyrinth of small irregular salons and narrow twisting passages.

Walking through yet another door only to find herself for the third time in the library, Sylvestra let out an exclamation of disgust, and plumping herself down on the nearest chair resolved to deal with the trailing flounce in a brutal but effective manner. It was only when she had the stitching holding the ruffle of pink tulle to the hem of her gown gripped firmly between her strong white teeth that some sixth sense warned her she was not alone. Looking up sharply, she met the amused gaze of a pair of startling blue eyes. They belonged to a gentleman, who, when he emerged from the shadows, proved to be both tall and well built. He was also, Sylvestra found herself thinking, quite irrelevantly given the circumstances, the most attractive man she had ever seen. For a few moments, his hooded blue eyes held her transfixed and then they left her face and travelled lazily and insolently down the length of Sylvestra's long and shapely legs, which she had inadvertently exposed in her impatience to deal with her gown.

Released from his hypnotic gaze, Sylvestra abruptly let go of the hem of her gown, and flushed to the roots of her hair. The gentleman's eyes returned to her face, but his countenance betrayed no embarrassment at his decidedly *de trop* presence. Sylvestra quickly got to her feet, determined to deliver this insufferable coxcomb a freezing set down. She found that even then she was forced to tilt her head upwards to meet that mocking gaze. For some reason this only served to compound his wrongdoing.

'Sir, if you were any sort of a gentleman you would have excused yourself as soon as you realized my predicament.'

The gentleman's well-shaped lips twitched infuriatingly. 'It would be a poor gentleman who deserted a damsel in distress.'

'I would hardly describe a torn flounce as "distress". Besides I am quite able to manage, so you may leave with a clear conscience,' responded Sylvestra with heavy irony.

The gentleman threw back his head and laughed aloud. 'You are clearly a resourceful young lady. Tell me, is that the usual method by which you ladies deal with these little misfortunes? I would never have guessed. It seems I have underestimated your sex.'

The vision his words conjured up, of the high and mighty ladies of the ton wrestling violently with their apparel behind closed doors before emerging serene and perfect into the ballroom was too much for Sylvestra and she gave a choke of reluctant laughter.

'If you must know, sir, we ladies are very well provided for in these circumstances.' She added ruefully, 'Or would be if we had the least notion where to find the retiring room.'

The gentleman smiled at her in sympathy and to her chagrin, Sylvestra felt colour suffuse her cheeks once more. Really, she chastised herself, you are behaving like the veriest simpleton, blushing like a schoolgirl just because a handsome man smiles at you! But he was doing more than just smile at her, he was moving towards her and his sudden proximity startled Sylvestra into taking a step back. A mistake, as the chair she had risen from so hastily was directly behind her and, just as quickly, she found herself sitting again, consequently putting herself at an even greater disadvantage with this disturbing man who now towered over her.

'What are you doing?' demanded Sylvestra, unable to keep a note of panic from her voice.

The blue eyes danced wickedly. 'Why, rescuing the damsel in distress, of course,' he murmured provocatively, as he leaned towards her. Sylvestra shrank back in her chair thoroughly alarmed, but his attention was not focused on her but on the desk top behind her. For a brief moment her nostrils were filled with the masculine aroma of sandalwood and clean linen before he stepped back, a pair of scissors in his hand.

'I think these will serve the purpose better, don't you?'

Sylvestra nodded dumbly and could only watch helplessly as he sank to his knees before her and, with deft fingers and judicious use of the scissors, removed the offending flounce. The gentleman then sat back on his heels and looked up at Sylvestra saying mournfully, 'I am afraid it is beyond repair.'

Sylvestra snatched the sorry strip of fabric from him, now limp and dusty from her perambulation through the corridors of the Leimster house. 'What a shame,' she sighed, matching his tone. 'And I declare it was quite my favourite gown.' She darted him a challenging look from beneath demurely lowered eyelids. Let us see how the silver-tongued rogue copes with that. Doubtless he would pay her some trite compliment just like all the other posturing fools she had encountered that evening.

He succeeded in surprising her, responding promptly and with deceptive sincerity, 'Oh, you may take my word for it, the loss of one little ruffle does not detract one jot from the overall effect.'

Sylvestra's eyes flew open and a gurgle of laughter rose to her lips, the gentleman smiled at her encouragingly and all of a sudden she felt herself relaxing. It was impossible to withstand the warmth of that smile. But she had not completely surrendered.

'Several gentlemen have complimented me on my appearance this evening,' she announced airily.

The gentleman sank his chin in his hands and studied her face with frowning concentration. 'Ah, then you must be Miss Harvey. Am I right?'

'You are indeed! But I am at a loss as to how you arrived at that conclusion!' exclaimed Sylvestra.

'Oh, it is really very easy to deduce. You see, my dear, heiresses are *always* beautiful.'

It was Sylvestra's turn to surprise her companion, for instead of bridling at this most ungentlemanly remark, she laughed aloud with genuine amusement. 'And from that I must deduce that you are as rich as Croesus to be able to afford such plain speaking!'

He joined in her laughter, grasping her hands and pulling her to her feet. 'Come, you must return to the ballroom or your reputation as well as your gown will be in tatters!'

Sylvestra shrugged. 'If it would drive my supposed suitors away then it would almost be worth it.'

'Ah! Does this explain the choice of ball gown?'

'Well, no,' admitted Sylvestra. 'My Aunt Julia's appalling taste is solely responsible for that. But I must own I had rather hoped it would frighten them off!'

The gentleman shook his head decidedly. 'No. You might go to Almack's in a potato sack and still be admired.'

Sylvestra laughed at this. 'You have no very high opinion of your peers, sir,' she observed. 'Is this why you hide yourself away in the library at the height of a ball?'

A shadow seemed to pass fleetingly across his handsome face, but he merely answered lightly, 'You have caught me out. You see, I know for a fact that old Leimster keeps a bottle of his best claret in here and I have come in search of it.'

Sylvestra sensed she had touched a nerve and wisely did not pursue the point, but allowed him to lead her unerringly in the direction of the ballroom. He halted outside the door saying, 'It would be better for you not to be seen entering on my arm, so I shall bid you good night, Miss Harvey.'

'Thank you. . . . Oh, I don't even know who you are!' exclaimed Sylvestra laughingly.

The gentleman gave her a crooked smile. 'My name is Evelyn Carston. As to who I am and what I am . . . well, you will discover that soon enough.' And with that enigmatic remark he was gone, leaving Sylvestra nothing to do but enter once more into the fray of Lady Leimster's ball.

Four

Sylvestra fidgeted restlessly on the hard, backless sofa and with an impatient sigh tossed aside her novel to join her already abandoned embroidery. Entertaining as Mrs Radcliffe's prose was, Sylvestra did not share her cousin's acute sensibilities and so could find little sympathy for a heroine who, if she was not succumbing to the vapours, was composing verse more awful than her fate.

The Harveys were 'At Home' to callers. Mrs Harvey had informed her daughter and niece, with a good deal of satisfaction, that they could expect to receive calls from all the gentlemen with whom they had danced the night before. This was not a prospect designed to appeal to Sylvestra who had not the slightest desire to further her acquaintance with any of the gallants she had met. Well, perhaps there was one. An involuntary smile touched Sylvestra's lips as she thought of the mysterious Evelyn Carston. He, at least, had not insulted her intelligence with shallow protestations of admiration. But then as he had not asked her to dance there was little likelihood of his calling upon them.

Sylvestra sighed again, rose to her feet and crossed to the window. It was a fresh spring morning, the sun shone in a cloudless sky and in the square opposite, daffodils nodded their heads in the gentle breeze. Sylvestra thought longingly of Earlam Park and her feisty little mare, Conny. A morning like this should be spent galloping across the downs. Sylvestra closed her eyes, she could almost feel the cool wind against her face, the exhilarating sensation of speed as the rolling grassland sped beneath her horse's flying hooves.

'Sylvestra, come and sit down at once! Really, there is nothing so ill bred as to be gawping out of the window for all the world to see.'

Mrs Harvey's words rudely jolted Sylvestra back to reality. Without bothering to argue, she returned to her uncomfortable chair casting a jaundiced eye over her surroundings. In the unforgiving morning sunlight, the splendours of the Nile room had taken on a rather tawdry appearance, a poor substitute in Sylvestra's opinion for the uplifting beauty of the English countryside on a spring day.

The sound of activity in the hallway heralded the arrival of their first visitors. 'Don't slouch so, Sylvestra!' whispered her aunt fiercely, before rising majestically to her feet, a smile of welcome pinned to her plump features.

'Mrs Clive and Mr Frederick Clive,' announced the butler.

'Alicia! My dear sister! Come in, come in! And Frederick too. What a lovely surprise!'

Mrs Alicia Clive was a younger and more attractive version of Mrs Harvey. They shared the same features but where Julia Harvey's countenance was marred even in repose by a permanent look of discontent, Mrs Clive's expression was altogether more placid. Alicia had never shared Julia's burning ambition to make a mark within society. She would have been very happy to move in the first circles as long as it did not demand any extraordinary effort upon her part. She was essentially an idle woman and it was only her genuine attachment to her son Frederick that had caused her to bestir herself and come to London that he might court her sister's wealthy niece. Neither was she a woman of high intellect as could be judged by her puzzled response to her sister's greeting.

'Well, I don't know how you can say it is a surprise, Julia, when it was you who especially requested us to call.'

'The pleasure is all ours, Aunt,' intervened Mr Clive smoothly, earning himself a warm smile of approval from Mrs Harvey.

'Why Alicia, I must congratulate you. Your son has grown into a fine young man. Isn't that so, Emily?'

Emily was spared the necessity of responding by Mr Clive's exclamation of feigned surprise. 'Surely this fashionable young miss cannot be my little Cousin Emily? It is I who must congratulate *you*, Aunt Harvey. To have not just one – here he directed a smug bow in Emily's direction – 'but two' – the obeisance was repeated for Sylvestra's benefit – 'beautiful young ladies beneath the same roof is an achievement indeed.' Mr Clive rocked back on his heels and smiled unctuously, evidently pleased with his attempt at gallantry.

Mrs Harvey gave a trill of false laughter, saying with terrible archness, 'Girls, you must beware! Cousin Frederick is clearly an accomplished flirt!'

This playful remark brought a frown to Mr Clive's heavy, square features and he said in tones of mild reproof, 'I hope I would never *flirt*, Aunt Harvey. I have always considered flirting an activity unbecoming in a gentleman of honour. Particularly in one whose intention it is to join the ranks of the clergy.'

There followed a pregnant pause during which Mrs Harvey wrestled with her desire to promote a match between Mr Clive and her niece and her instinctive urge to deliver a stinging set down to her pompous nephew. In the end, the more deep-seated resolution to secure Sylvestra's wealth for her family won out, and with a restraint that astonished her daughter and niece she said with determined cordiality, 'I am sure your sentiments do you great credit, Frederick. Don't you agree, Sylvestra?'

'What? Oh, er, very . . . very commendable, Mr Clive,' said Sylvestra, taken off guard by this unprecedented solicitation of her opinion.

Mr Clive smiled at her benignly. 'Miss Harvey – dare I say, Sylvestra? After all we are cousins of a sort. It is a great pleasure to meet you at last; my Aunt Harvey has spoken very highly of you to my mother.'

Sylvestra's eyes widened in disbelief, and even Mrs Harvey had the grace to look discomfited at this palpable untruth. She hastily intervened before Mr Clive could enlarge upon this theme.

'How remiss of me! Sylvestra, dear, this is my sister Alicia Clive and her son Frederick. As you have so astutely guessed, Frederick, this is my niece, Sylvestra Harvey. There! Now that we all know one another we can sit down and have a comfortable coze! Emily, my love, will you ring for some tea?'

Mr Clive, who was an enthusiastic collaborator in the plan to tie him to a wealthy wife, took the opportunity to seat himself beside Sylvestra with the intention of engaging her in conversation. His opening gambit did little to recommend him to his companion, saying as he did in a manner intended to be jocular, 'Well, now, Sylvestra, I hope you are not letting all this gay dissipation go to your head.'

In a gentleman of more mature years this might just have been forgivable; in someone no more than two or three years her senior Sylvestra found it unbearably patronizing.

'I shall endeavour not to let it,' she replied silkily. Sarcasm was apparently wasted upon Mr Clive who beamed at her approvingly and said he was glad to hear it. He then launched into an extremely tedious monologue on the evils of idleness and frivolity which had she bothered to attend, Sylvestra would doubtless have found very instructive. She was, however, unashamedly eavesdropping on the conversation between her aunt and Mrs Clive, which was proving far more interesting than anything Mr Clive had to say.

Sylvestra was quietly enjoying Mrs Harvey's grossly exaggerated account of the magnificence of Lady Leimster's ball and the effusiveness of the hostess's welcome, which was being listened to with gratifying envy by Mrs Clive.

That lady presently intervened to ask eagerly, 'Then you will have met Lord Evelyn Carston?'

The presence of Mr Clive was instantly forgotten as Sylvestra strained to hear more.

'Lord Evelyn Carston?' repeated Mrs Harvey, in a tone of voice which suggested that since she had never heard the name, its possessor could hardly be worthy of her notice.

Mrs Clive was very happy to elaborate; after all her sister's boasting it was not dissatisfying to discover Julia was not quite so at the hub of fashionable life as she professed.

'I am sorry, I should have said the Marquis of Derwent. Last night was his first appearance in public since his return from the Continent.'

Mrs Harvey greeted this information with a dismissive wave of her hand. 'You are out there, Alicia. As I understand it the Marquis of Derwent and his wife were drowned in a boating accident several months ago.'

'You are talking of *Vincent* Carston, Julia. The Duke of Were has another son, Lord Evelyn, and he has inherited the title.'

Mrs Harvey was still not convinced. She prided herself upon her knowledge of the intricate network of relationships which bound together the English nobility; she could not believe that the son of a duke, even a younger son, would have escaped her notice.

'Really, Alicia, I think you are getting muddled. You have no doubt misunderstood. Depend upon it, I would have known if that were the case.'

But Mrs Clive was insistent. 'I assure you it is true. Of course, he has been out of the country for years on account of the scandal. I have heard it said that the duke forbade his name to be mentioned in his presence! But now he is the heir, so His Grace is obliged to accept him.'

'What scandal?' demanded Mrs Harvey, immediately homing in on the crux of the matter. 'I suppose it was a duel. Did he kill the man?'

Alicia Clive shook her head. 'Oh no! It was much worse than

that.' She leaned forward and whispered conspiratorially, 'It was a woman.'

Mrs Harvey refused to be shocked by this revelation. 'Good Lord, Alicia. Is that all?'

'But, Julia, she was not a – that is to say she was not one of *those* women. She came from a good family.'

'Mother!' Mr Clive had also been monitoring his parent's conversation, but for different reasons to Sylvestra. 'Mother, I hardly think this is a suitable subject for the drawing-room. You would not wish to sully innocent ears with such a sordid tale I hope.'

'No indeed, Frederick,' acquiesced Mrs Clive looking deflated. There was nothing she enjoyed more than a good gossip, but since her husband's death, her son had gradually taken over as head of their little household to a point where Mrs Clive now naturally turned to him for guidance in every matter. Sylvestra could have screamed aloud with frustration. So near and yet so far from discovering the truth about the mysterious Evelyn Carston. Mrs Harvey, however, was not put off so easily. Having had her appetite whetted she would not be satisfied until she had heard the whole. Besides, it was clearly high time her nephew was put in his place.

'Frederick, much as I appreciate your concern, I think you should allow your mother and me to be the best judge of what is suitable. As the chaperon of two young ladies about to make their entrance into the world, it is my duty to be aware of all the dangers that await them.'

Mr Clive was as little used to having his opinion challenged as Mrs Harvey, but he also prided himself on his good manners, and he conceded defeat with a stiff inclination of his head. 'Naturally then, Aunt Harvey, I shall say no more.' He then turned his attention back to Sylvestra, pointedly turning his shoulder on his mother and aunt and their shocking conversation, and slightly raising his voice in a futile attempt to shield the innocent ears of

Sylvestra and Emily. It would have taken a far more enthralling orator than Mr Clive to hold the interest of two young ladies when the alternative was the scandalous tale of a handsome young lord, disowned by his family for some yet undisclosed but doubtless heinous crime.

Mr Clive's opinion on the beneficial effects of rigorous exercise on both the body and mind were, therefore, destined never to receive the attention they deserved, whereas a far more unsavoury topic of conversation was being recalled, recounted and embellished in every drawing-room in the capital.

'Her name was Marianne Devenish,' began Mrs Clive, before pausing, partly for dramatic effect but essentially to avail herself of one of the excellent macaroons sitting invitingly upon the tea tray. Her appetite satisfied and her audience hooked, Mrs Clive continued, 'Marianne was quite the most ravishing beauty of the season, though, of course, I believe blondes were all the rage that year. She was the daughter of Lord and Lady Devenish, but both her parents died whilst she was still in the nursery. She was brought up by her grandmother, old Lady Devenish, and a more spoilt and indulged child it would be hard to find. I don't believe she was ever denied anything and she teased her poor grandmother relentlessly until she was permitted to make her debut when she was scarcely sixteen years of age, which I think you will agree, Julia, is far too young.'

'Indeed it is. I am surprised at Lady Devenish allowing such a thing. Even with the benefits of the education my dear Emily has received – Miss Pinner's establishment was very select, you know – I would hesitate.'

'Quite. And you may be sure you would not have found a lady to disagree with you. The gentlemen were not so discerning. What we would condemn as unbecoming boldness, they were pleased to describe as innocent youthfulness. Not even her lack of fortune served to deter her suitors, of which, I might add, she had an almost indecent number. Why if I had been the mother of a daughter I dare say I would have wept at the injustice of it.'

'But what of Evelyn Carston?' demanded Mrs Harvey impatiently, unknowingly asking the question uppermost in the mind of her niece.

'Well, that is what made it all the more shocking, for Lord Evelyn Carston never formed one of her court. Oh, I dare say he stood up with her at Almack's once or twice but no one would have suspected that— but I am getting ahead of myself. The season progressed and the gentlemen, in their odious way, were placing bets as to who would win the hand and heart of the fair Marianne.' Mrs Clive gave a self-conscious titter. 'I believe the term to describe the betting is "open". Miss Devenish, although the most atrocious flirt, had never shown the least partiality for any of her admirers—'

'Really, Alicia, I wish you would spare us these cant expressions and get to the point,' interposed Mrs Harvey irritably.

Mrs Clive, who was relishing her rare moment of glory and was not about to be hurried, ignored this rude interruption, and after a dignified pause, continued. 'The season was at its height when all of a sudden the Devenishes left town. The official reason was an indisposition of Lady Devenish, the rumour was that it was Miss Devenish who had caused the unseemly haste of their departure.

'Well, months went by and Marianne Devenish was all but forgotten. The ton were looking forward to the most dazzling event of the year, the marriage of Vincent Carston, the Marquis of Derwent, to Lady Elizabeth Versoe. The ceremony was to take place at the chapel at Were and everybody who is anybody was there. Then, just as the vows were about to be taken, who should walk in but Marianne Devenish!' Mrs Clive dropped her voice to a theatrical whisper. '*With child.*'

She was not disappointed with the reaction this disclosure provoked. Mrs Harvey gave an affronted gasp. 'Surely not!'

Mrs Clive nodded her head vigorously. 'It is the truth, Julia, every word!'

'What happened?'

Mrs Clive was happy to satisfy her curiosity. 'Silence fell in the church. Then, quite clearly and distinctly, Vincent Carston said, "For God's sake Eve, what can have possessed you to invite your whore to the wedding of Lady Elizabeth".'

'Alicia!' exclaimed Mrs Harvey, clapping her hands to her ears.

Mrs Clive blushed. 'Well, I am only telling you what was said,' she argued defensively.

'Well, I should prefer it if you limited yourself to the bare facts, I am not used to such language under my roof.'

'Indeed, Mother, I am shocked,' interpolated Mr Clive, rigorous exercise momentarily forgotten. 'You know how I abhor this kind of scandalmongering. All Aunt Harvey need know is that Lord Evelyn was obliged to resign his commission and he and the unfortunate young woman left these shores and entered a life of shame and exile on the Continent. The fact that the man is now Marquis of Derwent will not elevate him in my esteem, nor I would hope in that of any person of sound morals and Christian principles. And now, with your permission, Aunt, this unpleasant subject may be dropped.'

Having learned all she needed to know, Mrs Harvey was content to let the conversation move on to less controversial ground. But although she would certainly have claimed as many Christian principles as her nephew, in her view a marquis was still a marquis and not to be sniffed at however shady his past. In fact, that might even work to her advantage, for surely Derwent would want to firmly quash any lingering rumours of his rakish lifestyle by marrying some unexceptional young lady. It was a short step in the workings of Mrs Harvey's logic to see Emily as the new Marchioness of Derwent. This happy thought brought a slight satisfied smile to her thin lips.

Breakfast at Derwent House the morning after the Leimster ball was a subdued affair, remarkable only for a lack of conviviality. It was Marianne's usual custom to take the first meal of the day in her own rooms, but on this occasion she was determined Evelyn should not suspect her of childish sulking following their contretemps of the previous evening. Furthermore, though she would never have admitted to it, Marianne was agog to hear Evelyn's account of the ball. So starved was she of the social life she loved above all else, even a second-hand report was something to be seized upon. On the other hand, it would not do for him to interpret this deviation from her usual habits as a sign of surrender. Marianne, therefore, preserved a dignified silence as she poured her chocolate and buttered two thin slices of bread. Since Evelyn limited his own conversation to a perfunctory greeting before returning to his paper, this strategy was not a great success.

Marianne sipped her chocolate and nibbled her bread and covertly watched her companion. His attention appeared to be equally divided between *The Times* and a plate of devilled kidneys. Marianne felt her temper rising. There was nothing she hated more than to be ignored. All her life she had known there were two certain ways of getting her own way – tears and tantrums. Evelyn had proved himself indifferent to both. Beneath the table, Marianne's hands clenched into angry claws, and it was only with a supreme effort of will that she maintained her serene expression. But, as the silence lengthened and her companion showed not the slightest inclination to break it, Marianne's curiosity inevitably got the better of her.

'I am surprised to find you up and about so early after last night's ball, Eve. I swear I never rose before noon during the season.'

Evelyn looked up from his paper and smiled sympathetically. Despite her attempts at superb indifference, Marianne could not prevent a wistful note from creeping into her seemingly casual remark.

'I dare say, Marianne, that you would have danced 'til dawn, and been among the last to leave. I, on the other hand, did not take to the floor once and left before the more fashionable guests had even deigned to make an appearance.'

Marianne set her cup down with a clatter, exclaiming indignantly, 'Oh, what a waste! I don't believe you even wanted to go! Why, I think you only went to spite me!'

This made Evelyn laugh. 'I am glad I have managed to convince you that I have no taste for the fashionable pursuits you rate so highly, but my dear, do you really think I would put myself out to such a degree purely to spite you?'

Marianne flushed angrily. 'I am sure I would not put anything past you, Evelyn. What am I supposed to think when you have never entered into my feelings on any subject? All you ever do is laugh at me or ignore me.'

'Does it seem that way? I am sorry for it. Believe me, I have a great deal of sympathy for your plight. I know you find it intolerable and if I could go back in time I should do things very differently. But it is useless to repine. All I can do – we both can do – is make the best of the situation until all is put to rights.'

'Oh, very well,' said Marianne, slightly mollified. 'But I wish it didn't take so long! I believe I shall go mad if I spend many more days cooped up in this house, and Edward is so demanding it quite wears me to a thread trying to keep him entertained.'

'Ah, now there I can help,' said Evelyn cheerfully. 'I have engaged a nurse, a Mrs Pierce. She will be with you sometime this afternoon.'

Marianne visibly brightened at this piece of news. She was, as she would willingly tell anyone who cared to listen, a devoted mother, and quite happy to have her darling Edward at her side if only he could be brought to sit quietly. Edward, a lively and inquisitive five year old, understandably thought this very poor sport, and had discovered that the kitchens and the stables offered far more scope for his talents than the rarefied atmosphere of the drawing-room.

'Well, I am glad at least one of my requests has not fallen on deaf ears,' said Marianne, not entirely graciously. Adding, 'Though

I must say I think it very high-handed of you to engage the woman without consulting me first. I am the child's mother after all.'

'Under normal circumstances I would have happily left the job to you, Marianne, but you could hardly have interviewed a string of candidates, could you? By lucky coincidence, the housekeeper was able to recommend Mrs Pierce, a relative or close friend, the exact connection escapes me. You may find her a trifle dour and she is perhaps a little old for such a lively young imp as Edward, but her references are excellent and I think she will be discreet.'

In no mood to be pleased by anything Evelyn said, Marianne would have argued the point further had the butler not entered at that moment to inform his master that a Mr Giles Cameron was in the hall.

'Giles Cameron!' exclaimed Marianne, instantly diverted. 'Why he was quite one of my favourite admirers. He was used to say some vastly pretty things. Show him in, Benton, show him in!'

The butler looked to Evelyn for guidance, who said repressively, 'You may take Mr Cameron to my study, Benton, I will be with him directly.' He waited for the butler to exit the room before addressing Marianne, who was looking decidedly mulish.

'Don't even bother to argue, Marianne. You may renew your acquaintance with Giles at a later date. Now, oblige me by staying out of sight until he has left.' And with that he was gone before Marianne could even think of a convincing argument.

'Giles, this is an unexpected pleasure.'

Mr Cameron, who had his back to the door when Evelyn entered the study, spun round, a belligerent frown marring his usually amiable features.

'And what is so damned unexpected about it?' he demanded, his slender figure fairly bristling with indignation.

Far from being put out by this aggressive greeting, Lord Evelyn looked if anything faintly amused. 'Or indeed pleasant, for that matter,' he murmured.

This provoked a snort of reluctant laughter from Mr Cameron. 'Damn you, Carston, you have not lost that devilish sharp tongue. But what I want to know is why you didn't come and see me the minute you arrived in London? Blast it all, Eve, a chap don't want to hear it off the gossips that his best friend – whom he has not set eyes on for the best part of six years *and* who has not even had the decency to let him know if he is alive or dead – is in town!'

Evelyn could not help smiling at this convoluted catalogue of Mr Cameron's grievances. He said simply, 'I did not want to presume upon our friendship, Giles.'

'Presume?' repeated Mr Cameron in disbelief. '*Presume?* I have never been so insulted in my life! A fine fellow you must think me.'

'Yes. A fine fellow, and the best of friends, which is why I would never take advantage of your good nature, Giles,' argued Evelyn earnestly. 'I would not drag you down with me.'

'Drag me down where? The depths of depravity?' put in Mr Cameron with heavy irony. 'Credit me with a grain of intelligence, Eve! The scandalmongers may say what they like, I know better. I know you have never done a dishonourable thing in your life.'

Evelyn gripped his friend's shoulder, visibly moved by such staunch loyalty it was a moment before he could bring himself to speak, and then it was haltingly, his voice thick with emotion. 'Giles, what I did . . . what I did, well, it may not have been dishonourable but it was foolish, foolish beyond permission. And the consequences. . . .' He shook his head helplessly. 'If what I begin to suspect is true, then the consequences are far worse than anyone imagines.'

Giles Cameron was shaken, as much by the bleak expression in his friend's eyes as by the intensity of his words. He longed to ask more, but already Evelyn had moved on, speaking of other matters in that faintly bantering familiar way of his.

'Well I am back, Giles, and sadly behind the times. I rely on you to fill me in or I shall look a regular flat before I am much older!'

Giles recognized the signs; he would learn no more today. With an effort he matched Carston's lighter mood and obliged him by updating him on the various crim. con. stories presently circulating the ton.

'There is a new heiress in town. I have not myself had the honour, but the word is she is something of a quiz. Was there ever an heiress otherwise?'

'Ah, now there you have been misinformed" interjected Evelyn. 'Not a quiz, just burdened with an aunt, who, if my theory is correct, does not wish her rich niece to outshine her less-well circumstanced daughter.'

'And where did you have the opportunity to form such an opinion?' asked Giles laughingly.

'Why at the Leimster Ball, naturally,' responded Evelyn.

'You went to the Leimster Ball!' exclaimed his friend in thunderstruck tones, the merits or otherwise of the latest heiress instantly forgotten.

Evelyn laughed in genuine amusement at Giles's reaction. 'But of course. Did you think I would not receive an entrée into polite society? Believe me, a marquis is forgiven a good deal more than a commoner!'

'You need not tell me that! I don't doubt you were fawned upon to a nauseating degree; after all, you are quite a catch. What surprises me is that you choose to pander to such hypocrisy,' responded Giles with some warmth.

'Strange, isn't it? Perhaps I gain some perverse pleasure in watching that inner struggle between morality and avarice,' said Evelyn whimsically.

Mr Cameron snorted derisively. 'I'll warrant morality put up a poor show.'

'Oh, indeed. But the ton have not quite succeeded in squaring me with their collective conscience. I suspect I am invited purely for my value as a freak. I believe I would probably rate above the strong man but below the bearded lady. As with those poor creatures they whisper and stare, but only the brave dare approach.'

'And the heiress was brave?' hazarded Mr Cameron.

'Why, Giles, age has lent you a perspicacity I never dreamt you could possess!' exclaimed Evelyn in mock admiration. 'But I fear it was ignorance rather than bravery which allowed me to insinuate myself into Miss Harvey's good graces. No doubt the good aunt will have been busy since.'

'Aye. She'll be throwing the chit at your head given the slightest encouragement,' opined Mr Cameron cynically.

'I wonder,' mused Evelyn, and then with purpose, 'Well, let us discover for ourselves. Come along, Giles! You are going to meet the heiress!'

'You surely don't mean to call upon her?' expostulated Mr Cameron.

'I see no reason why I shouldn't,' replied Evelyn calmly.

'But it would stir up just the sort of speculation I would have thought you'd be at pains to avoid – tongues will already be wagging after you singled her out at last night's affair.'

'Now, there you are wrong, Giles. My encounter with Miss Harvey went entirely unnoticed.'

Mr Cameron shook his head. 'The latest heiress and the most notorious rake in town? It will be all over London by noon!'

Evelyn looked amused. 'The most notorious rake in town? Well, that's a title to live up to at any rate.'

'I'm only saying what the gossips will say, Eve. Take my advice and steer well clear. That Harvey woman will have you in the parson's mousetrap before you can blink!'

It was Evelyn's turn to shake his head. 'Believe me there is no danger of that, my old friend. Besides, you are wrong. My er . . . tête-à-tête with Miss Harvey was well out of sight of prying eyes.'

This made his friend eye him suspiciously. 'There's something you're not telling me Carston, cut line!'

The blue eyes twinkled wickedly. 'Nothing of note, Giles, I promise you. I chanced to encounter Miss Harvey in the library at Leimster House rather than the ballroom, that is all.'

'Well she sounds a havey-cavey sort of girl to me, meeting men she don't know in libraries!' pronounced Mr Cameron.

Evelyn laughed and said, 'Have I offended your sense of propriety, Giles? 'Twas totally innocent I promise you.' And with that he favoured Mr Cameron with a truncated version of his meeting with Sylvestra.

Giles listened in silence and then said triumphantly, 'Well, that settles it, you cannot possibly go calling on a girl whom you ain't been properly introduced to. Simply isn't done!'

'But surely "the most notorious rake in town" would not let such considerations weigh with him? Besides, if what you say is true, Mrs Harvey will be in such high alt to see me under her roof that my unconventionality will be overlooked!'

Five

Lord Evelyn had his way and within the half-hour the two men were mounting the steps of the house in Green Street. The morning was by then considerably advanced and the company in Mrs Harvey's drawing-room had been swelled by several new arrivals. Mr Wynchip had been the first, clutching an untidy sheaf of papers covered with the results of his recent poetic exertions. Sir Horace, yielding to the promptings of his sisters, was not far behind bearing a more conventional offering in the form of a posy of spring flowers. Sylvestra accepted these tributes with equal expressions of gratitude, not wishing either gentleman to think himself particularly favoured. Emily, too, had her callers in the shape of two shy and inarticulate young men fresh up from Oxford. These gentleman on their first foray into London society, and as their fond parents were wont to say, not quite up to snuff, finding the dazzling and fashionable beauties of the ton rather intimidating and unapproachable, had immediately been attracted by Emily Harvey's gentle, unassuming disposition.

Needless to say this influx of young men, none of whom had either wealth or particular social standing to recommend him, found little favour with Mrs Harvey. Lord Evelyn Carston was therefore guaranteed the warmest of receptions whatever his pretext for calling. In the event, the vague and totally fabricated reference to a mutual acquaintance was barely attended to as Mrs Harvey hastened to usher in her new guests.

'Lord Carston, you are more than welcome. Won't you join us for tea? I was just about to ring for the tray,' she gushed, before performing the most perfunctory of introductions. Then, with a skill peculiar to the mothers of marriageable daughters, she endeavoured to manoeuvre Lord Evelyn into a chair beside Emily, saying sweetly, 'I shall leave it to Emily to entertain you. Now, Emily dear, make sure his lordship gets one of cook's macaroons before they all disappear.' With that she took herself off, satisfied that she had given her daughter the perfect opportunity to ensnare her marquis.

'Would . . . would you care for a macaroon, Lord Carston?' asked Emily obediently, but a little weakly. It seemed to an over-awed Emily that a man of the marquis's overpowering physical presence and rakehell reputation would surely be more than capable of securing cakes for himself if he so desired.

'Thank you no, Miss Emily, tea will be quite sufficient,' responded Lord Evelyn kindly, laughter dancing in his blue eyes. He had encountered many match-making mothers in the past, but he rather thought Mrs Harvey was going to prove something out of the ordinary. He chanced to look up and meet Sylvestra's gaze, the unholy glee in those green eyes clear evidence that she had heard and appreciated every word.

'Miss Harvey, you have an unusual name, does it have any significance?' he asked. His voice was deep and pleasant and had the effect of capturing the attention of everyone in the room.

'Sylvestra is named after my sister-in-law's father, Sylvester, Earl of Beckham, you know,' pronounced Mrs Harvey, disliking the attention her exalted guest was giving her niece but not about to let an opportunity to boast of her grand connections go begging.

'Your sister-in-law's father,' repeated Lord Evelyn with a slight frown. 'Ah, I see, Miss Harvey's grandfather!' he exclaimed, his brow clearing as if he had just fathomed out Mrs Harvey's rather distant and convoluted connection to the earl. Mrs Harvey flushed with annoyance and regarded him with suspicion. She was rewarded with a bland, lazy smile that left her doubting the mischievous intent behind his words.

Mr Wynchip meanwhile, who was torn between reluctant admiration for the wicked marquis and a determination to protect Miss Harvey from any possibility of dishonourable advances, had taken offence at the term 'unusual' when applied to his beloved's name.

'Sylvestra is a noble name, worthy of a warrior queen. Only someone of Miss Harvey's Amazonian beauty and bearing could carry off such a proud name!' he announced hotly, eyeing Lord Carston challengingly.

This declaration was greeted with a stunned silence, interrupted only by a derisory snort from Sir Horace.

'Well said, Wynchip,' approved Lord Evelyn. 'Come Miss Harvey, such a flattering description surely deserves a response.'

Sylvestra laughed lightly, simultaneously shooting a dagger glance in Evelyn Carston's direction. 'I think it is a little unkind of Mr Wynchip to draw attention to my height; it has always been such a sad trial to me.'

Horrified that his words should be so misconstrued, Mr Wynchip was eager to make amends. 'Miss Harvey, I forbid you to talk so! Why your stature, grace and beauty are beyond compare!'

'Nothing wrong with a tall girl. Like a woman with a bit of meat on her bones,' put in Sir Horace, feeling that if he were to have any chance in the battle for Miss Harvey's affections his position on the matter must be made clear. It then only remained for Mr Clive to say in tones of strong disapproval that surely a well-informed mind and a modest disposition were worth more than mere physical attributes, for the issue to be thoroughly done to death.

Mrs Harvey certainly thought so. In her opinion, the conversation had revolved around her niece for far too long, and she said with a hard tinkling laugh, 'Lord Carston must be wishing he had not raised the subject, such contention as it has caused. I'll warrant there would not have been such disagreement on the merits of my dear Emily's figure, what say you, My Lord?'

'You are most fortunate in both your charges, Mrs Harvey,' replied Lord Evelyn diplomatically. A glance at Emily Harvey's flushed countenance and lowered eyes told him that the poor girl was completely mortified by her mother's blatant attempts to bring her to the fore, and he added, 'But I fear we are embarrassing them with our admiration. Should you like us to spare your blushes and turn to another topic, Miss Emily?'

He was rewarded for his kindness by a grateful if tremulous smile. But Mrs Harvey was not done. 'Oh, you need not worry upon that head, Lord Carston. My Emily is a sensible, modest girl and would not allow her head to be turned by a gentleman's compliments, I hope!'

Lord Evelyn was enjoying Mrs Harvey's militant approach to match-making hugely, but he knew that for the daughter's sake he must bring it to an end. He did not doubt his ability to avoid Mrs Harvey's crude snares, but if he did not nip her expectations in the bud it was clear that Miss Emily would be the one to suffer. He, therefore, neatly called her bluff by saying with feigned concern, 'Miss Harvey on the other hand is quite pink with embarrassment. Perhaps, Miss Harvey, you would allow me to take you for a turn about the park to cool those cheeks?'

Sylvestra, whose heightened colour was, as she suspected Lord Carston knew full well, more the result of suppressed mirth than maidenly modesty, gladly seized upon this opportunity to escape the increasingly unbearable confines of her aunt's drawing-room.

'That would be most pleasant,' she replied promptly before her affronted aunt could raise any objection. 'If you would not mind waiting a moment while I change my attire?'

'Not at all! Please, take your time, Miss Harvey.'

The memory of his remarks regarding her ball gown fresh in her mind, the underlying note of mock entreaty was not lost on Sylvestra and she was forced to exit the room at some speed before her giggles overcame her.

Still chuckling, she reached her bedroom and threw open her wardrobe. Its contents caused her to grimace. For all her past indifference to personal adornment, the idea of sitting in an open carriage beside the handsome and elegant figure of Evelyn Carston in one of these monstrous creations was enough to make her blush in genuine shame.

When Duffey entered the room it was to find her young mistress sitting cross-legged and disconsolate upon the floor, her chin in her hands, glowering fiercely at the ruthlessly discarded gowns about her. The maid folded her lips in disapproval at this unladylike pose, but had no word of remonstrance for the cavalier treatment of the garments. The news that Miss Sylvestra had been singled out for the most flattering attention by the Marquis of Derwent had quickly spread through the lower quarters. The young maid whose duty it was to take in the tea tray had been privileged to hear the charmingly phrased invitation, and to witness Mrs Harvey's chagrin. She had taken great pleasure in recounting this tasty morsel of household gossip to her young man, the second footman, who had in turn shared it with the butler, Mosely, and so on and so forth. The universally held feeling was one of malicious satisfaction, for Mrs Harvey was not popular with her servants.

Julia Harvey was an exacting and intolerant mistress, but her greatest sin in her servants' eyes was her total disregard for the subtle yet rigid social hierarchy which prevailed below stairs. In treating each of her household with equal contempt Mrs Harvey wrongly assumed herself to be acting the part of the great lady. In fact, the reverse was true and the contempt was mutual, Mrs Harvey's behaviour advertising her inexperience in managing a large fashionable residence. On the other hand, Sylvestra, whose manner of easy unaffectedness showed her to be perfectly at home as mistress of a gentleman's house, was looked upon with approval. She would have been surprised and amused to learn that she had a silent band of allies amongst the Green Street household.

Professional pride was also on the line in Duffey's case, and even before she entered her mistress's room her mind had been busy with the problem of what Miss Harvey would wear. She said not unkindly, 'Now, miss, it won't do to keep His Lordship waiting.'

The sound of her maid's voice roused Sylvestra from her uncharacteristic melancholy and she scrambled to her feet. 'You are right, of course!' she said with determined brightness. Really this vacuous lifestyle must be starting to affect her. A month ago she would have laughed heartily at the thought of herself falling into a brown study simply because she had not a pretty gown to wear! 'As you see, Duffey, I am so woolly headed I cannot make a decision! You must choose.'

The maid cast only a cursory glance at the crumpled finery before moving to the wardrobe, saying as she did, 'Although the weather is fine, there is still a chill in the air. I think it would be perfectly acceptable for miss to wear the velvet habit.'

'Really?' asked Sylvestra eagerly, her brow clearing. The riding habit had been a gift, prompted by a guilty conscience, from her uncle before they had left Brimpton Mewsey. Since her Aunt Julia had no intention of keeping a stable in town (Emily was a poor horsewoman and would certainly appear to disadvantage beside her intrepid cousin), Sylvestra had been given a free hand. The habit had been designed more with comfort and utility in mind than with fashion, but the severe military cut of the jade green velvet gown with its minimal adornment of black frogging and fringed epaulets was the perfect foil for Sylvestra's striking colouring. A mannish black shako set at a jaunty angle upon her copper curls completed this dashing ensemble, and it was with her head held high and a defiant gleam in her green eyes that Sylvestra re-entered the drawing-room.

The company had been considerably depleted. Sir Horace, never particularly comfortable in female company, had gladly made his escape – not even his sisters could expect him to sit maudling his insides with tea and doing the pretty when the girl was not even there to be courted. Mr Wynchip, spurred on by purer motives, was more tenacious, and showed no inclination to take himself off despite the glaring hints of both his hostess and Mr Frederick Clive. The two shy young men, at a loss to understand, but acutely aware of the underlying tension in the atmosphere, had also taken their leave, along with Mr Cameron, who had at the same time washed his hands of Carston since his friend had clearly taken leave of his senses.

Seeing the breathtaking vision of Sylvestra Harvey, the plush fabric of her gown hugging each perfect curve of her slender figure, Lord Evelyn would not have disagreed with his friend. A mischievous desire to take the wind out of Mrs Harvey's sails had prompted him to make the invitation, or so he thought. Now, seeing this statuesque beauty before him, Evelyn had a disturbing sensation that he was playing with fire. But, like the moth, he was drawn irresistibly to the flame, and he could not regret his impulse.

'Shall we go, Lord Carston? I would not like to keep your horses standing,' prompted Sylvestra, a little self-consciously, for she was uncomfortably aware that every eye was upon her and not all held approval.

Lord Evelyn bowed silently, finding himself momentarily bereft of speech. Mrs Harvey was not so afflicted; she had been forced to accept with a semblance of tranquillity the proposed drive, but the sight of her niece looking every inch the fashionable beauty was too much for her to swallow.

'What on earth are you wearing, Sylvestra, you are not out hunting now.' She gave an angry titter. 'I'm afraid my niece has not quite got to grips with London fashions.'

The loyal Mr Wynchip immediately fired up in his idol's defence and during the impassioned if barely coherent homage to her divine beauty that followed, Evelyn and Sylvestra slipped unobtrusively from the room.

The first few minutes of their drive passed in silence. Lord

Carston was obliged to concentrate on his horses, who, having spent fifteen minutes dawdling around the square, were keen to show their paces. After the empty chatter of her aunt's drawing-room Sylvestra was quite content simply to enjoy the fresh air and admire her companion's skill as he deftly wove a path through the congested London streets.

Only as the phaeton turned through the Stanhope Gate into Hyde Park was the comfortable silence broken. Lord Evelyn cast an amused, sidelong glance at the lady by his side.

'Miss Harvey, you are certainly unique! You are the only debutante to my knowledge who does not feel it her bounden duty when in a gentleman's company to entertain him constantly with examples of her lively wit!'

Sylvestra sighed mournfully. 'Alas, I am no great hand at polite chit chat, My Lord. It is one of my greatest failings if Aunt Julia is to be believed. Though, on balance, I think she prefers my silence to anything I might choose to say, seeing as I can barely open my lips without breaching some code of correct behaviour.'

'I am sure you do your best, Miss Harvey.'

Since Sylvestra's piteous speech was accompanied by a look as mischievous as it was bewitching, Lord Evelyn's response was heavily laden with irony and it prompted her to reply candidly, 'I must confess I have little patience with society's conventions. It seems to me that the ability to talk a great deal and say nothing at all is hardly a talent worth acquiring.'

'Then I hesitate to subject you to my wretched conversational skills!'

Sylvestra laughed. 'On the contrary! I am deeply in your debt, My Lord. You have gallantly rescued me from the most interminable morning of my life!'

'It seems I am falling into the habit of coming to your aid, Miss Harvey. I look forward to the day I might claim my reward.'

His tone was wickedly sensuous and the inference was clear. Sylvestra blushed, but to her shame it was not so much modesty as the fleeting images that his words provoked that brought warmth to her cheeks. Determined to show him that she was quite capable of dealing with one who was clearly an unprincipled flirt, she reminded him in her best schoolma'am voice, 'We are here to *cool* my cheeks, My Lord.'

Lord Evelyn was a picture of innocence. 'Now, what can I have said to make you blush? I have been out of society for some time but surely one may express one's wish to dance with a lady without causing her embarrassment?'

'*Dance!*' exclaimed Sylvestra without thinking.

Lord Evelyn raised his eyebrows questioningly. 'But of course, Miss Harvey. What else?'

Sylvestra had by now gained control of her wayward tongue if not her thoughts, and she had no intention of satisfying his curiosity; indeed, she doubted if she could find words to describe the images that had leapt unbidden into her mind. Instead she said reprovingly, 'I hardly think the motive behind your invitation is worthy of any reward.'

'Am I so transparent? I admit it was a ruse. But how else was I to get the attention of the beautiful Miss Harvey surrounded as she was by such a coterie of admirers?'

Sylvestra could not allow him to get away with such a blatant untruth. 'What flummery! You know very well that you thought only of putting my aunt at a stand! Now you dare not deny it!'

Lord Evelyn shrugged and shook his head in comic despair. 'Under the gaze of those magnificent eyes what can I do but confess my guilt.'

Sylvestra laughed and blushed, hiding the confusion even this slight compliment threw her into by exclaiming with mock displeasure, 'Twin pools of emerald light, if you please, sir!'

'Ah, then the poet is favourite.'

'Favourite?' queried Sylvestra, puzzled.

'Why, to win the much coveted hand of Miss Sylvestra Harvey, heiress.'

Sylvestra shook her head firmly. 'Miss Sylvestra Harvey, heiress, has no intention of marrying anyone!' Then, as she rather belatedly remembered her engagement to Captain Maynard, qualified this assertion by adding, 'Well, certainly none of the silly gudgeons I have met since I came to London.'

'If that is an example of your candidness, I begin to have sympathy with Mrs Harvey!' said Lord Evelyn, considerably amused.

'Oh, my wretched tongue!' exclaimed Sylvestra contritely. 'I have never learned to think before I speak! Of course, I did not mean to call *you* a silly gudgeon! Indeed, you are the only sensible man I have met – not that I am saying I wish to marry you – oh dear, what *am* I saying?' She came to a stumbling halt, her face a picture of comical confusion.

By this point Evelyn Carston was laughing so much he was forced to rein in his horses. Now he turned to face her, saying, 'I beg of you, Miss Harvey, don't ever curb your tongue in my presence. Your devastating observations are like a breath of fresh air.'

His blue eyes were smiling warmly down at her and Sylvestra felt colour suffuse her face. It was quite ridiculous and inexplicable that while the wildly extravagant compliments of other gentlemen left her unmoved, the slightest hint of approval from this man should so discompose her.

'Let us hope you are in the minority then! I had hoped my outspokenness would act as a deterrent to prospective suitors,' she managed to reply.

'Are you so determined to repel any admirers?' asked Lord Evelyn seriously. 'What have you against the married state?'

'Nothing . . . that is I have no great liking for being courted for my fortune.' Sylvestra found herself strangely reluctant to tell him of her attachment to Perry. Well, it was a private engagement, she reasoned, it would be wrong to publicize it.

'London is not populated entirely by scoundrels and adventurers you know. Give our poor sex a chance. And you shouldn't believe everything that aunt of yours says. Not every man is looking for a pattern card of feminine propriety.'

Sylvestra looked sceptical but said nothing. He might have given her *carte blanche* to say whatever came into her head, but she judged it would be indelicate in the extreme to suggest that since Lord Evelyn Carston's preference for decidedly *improper* females was already well documented he was hardly in position to offer an unbiased opinion of the tastes of the average gentleman.

Her face apparently said it all, however, since after a pregnant pause, Lord Evelyn adroitly changed the subject, only the slightest quiver of his lips betraying his very accurate reading of Sylvestra's thoughts.

'It seems to me, Miss Harvey, that you are going about this all wrong,' he said, briskly setting his impatient horses once more in motion. 'Has it never occurred to you that your Aunt Julia would not dress you like a dowd and put you down in public if she was interested in contracting an eligible alliance for you?'

'My Lord, you have seen my aunt's drawing-room. Surely I need only tell you it was designed to her own specifications for you to realize that nothing but bad taste lies behind my wardrobe. As to her criticism of me. . . .' Sylvestra shrugged philosophically. 'Well, I daresay it has become such a habit with her that she scarcely realizes she is doing it.'

Lord Evelyn shook his head. ' No, I don't think so. Mrs Harvey strikes me as a woman very much aware at all times of what she is doing. Tell me, who was that pompous fool in the brown coat?'

Sylvestra giggled involuntarily; she would have been able to recognize this as a reference to Mr Clive even without mention of his attire. 'Frederick Clive. I suppose he is my cousin of sorts, at any rate he is my aunt's nephew.'

'The picture becomes clear!'

'It does?' asked Sylvestra, completely at a loss.

'Really, Miss Harvey, I took you for a young lady of above average intelligence. You are clearly earmarked as the future Mrs Clive.'

'Good God, no!' exclaimed Sylvestra, in appalled accents.

'Exactly,' said Lord Evelyn with feeling. 'And unless I am mistaken, in your determination to repel any man who shows the slightest interest in you, you will be playing right into your aunt's hands.'

Sylvestra sat in frowning silence for a moment as the undeniable logic of his words sank in. It certainly would explain her aunt's odd behaviour. Even so, it seemed fantastic that Mrs Harvey could possibly imagine that her niece – or for that matter her nephew – would fall in with such a preposterous scheme. No! It was too ridiculous. Sylvestra shook her head decidedly.

'You must be mistaken. I may have only made Mr Clive's acquaintance for the first time this morning, but I can say categorically that we would not suit. My aunt, more than anyone, must see that!'

'But you are forgetting your greatest asset, Miss Harvey,' argued Lord Evelyn. 'I am confident your fortune will suit Mr Clive admirably.'

Sylvestra was still unconvinced. 'He may be an intolerable bore, but from what I have learned of Mr Clive such venal considerations are quite beneath him! He positively abhors any form of extravagance or frivolity – which I suppose one should applaud as I gather he intends to follow his father into the church.'

Lord Carston disagreed. 'You will think me harsh perhaps, but in my view he is overflowing with just the kind of pompous hypocrisy which gives the clergy a bad name. I strongly suspect that his condemnation of a life of ease and extravagance springs out of envy rather than any more admirable principle.'

Sylvestra was ready to concede that this might indeed be the case. 'For I have often noticed that those who make the greatest noise about Christian duty and charity have a tendency to become suddenly very silent when an act of personal sacrifice is required. That said,' she added, on a more positive note, 'I think, indeed I know, I would make Mr Clive a very uncomfortable wife, for I gain the impression that he sets *great* store by the proprieties. I shouldn't wonder if my eagerness to accept your invitation has lowered me considerably in his esteem. You see, he has a very poor opinion of you!'

'Does he now,' replied Lord Evelyn, with no visible signs of chagrin.

'Oh yes! And the fact that I have shown myself to prefer the company of a renowned libertine to that of a man of Mr Clive's stainless reputation only goes to prove just how unsuited I would be to the role of parson's wife,' reasoned Sylvestra artlessly.

'You would certainly set any parish by the ears, Miss Harvey!' responded Lord Evelyn with feeling.

Sylvestra clapped her hand to her mouth with an exclamation of consternation. 'Oh dear, that was an unforgivable thing for me to have said! I do beg your pardon!'

'Not at all. You cannot imagine what a comfort it is to know I am better company than Mr Frederick Clive.'

Sylvestra gave an involuntary giggle, but quickly became serious, saying resolutely, 'No. I do not deserve such tolerance. It was a very unmannerly thing to say and I am sorry. I was determined not to make any reference to what you had – I mean, your past.'

Lord Carston grinned appreciatively at this singularly unsuccessful attempt at tact and said, 'But why? You have entertained me greatly with your views on a variety of subjects, I await your opinion of me with a combination of anticipation and trepidation, please don't disappoint me!'

'You make me sound quite odiously opinionated,' objected Sylvestra. 'Believe me, I do not rate myself a shrewd judge of human character.'

'Hence your lamentable preference for renowned libertines,' interposed Lord Evelyn wickedly.

Sylvestra's lips twitched but she lifted her chin, saying with dignity, 'It was very wrong of me to call you that but I think it ungentlemanly of you to throw it at my head.'

'But surely you must have heard, Miss Harvey, I am not a gentleman.'

'I never listen to gossip, Lord Carston,' she replied grandly.

This made Lord Carston laugh heartily. 'Well, of all the bouncers!'

His laughter was infectious and Sylvestra found it impossible to maintain her haughty demeanour. 'Well, perhaps that is not quite true,' she conceded ruefully, 'but it doesn't mean to say that I believe every word I hear.'

'But in my case the evidence is pretty damning, wouldn't you agree?' persisted Lord Evelyn.

'Certainly! But although it might be an old cliché, I firmly believe there are always two sides to any story.'

Sylvestra eyed him expectantly, surprised at how much she wanted him to deny all the scurrilous rumours that surrounded him. He didn't, only saying lightly after a short pause, 'Well if you will not oblige me by giving your opinion, we shall return to discussing your future as the envied wife of the Very Reverend Clive, rather than my past.'

Sylvestra was disappointed but instinctively she knew it would serve no purpose to tease this man for confidences he was not willing to give, and so she allowed him to change the subject, replying, 'I think we were actually discussing how I might avoid that particular honour.'

'Well, that is simple enough. You do not strike me as the kind of shrinking violet who would permit herself to be bullied into a union that is repugnant to her.'

'True. But the prospect of Mr Clive dancing constant attendance for the duration of our stay is enough to throw me into strong hysterics.'

'Then you must surround yourself with so many ardent admirers that poor Mr Clive cannot get a look in.'

'But of course! What could be simpler!' exclaimed Sylvestra with heavy irony.

'I am serious. I very ungallantly – and inaccurately – suggested that your fortune was your greatest asset, but you may take it from me, you will attract as many men with your beauty and wit as with your wealth.'

Sylvestra blushed and demurred, suddenly feeling a little shy and self-conscious under his appreciative gaze. Evelyn realized with surprise that for all her apparent self-confidence she really was totally unaware of her very real charms.

'Take my advice, Miss Harvey. You would be better placed to foil your aunt's schemes if Mr Clive was just one among many. I take it you are well supplied with pin money?'

'Pin money? Yes . . . yes, my aunt has no control over that,' replied Sylvestra, bemused by this seemingly unconnected query.

'Then visit Madame Suresne in Bruton Street,' instructed Lord Evelyn. 'She is a modiste, and a very adept one too,' he supplied, in response to Sylvestra's puzzled expression.

Sylvestra did not see how a modiste could solve her predicament, but by that time the phaeton had pulled up once more outside the house in Green Street, and since her aunt was waiting to greet their return, she had no opportunity to interrogate Lord Carston any further.

Mrs Harvey's timely appearance was by no means a coincidence. Despite her earlier animadversions on the unseemliness of such behaviour, she had been for the past thirty minutes stationed in the bay window at the front of the house, her sharp eyes on the look out for Sylvestra and her escort, her sense of indignation growing stronger by the second.

Now she exclaimed in a waggish manner that disguised imperfectly the malicious intent behind her words, 'Why, what an age you have been! It is a wonder you have not bored poor Lord Carston to death, Sylvestra!'

'As you see, ma'am, I still live,' replied poor Lord Carston at his driest.

Mrs Harvey tittered a little uncertainly. 'You see what wits these

London beaux are, Sylvestra?' And then added in a confidential manner, 'You will have discovered that my niece takes no interest in the latest *on dits*. I fear she will always be a country girl at heart, the role of society hostess would be quite beyond her, I believe.'

'Really?' queried Lord Evelyn innocently. 'I had gained the impression that Miss Harvey was equal to anything!' and with exaggerated gallantry he handed Sylvestra down from his carriage.

Mrs Harvey's eyes narrowed suspiciously as she observed the brief glance that passed between them. She did not know what silent message it held, but the mere fact that Sylvestra had succeeded in establishing a degree of intimacy with the marquis was enough to bring her simmering discontent with the morning's events bubbling to the surface.

Six

The house was now free of guests, none of those remaining choosing to linger for very long after Sylvestra's departure. Not even Mr Wynchip could continue impervious to his hostess's antipathy and, with a stiff farewell, he had made a strategic retreat, his mind buzzing with fantastic scenarios in which he would not only woo his Cleopatra from under the nose of the wicked marquis, but rescue her from the cruel oppression of her aunt.

Happily unaware of her perilous position between domestic tyrant and heartless seducer, Sylvestra followed her aunt into the house with something like a spring in her light step. The uncharacteristic lowness of spirits to which she had been subject since rising from her bed had miraculously vanished, blown away, she supposed, by the fresh spring breeze. If she had chosen to examine more profoundly her sudden change of humour, she would have been obliged to own that the company and conversation of Lord Evelyn Carston had proved at least as exhilarating as the May sunshine. In the event Sylvestra was given little opportunity to question the cause or indeed enjoy the effect, for as soon as the door had shut behind them, Mrs Harvey ominously pronounced her desire to 'Have A Word' with her niece.

Sylvestra, who knew from long experience that Mrs Harvey's 'Word' would certainly stretch to a lengthy diatribe, unpinned the jaunty shako, stripped off her York tan gloves and handed these items of apparel, with a rueful twinkle in her eye, to the silently sympathetic butler, before followinq her aunt meekly into the empty drawing-room.

'Never have I witnessed such a brazen display!' Mrs Harvey's voice throbbed with indignation. Sylvestra raised her eyebrows in surprise; true, her own views and those of her aunt were unfailingly poles apart, but even so she was at a loss to account for this distorted interpretation of her actions.

To Mrs Harvey, who could never be brought to believe that her niece's behaviour was not deliberately calculated to cause her maximum annoyance, Sylvestra's expression of bewildered innocence was like a red rag to a bull.

'You don't fool me with your innocent looks, miss! I know what is o'clock, let me tell you! Can you deny that you were quite blatantly casting out lures to the marquis from the moment he arrived?'

'Emphatically!' protested Sylvestra. 'Why, I barely exchanged two words with Lord Carston.'

'Indeed.' Mrs Harvey's disbelief was patent. 'And I suppose you will also have me believe you did not set out to make yourself the centre of attention by encouraging that half-wit Aubrey Wynchip's absurdities.'

Sylvestra, her own temper rising at the injustice of her aunt's accusations, was stung into replying heatedly, 'But that is nonsensical, Aunt Julia! Mr Wynchip's attentions are more likely to make me an object of ridicule than of admiration!'

Mrs Harvey's formidable bosom swelled with indignation. 'Oh, I see how it is! You have set your sights higher! Well, let me tell you, my girl, the Marquis of Derwent will not choose a vulgar flirt for his wife!'

'I have not the slightest desire to wed the Marquis of Derwent!' declared Sylvestra, but she might as well have saved her breath. Mrs Harvey was in full flow and in no mood to listen to reason.

'Why do you suppose Lord Carston invited you to go driving? Answer me that.'

'I have no notion,' lied Sylvestra. The truth, she reflected, would hardly improve her aunt's temper.

'I will tell you why! Mark my words, he thinks you another Marianne Devenish! And we know what became of *her*!' Mrs Harvey ended on a triumphant note. She had almost succeeded in convincing herself that it was her niece's bold behaviour that had caused her to be singled out by Lord Carston. The possibility that he might really prefer Sylvestra to her own daughter was not to be entertained.

Sylvestra was on the point of hotly refuting her aunt's insulting aspersions when the germ of an idea caused her to pause, a thoughtful frown creasing her smooth brow.

'Would that be the general opinion if I were to be seen in the marquis's company?'

This brought Mrs Harvey up short. She would have liked to encourage her niece in this belief, but at the same time she was hoping Emily would soon be seen very frequently in the marquis's company. She said by way of a compromise, 'If you insist on behaving with such a lack of modesty, yes. To allow a man of the marquis's reputation to set you up as his flirt would instantly label you as fast.' Adding, by way of example, 'Mr Clive was very disappointed by your obvious eagerness to accept Lord Carston's invitation. Any well-bred young lady knowing what you do of Lord Carston's past would have been exceedingly hesitant to spend time alone in his company. It is unfortunate, for Mr Clive I think was disposed to look kindly upon you, but I fear he is now quite disillusioned.'

Sylvestra cast down her eyes and catching her lower lip between her teeth, said with the barest tremor in her voice, 'Oh, dear! I would not have that for the world!'

This apparent remorse greatly mollified her aunt, who said on a more encouraging note, 'Well, I am sure he will come round.

Frederick has kindly offered to escort us to the theatre this evening so you will have an opportunity to make amends. Pray do not waste it.'

Mrs Harvey preserved a moment's silence to allow the wisdom of her words to take effect before majestically dismissing her niece, very satisfied by the signs of penitence she had succeeded in inducing.

She would have been less complacent had she seen how speedily abject repentance magically disappeared once the drawing-room door closed behind her niece. Sylvestra, her eyes brimful of mischief, mounted the stairs with her usual unladylike haste and bounced into her cousin's bedchamber exclaiming cheerfully as she did, 'Heavens, Em, Aunt Julia has just given me the most tremendous jawbation!' The sight that greeted her brought her to an abrupt halt. Upon her cousin's entrance into the room, Emily had surreptitiously dried her eyes with an already exceedingly damp handkerchief and attempted to compose her ravaged features into a bright smile. It was a pathetic attempt. The swollen eyes and drooping shoulders told their own tale.

'Why, Em, what on earth has happened?' Sylvestra sank down next to her cousin, taking her trembling hands between her own.

Emily shook her head mutely, tears starting once more in her brown eyes. 'Oh, Sylvie, you will think me dreadfully weak and foolish, but the thought of— to be married to such a man! Mama says it is my duty, but I do not think I could bear it!' And with these disjointed words she dissolved into tears once more.

Sylvestra patted her hands, saying in bracing accents, 'There now, Em, your mama cannot force you to do anything you don't wish to, you know.'

Emily took a deep shuddering breath in an attempt to bring her sobs under control, and said more calmly, 'You are right I know, but after all Mama has done for me, all the sacrifices she has made to give me a season, I cannot help but feel it would be wickedly selfish of me to disappoint her.'

'Humbug!' exclaimed Sylvestra forcibly. 'What sacrifices? I am sure I have seen no sign of them.'

'Well, you know Miss Pinner's was very expensive. Mama must certainly have been obliged to forgo any number of things to pay for my education.'

Sylvestra looked sceptical. 'I think you are refining too much upon it, Emily. The only thing I can remember Aunt Julia forgoing was crimson flocked paper for the walls of Uncle William's study, and you may be sure he did not regard it as a sacrifice!'

'No, but—'

'But nothing,' interrupted Sylvestra ruthlessly. 'You cannot marry simply to oblige your mother. Indeed it is infamous that she should expect you to make such a sacrifice.'

Emily sniffed disconsolately and looked anything but convinced. 'But it is not as though I have given my affections elsewhere. If that were the case then I think I might be able to oppose Mama. But I have not, and it would be dreadfully ungrateful of me to turn down such an advantageous match.'

'What advantageous match?' asked Sylvestra puzzled, for she could not imagine when this flattering proposal could have been made or indeed who was behind it.

'The marquis, of course,' gulped Emily.

'The marquis? You mean Lord Carston? But he has not asked you to marry him.'

'No, and I pray that he will not! But you know what Mama is! She has set her heart on seeing me as the Marchioness of Derwent, and you know she always gets her way.'

'Good Lord, Em, fancy getting in such a state about something that will almost certainly never happen! Aunt Julia may rule the roast in her own household, but you surely don't imagine she could make Lord Carston do anything he didn't want to?'

'Do . . . do you think so?' asked Emily more hopefully.

'Heavens yes! Besides, you know I don't think it would be so very bad to be married to Lord Carston, it is certainly nothing to cry about.'

'Oh, Sylvie, how can you say so?' exclaimed Emily appalled.

Sylvestra coloured slightly. 'You cannot deny he is very handsome. And you know if you married him I am sure he would not let Aunt Julia bully you any more.'

'But his reputation. That poor young girl!' Emily gave an eloquent shudder.

'Really Em, you make him sound the worst beast in Nature. He is not a murderer!'

'But Sylvie, how can you defend him? Imagine if it had been you or I, imagine how you would have felt then.'

'But it wasn't,' argued Sylvestra, 'simply because I would hope we both have more sense than to allow ourselves to get into such a situation. I am not saying I have no sympathy for Miss Devenish, for I have, but you know the blame cannot be laid entirely at the marquis's door.'

Emily looked far from convinced. She had a great deal of admiration for her daring cousin, but she found she could not agree with her in this instance. Men of Lord Carston's ilk were to be feared and avoided at all costs, Miss Pinner had been very precise upon that point.

'I can see you are determined to brand him an ogre, but really he is nothing of the sort.'

Emily looked troubled. 'Oh, Sylvie, pray do not allow yourself to be taken in. I dare say he can be very charming, indeed I suppose he must be, for how else could he—' Emily blushed vividly but persevered. 'What I mean to say is, well, you seemed very happy to go driving with him.'

Sylvestra grinned wickedly. 'So you fear I might be bowled over by his devastating charm? Oh, Emily, you widgeon! Indeed, I was very happy to go driving with him; anything to escape Cousin Frederick's sermonizing!'

This provoked a watery smile from Emily, who said with feeling, 'It is very wrong of me I know, but I cannot bring myself to like him. He visited us once when I was a child, and even then he was the most odious little sneak imaginable!' Her soft brown eyes kindled at the memory.

Sylvestra was amused, it was so unlike her gentle cousin to take anyone into dislike. 'I can well imagine! Age has not improved him it would seem.'

'Well, I would not suppose he would now throw one's favourite doll into a muddy stream,' said Emily, with scrupulous fairness, 'but then,' she added, a mischievous smile quivering on her lips, 'I don't suppose I would respond by pushing him in after it.'

'You didn't?' exclaimed Sylvestra, clapping her hands together in delight.

Emily blushed rosily and nodded her head, saying defiantly, 'I know it was very bad of me but I *cannot* bring myself to regret it, even if it did ruin his best nankeen breeches, and earn me the most dreadful scold.'

'I should say not! A few duckings is just what our saintly cousin is short of! But Emily, I never suspected you had such a temper.'

'Well in general, you know, I don't,' replied Emily seriously, 'which only goes to show what a very irritating person Cousin Frederick is.' A giggle escaped her. 'Oh Sylvie, I wish you could have seen him. Standing in the middle of the stream dripping muddy water and covered in pond weed, and *still* with that pompous expression on his face.'

The vivid image this provoked had the effect of reducing the two girls to fits of helpless laughter, and it was some minutes before Sylvestra, mopping her streaming eyes could say, 'And Aunt Julia expects me to marry him!'

This had the effect of sobering up the cousins very quickly. For a moment each pondered in silence the nightmarish prospect of being Mrs Frederick Clive.

'But why?' asked Emily presently. 'After all, Frederick is hardly an eligible match. Indeed I know Papa has been obliged to help out Aunt Alicia on more than one occasion.'

'Uncle William would be relieved of that burden if Mr Clive found himself a wealthy wife,' suggested Sylvestra, as tactfully as she could.

'Surely not!' exclaimed Emily, and then blushed miserably as she recognized the truth in her cousin's words. 'Mama wasn't always so . . .' she said hesitantly. 'Indeed before I went to Miss Pinner's we were very happy at Mewsey Grange.'

Sylvestra squeezed her hand sympathetically. 'I am sure my aunt is only doing what she believes is best for her family,' she said, finding herself in the unusual position of defending Mrs Harvey's behaviour.

But Emily shook her head sadly. '*You* are family, Sylvie. And no one could possibly imagine that marriage to Cousin Frederick would be best for you.'

'Or best for Cousin Frederick, for I would certainly lead him a dog's life!' exclaimed Sylvestra, in an attempt to bolster Emily's spirits. But the smile she achieved was weak and it very quickly faded. It was clear she was pondering her own fate as Marchioness of Derwent.

'Come along, Emily! Do not be falling into the doldrums. I promise you will not have to marry anyone you don't want to,' asserted Sylvestra with rash confidence. But while Emily had a great deal of faith in her cousin's resourcefulness, she had an even greater respect for her mother's capabilities.

Sylvestra sighed and fell to thinking. It was clearly no good telling Emily she need only refuse to marry the marquis; she could as well swim the Channel as go against her mother's express wish. Clearly the proposal must never take place.

'You know, Emily, for all you think him a monster of depravity, I believe Lord Carston to be a reasonable man. I am sure I would only have to give him the hint—'

'Good gracious, no!' intervened Emily appalled. 'Indeed you must not! I would die of mortification! Why, he has never spoken to me beyond mere civilities. To hint him away when for all we know he has not the least intention of courting me, why it would seem like the most odious conceit! No, I implore you Sylvie, do not even think of it!'

'Very well. But you know you have put your finger on the crux, Emily. We have not the slightest reason for supposing he does want to marry you. I think you are getting yourself in a flap over something and nothing,' argued Sylvestra.

This eminently sensible view did not, however, have the beneficial effect Sylvestra had hoped for. Indeed, if anything Emily looked even more dejected. 'Of course, I have thought of that. And indeed I think you are right, for it seems to me that the marquis is clearly more taken with you. But Mama has made it quite clear that I must make the effort to . . . to engage his interest.'

Sylvestra frowned. It seemed they had reached *point non plus*. Poor Emily's life would be made miserable whether or not she married the marquis. And then Sylvestra remembered the half-formed plan her aunt's words had unwittingly prompted, and a slow impish smile spread across her features.

'I have it! Emily, if the marquis was to do something quite dreadfully scandalous, Aunt Julia would not expect you to marry him, would she?'

Emily looked doubtful. 'But he has done something dreadfully scandalous—'

'Oh, I know, I know.' Sylvestra dismissed Lord Evelyn's iniquitous past with an impatient wave of her arm. 'But that was years ago. If he were to do something now, something for which my aunt could not forgive him, then she would not wish you to be married.'

'Well, no, I don't expect so, but what could he possibly do?'

Sylvestra grinned wickedly, her green eyes dancing like little devils. 'If he were to blatantly set up a well-bred young lady as his *chère amie*, not even Aunt Julia could sweep that under the carpet.'

'No. But there is not the least likelihood of that happening—

Oh my goodness, Sylvie, no! No, you cannot!' Emily stared at her cousin in round-eyed horror.

'Stoopid. Of course I won't! But you know what the gossips are, it would not take very much to convince them that the marquis and I were, well, you know.'

'But you would be left without a shred of reputation, and think of poor Captain Maynard. Imagine what his feelings would be,' protested Emily.

'Oh, Perry won't mind,' said Sylvestra airily. 'Besides I am doing it for his sake as well. If anything will stop Cousin Frederick in his tracks, and all the other fortune hunters I am like to be plagued with, the rumour that I am the Marquis of Derwent's mistress will!'

Unaware of Miss Harvey's plans to embroil him in her scandalous schemes, Evelyn Carston drove away from Green Street in thoughtful mood. It struck him forcibly that for perhaps the first time in five years he had for a brief half-hour forgotten his troubles and simply enjoyed the company of a beautiful and captivating woman. Paradoxically, this did not infect him with the same innocent *joie de vivre* Sylvestra had experienced, rather it made the problems that beset him chafe all the more, and left him reluctant to return home. It would, of course, give Marianne an excellent excuse to accuse him of abandoning her to her enforced seclusion, but since on the other hand she was wont to regard his company as a persecution in itself, the struggle with his conscience was of short duration and instead of turning his horses into Grosvenor Square, Evelyn continued along South Audley Street towards Curzon Street and the bachelor residence of Mr Giles Cameron.

Mr Cameron's welcome was pointedly cool and his square features wore a frankly disapproving expression, provoking Evelyn to exclaim laughingly, 'Good Lord, Giles, why the long face?'

'As if you didn't know!' was the indignant reply. 'Abandoning me in the dragon's lair. I call that damned shabby!'

Evelyn was openly sceptical. ‘Coming it a bit strong, Giles. You made your escape sharp enough,’ he added cheekily. ‘Besides you ain’t plump enough in the pocket to catch Mother Harvey’s eye.’

‘Believe me I have never been more glad of it,’ responded Mr Cameron with a good deal of feeling. He cocked a quizzical eyebrow at his friend. ‘But you’re sailing pretty close to the wind, aren’t you?’

‘One morning call and a drive in the park hardly amounts to a declaration!’ protested Evelyn.

‘Maybe not. But to single the girl out when you have only been back in the country five minutes, well. . . .’ Mr Cameron shrugged eloquently.

‘Oh plague take the gossips!’ exclaimed Evelyn impatiently. ‘I’ll not order my life to suit their notions of propriety. Miss Harvey has no such expectations I assure you.’

Mr Cameron continued to frown, and Evelyn eyed his friend with mild exasperation. ‘Come on then, man, out with it! Let’s have the words with no bark on them.’

Mr Cameron hesitantly obliged. ‘It is rather that you might not have marriage in mind that will give rise to talk. The kind of talk that even if you are indifferent to it, would be very unpleasant for Miss Harvey.’

Evelyn gave a harsh, humourless laugh. ‘I was forgetting my wicked reputation. Seduction of innocents is, of course, my forte.’

Mr Cameron looked uncomfortable. ‘Now Eve, no need to look blue as megrim. Your friends know it ain’t so. Good Lord, I know you’ve never been in the petticoat line. If it were Vincent now. . . .’ He paused. Evelyn’s expression was far from encouraging. ‘Well, I’ll say no more on that head.’

‘Indeed. I think a great deal too many words have been wasted on this subject already. Just tell me, oh wise one, what would you have me do? I have no plans to marry anyone, so what must I do, live like a monk?’

Mr Cameron smiled. ‘For what it is worth, my advice would be to amuse yourself with a lady who understands the rules, not a young miss fresh up from the country.'

If Mrs Harvey had hoped to arrive at Drury Lane in fine style then she was destined to disappointment. At the appointed hour, it was not the smart town carriage she had fondly imagined that drew up outside the house in Green Street to take the ladies to Mr Kemble's performance of Hamlet, but a dilapidated coach, its paintwork faded and peeling, and drawn by two ancient animals who should clearly have been put out to pasture some years previously. Everything about the sorry equipage appeared to sag; its heavy, old-fashioned body between the wheels, the poor beasts in their harness, even the shabby coachman on his box.

'Great Heavens, Frederick! Where did you find . . . this!' For once Mrs Harvey was at a loss for words.

Mr Clive, who had stepped down punctiliously from his chariot in order to aid the ladies, oblivious to his aunt's horror, smiled smugly and said in self-satisfied accents, 'Where indeed! Let me tell you, Aunt Harvey, it was no easy task. The rates that are usually demanded for these vehicles are nothing short of robbery! But I fancy I am no flat when it comes to these little transactions. I beat the fellow down to a very reasonable price, very reasonable indeed. And including the horses!' He beamed proudly, evidently expecting a degree of acclamation. It was not forthcoming. Mrs Harvey, saying with awful sarcasm that was wasted upon her victim, that she trusted her nephew's notions of economy had not reduced them to watching the performance from the pit, allowed herself to be handed into the vehicle, fastidiously holding her skirts clear of the dusty floor and sniffing distastefully at the cracked leather squabs.

It was a far from comfortable journey. If the carriage had ever in its long history been sprung it was by now nothing more than a distant memory, and only the fact that the members of the party were squashed in so tightly prevented their being flung from their seats at every bump in the road. The ample proportions of Mrs Harvey and her sister would have made it a close fit in any event, but this was exacerbated to no minor degree by Mrs Clive's decision to dignify the occasion with an extremely outmoded gown of a powder-blue armozine arranged over hoops of alarming proportions. She had even gone so far as to powder her greying hair which was piled to such a height that the faded blue ostrich feathers with which she had chosen to adorn her startling coiffure brushed the ceiling of the carriage.

'Good Lord, Alicia! We are not attending a masquerade!' exclaimed her forthright sister scornfully. 'You look like a Bath quiz.'

'At least no one may accuse me of being mutton dressed as lamb,' returned Mrs Clive with great daring.

Mrs Harvey bridled. 'If you had the least notion, Alicia, you would know that my gown is the first stare of fashion.'

And so it was. But as Mrs Clive had cruelly pointed out, the prevalent style of low necklines, high waists and narrow skirts did little for a middle-aged matron of generous build. Nor was plum satin with an overdress of spangled cerise gauze a becoming foil for a mature complexion. Mrs Harvey's sole concession to her chaperon status was a magnificent satin turban decorated with a large paste ruby and giving her the appearance of a rather malevolent Buddha.

In fact, thought Sylvestra glumly, as the coach swayed and bumped along, with the exception of Emily, who was looking sweetly innocent in pale-pink jaconet, we look like a parcel of dowds. Nor were the schemes busily fomenting in her head going to be helped by her own appearance. She had little experience to guide her but she was fairly sure that *femmes fatales* did not achieve their disastrous notoriety wearing high-necked gowns of a particularly hideous shade of mauve.

The short journey did little improve their appearance. The cramped confines of the carriage had not only left the ladies' gowns sadly crushed, but their complexions unbecomingly flushed. Mrs Clive, encased in whalebone stays and the heavy stuff of her gown was perspiring visibly beneath her *maquillage*, while one of her ostrich plumes now drooped at a drunken angle over one eye. With the exception of Mr Clive then, who had beguiled the journey with further self-congratulatory exclamations on his shrewdness at striking such a good bargain, and seemed impervious to such sartorial predicaments as wilting shirt points, it was a disgruntled party that arrived at Drury Lane.

Mr Clive's cheeseparing ways did not, as Mrs Harvey feared, force the ladies to endure the discomfort of the pit, but the box he had hired was inevitably the cheapest to be had. Fortunately, the fact that a pillar largely obscured the stage was not felt to be a significant disadvantage by Mrs Harvey, who, along with the majority of the ton, had come rather to see and be seen than to enjoy the thespian delights on offer, nor indeed by Mrs Clive who, having settled her voluminous skirts about her promptly fell into a gentle doze, the occasional genteel snore ruffling the fronds of her errant ostrich plume. It was otherwise with Sylvestra, for whom the theatre was one of the few saving graces offered by a London season. She, therefore stationed herself in the one corner of the box where a virtually unimpaired view of the action could be obtained. It was not long before she realized this was a mistake, for it allowed her Cousin Frederick to sit at her side and effectively cut her off from the rest of the party. The hope that once the curtains had risen, her obvious enthralment in the performance would dissuade him from disturbing her was a vain one. Mr Clive considered it his duty to keep Sylvestra appraised of every twist and turn of the plot. She was obliged to endure this for the better part of the first act, since all her attempts to convince him she was in no need of such a service went unheeded.

It was much to her relief then when Mr Clive was diverted from his painstaking translation of events on stage by Mrs Harvey.

'Why, I do believe that is the Marquis of Derwent! There, in the box next to Lady Sephton's,' she exclaimed with an air of artless surprise for all the world as if she had not spent every minute since their arrival scouring the theatre for Lord Carston's handsome face. 'Yes, yes, I am sure of it. He is with the gentleman who came to call on us.'

'Mr Cameron,' supplied Sylvestra, following her aunt's gaze with interest. She had not expected such an early opportunity to put her scandalous plan into action, and indeed she had only the haziest notions of what she was going to do. It had seemed simple enough when she had confidently pronounced her intention to Emily earlier in the day. Now, looking across to where Lord Carston lounged casually in his box, the very epitome of a man of rank and fashion, Sylvestra felt a flicker of doubt.

'He is looking this way! Smile Emily! If we can succeed in catching his eye, he is bound to come to our box at the interval.' This was muttered urgently by Mrs Harvey through a wide smile, and accompanied by a great deal of nodding of her turbanned head and energetic plying of her fan. She was rewarded with no more than a slight inclination of the head, but when the curtains fell, Lord Carston and Mr Cameron did rise to leave their box.

Triumphantly, Mrs Harvey busied herself arranging the members of her party. Mrs Clive was unceremoniously poked in the ribs and adjured to make room so that the marquis could enter the box with ease. 'Sylvestra and Frederick you may stay where you are. Emily, for heaven's sake, what are you doing hiding in the shadows? Come and sit here where Lord Carston may speak to you.'

Mr Clive, who had been watching his aunt's manoeuvres with an increasingly censorious expression, felt obliged to make his feelings known. 'Aunt Harvey, I hardly suppose, given what we know of this man, that you would wish your daughter and Miss Harvey to be subjected to his company.'

Mrs Harvey eyed her nephew with disfavour and said rather sharply, 'Lord Carston's behaviour in the past is certainly regrettable, but I believe him now to be every inch the perfect gentleman. It would not be Christian of us, Frederick, to refuse him a second chance.'

'I beg leave to doubt that he has rejected his abhorrent lifestyle.' And with a degree of malicious satisfaction quite unsuited to one of his vocation, Mr Clive motioned significantly to the box directly opposite.

Mrs Harvey shut her fan with an angry snap. Lord Carston was following his friend's advice and conducting a lively flirtation with a ravishing brunette.

'Who is that?' asked Mrs Harvey darkly, her eyes flashing dangerously.

Mrs Clive, roused from her somnolent state, said placidly, 'She is Lady Annabel Swaffham, Sir John Swaffham's widow.'

Sylvestra, who had experienced a sense of nervous anticipation when her aunt had pointed out Evelyn Carston's presence, and was now feeling inexplicably deflated, said critically, 'She is not my idea of a widow!'

'Indeed not!' agreed Mr Clive eagerly. 'Her lack of proper feeling and her shameless behaviour are to be deprecated. She is not, I believe . . .' he paused delicately, 'a *virtuous* woman.'

Since the lady in question was arrayed in a clinging gown of scarlet satin, the plunging neckline of which exposed a tantalizing expanse of creamy-white bosom, upon which a heavy necklace of cabochon rubies glinted wickedly in the candlelight, this fact had already been assimilated by the whole party.

Lord Carston bent his head to murmur into Lady Annabel's ear. Whatever he said was outrageous enough to earn him a sharp rap on the knuckles from his companion's fan, but also complimentary judging by the seductive pout of Lady Swaffham's painted lips and the roguish glance she darted at him from under lowered lashes. Watching this intimate by-play, Sylvestra was aware she should be taking mental notes; after all Annabel Swaffham was surely the perfect role model for the charade she had in mind.

Unaccountably, Sylvestra found it impossible to observe the elegant dalliance between the dark-haired beauty and Lord Carston with the required detachment.

To her dismay, she found that she resented the evidently *very* amicable relationship Lady Swaffham shared with Lord Carston. Not that she was jealous, that would be quite ridiculous, but Sylvestra was feminine enough to have been flattered by Evelyn Carson's admiration and feminine enough to feel a certain amount of pique when it became apparent that his compliments were in no way reserved exclusively for herself.

Sylvestra would have died rather than admit as much, and to be fair, it was not simply wounded vanity that had made her feel so out of reason cross. In Lord Carston, Sylvestra realized, she had thought she had found a friend; someone who shared her own disregard for the conventions and contempt for society's artificialities and hypocrisies. Now she was struck by the lowering thought that Emily might have had the truth of the matter when she had expressed concern that Sylvestra had succumbed to Lord Carston's charm.

While Sylvestra had always felt sympathy for girls who found themselves in Marianne Devenish's situation, she had always privately thought them rather foolish; she would not be so gullible. Now she was obliged to own that the empty blandishments to which she personally was impervious, but which she had always supposed to be the seducer's stock in trade, were not, in fact, the only tools at his disposal. Clearly this particular rake was clever enough to adapt his charismatic skills to suit the personality of the lady he was pursuing.

This evidence of Lord Carston's dangerous charm might have deterred a young lady of lesser resolve, but it only made Sylvestra doubly determined to go ahead with her plan, with one important modification. She had foolishly imagined some kind of rapport between herself and Lord Carston, had stupidly supposed he would go along with her plans. Lord Carston, unprincipled

Lothario that he was, could certainly not be trusted not to take advantage of the situation. Indeed, she blushed with shame when she thought of the predicament she might have found herself in had she been so cockle-brained as to ask Lord Carston to conspire with her to deceive the ton into believing they were lovers!

Well, she had his measure now! He would not succeed twice in slipping beneath her defences. Lord Evelyn Carston had better look out for he was about to find himself in a new and unfamiliar role – not the seducer but rather the seduced!

Seven

While the entrance of Lady Swaffham into the equation had precipitated a radical alteration of Sylvestra's plans, Mrs Harvey was, on reflection, undaunted. Whatever relationship existed between the marquis and Lady Annabel Swaffham, marriage was certainly not on the agenda. Lady Swaffham could be safely dismissed.

'I do not wish to discuss Lady Swaffham,' she pronounced grandly. 'Thankfully, we are not obliged to move in the same circles as such as she. Men, I know, have certain weaknesses, but it is the duty of a well-bred lady to ignore their little peccadilloes.'

Mr Clive could not agree. 'You are too forgiving of my sex, Aunt Harvey. I would assure you that any lady who did me the honour of becoming my wife would not be expected to tolerate such humiliation.'

This speech was directed quite pointedly at Sylvestra, who could imagine nothing more unlikely than the spectacle of Frederick Clive with a dazzling barque of frailty upon his arm.

She responded, however, with perfect seriousness. 'Indeed I believe these arrangements are very expensive. I am persuaded they would not suit your strict notions of economy.'

The suspicion that he was being made fun of briefly crossed Mr Clive's mind to be speedily dismissed. There was no hint of mockery in Sylvestra's limpid gaze but Mr Clive privately began to wonder if the tone of Miss Harvey's mind was quite what one would hope for in the wife of a clergyman. He was given no opportunity to explore this theory further since Mrs Harvey had other plans.

Lord Carston and Mr Cameron were taking their leave of Lady Swaffham and Mrs Harvey had swiftly calculated that the gentlemen must perforce pass by the box occupied by the Harveys. It was a chance not to be missed and the whole party, with the exception of Mrs Clive who had fallen once more into a light doze, were reluctantly herded out into the corridor in time to intercept Julia Harvey's quarry.

In her anxiety not to miss Lord Carston, Mrs Harvey was a little precipitate. In consequence, they were obliged to mill around aimlessly in the corridor. Like so many sheep, thought Sylvestra, feeling unaccountably vexed. For the first time since their arrival in the capital she was embarrassed by her aunt's exceedingly obvious stratagems. Sylvestra had always watched Mrs Harvey's determined assault upon the inner sanctums of the *haut monde* with a kind of detached amusement. She had no desire to be accepted into the rarefied circles her aunt was so set on breaching simply because she had no great admiration for those who moved within them. But for all her resolutions, Sylvestra discovered she was not so indifferent to Lord Evelyn Carston's opinion.

At that moment it seemed insupportable that Lord Carston should suppose her to share Mrs Harvey's desperate eagerness to court his attention and Sylvestra abruptly turned her back upon his approach, saying with spurious concern, 'I am sorry, Cousin Frederick, were you addressing me?' An ill advised move, she realized almost immediately, since it instantly promoted her in Mr Clive's esteem, and caused him to say with warm admiration that he was glad she at least did not allow the hollow attractions of wealth and title to overcome her moral judgement. Since Sylvestra was unhappily aware of the rather more base motive behind her actions, namely pique at Lord Carston's preference for the company of Lady Swaffham, she was unable to derive any consolation from Mr Clive's praise. It was debatable which afforded her least gratification: Mr Clive's muttered denunciation of the wicked marquis's libertine propensities or her aunt's appalling obsequiousness.

The former need not be recorded. Despite Mr Clive's avowed wish to take Lord Carston verbally to task for his numerous infamies, he was careful to deliver his vituperation in a undertone barely audible to anyone but himself, and so it can be assumed he wished for no larger audience. It was otherwise with Julia Harvey, who was determined that the world and his wife should know upon what easy terms she stood with the Marquis of Derwent.

Sylvestra, inwardly cringing and hating herself for it, imagined rather than witnessed Lord Carston's weary resignation and impatient contempt. If he did indeed experience either of these emotions, Lord Evelyn was too much of a gentleman to allow it show. He expressed himself delighted at this opportunity to further their acquaintance, agreed with Mrs Harvey that it was indeed a remarkable and fortuitous coincidence that they should meet thus, and when Mr Cameron, who was no less the gentleman but expressed his pleasure in a more restrained fashion, rather pointedly drew the party's attention to the fact that the curtains were rising on the second act, even allowed himself to be urged to enter the Harveys' box.

His compliance stopped short of permitting himself to be manoeuvred into a seat between Mrs Harvey and her daughter. With a sublime disregard for the actual logistics of the box, Lord Evelyn declared he could not possibly deny his friend Giles, who had a particular liking for drama, the excellent view provided by that particular position. He would be quite happy to sit in a corner, upon which he promptly seated himself at Sylvestra's side.

Mrs Harvey would have been very happy to argue the point, but to Emily's profound relief, the actors chose that point to take once more to the stage, and the ensuing heckling and cat-calling from the pit made further discussion out of the question. Mrs Harvey was obliged to accept this far from satisfactory arrangement and content herself with frequent suspicious glances in her niece's direction. Sylvestra herself fixed her gaze firmly upon the stage and willed herself to ignore Lord Carston's presence. In normal circumstances, Mr Kemble's superlative performance would have held her enthralled, but this evening Sylvestra found it impossible to attend and had Mr Clive not been relegated to the rear of the box by their more illustrious guests she would even have been grateful for his laboured interpretations.

Lord Carston, without even saying a word, had thrown her thoughts into disarray, which for Sylvestra was a novel and not entirely pleasant experience. She had always thought herself to be possessed of an above-average measure of common sense; she was certainly not prone to excesses of sensibility. Angry at her own weakness and resentful of its cause, Sylvestra was doubly determined not to give Evelyn Carston – whom she suspected of amusing himself at her expense – the satisfaction of guessing her discomfort. It would have surprised her to know that Lord Evelyn was suffering from the same distressing inability to concentrate on the drama unfolding upon stage.

Sylvestra was sitting slightly in front of Evelyn and he found his eyes constantly drawn to her upright figure, the slender grace of her swan-like neck, the generous swell of her bosom beneath the concealing bodice of her dress. Even in that dreadful gown there was something infinitely more alluring about Miss Sylvestra Harvey than Lady Annabel Swaffham with her rather overblown charms. Indeed, it was as though the modest neckline with its prim ruffle of lace only exacerbated his desire to explore the undiscovered delights beneath. Enough of that! Evelyn inwardly chastised himself for these wayward thoughts. With Marianne and Edward at this moment concealed in Grosvenor Square, he should need no reminder that he must not allow his relationship with Miss Harvey to develop beyond mere acquaintanceship. What a fool he was! He could easily have depressed Mrs Harvey's pretensions; that had been his intention until Miss Harvey had quite deliberately turned her back upon him. That had intrigued him; after all, they had parted this morning on excellent terms.

He glanced towards the opposite box where Lady Annabel's opulent form had taken on a languorous pose. Even from this distance, the signals being sent out by the voluptuous beauty were unmistakable. Thoughtfully, he regarded Miss Harvey's aloof profile. Surely she was not jealous? If it had been any other lady of his acquaintance he would have been able to put this interpretation on her behaviour with more confidence. But Sylvestra Harvey was like no female he had ever encountered, and he was wary of jumping to the obvious conclusion. Still, said a cautious voice in his head, it would not do to encourage any hopes in that direction; in fact, all the more reason to sever his connection with the entire Harvey tribe. Besides, they hardly represented the kind of company he was used to keeping. Mrs Harvey was a harpy, her daughter an insipid mouse with scarcely a word to say for herself, and the Clives were just the sort of provincial gentry he invariably found a dead bore. And Miss Harvey? Evelyn could not dismiss her with such casual cruelty. She sat beside him, her exquisite face a mask of cool indifference. He wanted to pierce that indifference, see those slanting green eyes sparkle with wicked mirth as he knew they could, see those generous lips parted in laughter. The voice of caution was drowned by this more urgent desire and he leant forward to murmur in Sylvestra's ear, unconsciously confirming all her worst suspicions of him, 'I hope I have done nothing to offend you, Miss Harvey.'

His voice was low and sensuous, more amused than apologetic, and Sylvestra felt her cheeks grow warm. She was angry; with herself for being so susceptible to his slightest attention, with him for his intolerable audacity. The sheer arrogance of the man took her breath away! Not ten minutes since he had been whispering sweet nothings into the receptive ear of Lady Annabel, now he had the barefaced impertinence to try the same on her. Well, he would not find Miss Sylvestra Harvey so easy to charm, *she* was going to set the pace in this particular dalliance.

She took a deep breath and with the air of one just roused from profound absorption said, 'Oh, Lord Carston, did you say something? I am afraid when watching a performance of this calibre I am lost to the world.'

Lord Carston eyed her with appreciation. 'You have a great love of the theatre then, Miss Harvey. Your level of concentration amongst such a noisy audience almost defies belief. I fear I lost the thread of this particular tale some time ago. Perhaps you could enlighten me.'

There was a fleeting look of panic in those emerald eyes before Sylvestra replied smoothly, 'The plot is not complicated, Lord Carston. I feel sure it would not long remain a mystery for anyone of average intelligence.'

'*You* say so, Miss Harvey, but I can see that you have a very definite affinity for the dramatic medium. Should your circumstances ever require you to earn your bread, I am confident you would be a very accomplished actress.'

Sylvestra fought an almost overpowering urge to slap that smug face, but beyond a brief scorching glance she restrained her anger admirably, saying with a tolerable display of indifference, 'It seems highly unlikely that I should be reduced to such drastic measures.'

Before she knew what he was about, Lord Carston had possessed himself of one of her hands. Startled she looked up and found herself trapped by his mocking blue gaze. 'What a shame! Your presence on the stage would have guaranteed my full attention,' and he bent to press his lips upon her upturned palm, his shoulders shaking with silent laughter.

Sylvestra glared impotently at his dark head. Of all the insufferable, conceited . . . words were not equal to his infamy. So he fancied she was affecting her indifference. The fact that he was right only incensed Sylvestra all the more. Well, if Lord Carston wanted to see more of her acting ability she would not disappoint him, she vowed. She would convince the entire ton that she was on the point of casting her cap over the windmill for the wicked Marquis of Derwent; and no one would be more convinced than the impudent lord himself. And when she had succeeded in driving him to distraction, she would tell him just how she had used him and see if that did not rid him of his odious conceit!

The sight of her niece handfast with the Marquis of Derwent was a little too much for Mrs Harvey to bear in silence, and she wasted no time in bringing that undesirable tête-à-tête to a close.

'Lord Carston, will you not pull your chair over beside me? There is something I particularly wish to say to you.'

Faced with this direct assault, Lord Evelyn could do nothing but gracefully concede defeat. With a wry glance in Sylvestra's direction, to which she struggled not to respond for all she was out of charity with him, he obediently moved to Mrs Harvey's side.

This lady patted him on the arm in a confidential manner and said in a penetrating whisper, designed to reach his ears alone but which was in fact clearly audible to every occupant of the box, 'I am persuaded you will not mind my giving you the hint, My Lord. . . ?' Mrs Harvey raised her eyebrows coyly.

'Not at all, Mrs Harvey!' responded Lord Evelyn promptly, only hoping he would be able to preserve his countenance.

Mrs Harvey smiled ingratiatingly. 'I knew the moment we met, Lord Carston, that you were a gentleman of superior sense! Now, I am sure you have already observed that there is a degree of *understanding* between my niece and Mr Clive – indeed, I am sure only a perfect noddy could fail to! I declare I have never seen such a pair of lovebirds! Good heavens, if you could only have seen poor Frederick's face when you sat beside Sylvestra! I swear he would have run you through had he a sword about his person!'

'We must be thankful he has not, then,' observed Lord Evelyn dryly.

Mrs Harvey gave a trill of laughter. 'Oh, I do not mean you to take me *literally*, Lord Carston. After all, Mr Clive will soon be a man of the cloth! But you know what young people are when they are in love. Forever falling out over the most trivial misunderstandings. I am persuaded you would not wish to cause a breach between two lovers.'

'If Miss Harvey's feelings for her cousin are so strong I fail to see how I could be seen to pose a threat,' said Lord Evelyn reasonably, wondering what this enterprising woman would say if she were privy, as he was, to Miss Harvey's true opinion of Mr Clive.

Mrs Harvey was pressing onward. 'You are too modest, Lord Carston! A man of your address! Why, it would not be at all wonderful if you were to turn a girl's head. I know it is nothing more than politeness on your part, but young misses fresh out of the schoolroom are apt to take the silliest notions into their heads with the least provocation.'

'I must bow to your superior knowledge, Mrs Harvey. Be assured I shall do nothing to jeopardize Mr Clive's aspirations,' said Lord Evelyn gravely, privately thinking no one was more likely to do that than the gentleman himself.

Mrs Harvey gave a satisfied nod. 'Then I shall say no more, for I see you understand me.'

'Oh, perfectly, Mrs Harvey, perfectly.' This was said with touch too much feeling, and Mrs Harvey's eyes narrowed suspiciously. She was used to getting her own way, but she had not expected quite such a bloodless victory, and it made her uneasy. Still, it would not do to labour the point.

'Now we may talk of more pleasant things. We are getting up a small party to go to Vauxhall tomorrow evening – not my choice I assure you, but the young people will have their way and Vauxhall it must be. 'Tis very short notice I know, but it struck me that perhaps you and Mr Cameron might care to join us?'

'Tomorrow evening? How unfortunate. I am afraid we are already engaged, to dine, with er . . . with Sir Lawrence Snaithsby. Isn't that so, Giles?'

Apparently deaf to the desperate note of appeal in his friend's voice and blind to his frantic grimaces, Mr Cameron smiled sweetly and said. 'Well you know, Eve, I only saw Snaithsby this morning in White's and I distinctly remember him saying that he wasn't expecting you above half. I can easily make your excuses, very easy-going chap, won't take snuff I assure you.'

'That is settled then,' interposed Mrs Harvey, with a note of finality. 'It only remains for us to make the arrangements. Of course, I would offer to take you up in our carriage, but I fear it cannot hold more than five in comfort, though I suppose Frederick could take a hack. What do you think, Lord Carston, should we hire a box? I depend entirely upon your advice! Why, it is an absolute age since I was last in the capital and, of course, when I was a girl it was Ranelagh that was all the rage. . . .'

Some time later Lord Carston and Mr Cameron at last succeeded in escaping Mrs Harvey's clutches, Evelyn rather bemusedly wondering how it was that from politely excusing himself from the trip to Vauxhall, he was now not only fully committed to the party but had been induced to offer his own more commodious town carriage for the expedition and had undertaken to secure for them all a box in the Rotunda. A large portion of the blame he felt could justifiably be heaped upon his friend, whose heartless desertion had left him entirely at Mrs Harvey's mercy. Mr Cameron when taken to task was wholly unrepentant.

'You brought it upon yourself, Carston,' he declared callously. 'So I am a connoisseur of the stage, am I? It would be news to my friends! And you needn't think to persuade me to support you on this little pleasure jaunt. I've no fancy to spend another evening sitting bodkin between the old trout and her daughter while you conduct one of your flirtations with the niece!'

'I would not dream of it! After all, we must not rob poor Snaithsby of all his dinner guests, that would be too shabby.'

Mr Cameron immediately pounced upon this piece of frivolity.

'That's another thing. What in devil's name made you pick Snaithsby of all people?'

Evelyn shrugged helplessly. 'His was the first name that popped into my head. I think it was on account of that fellow playing Polonius, absolute double for the old boy, you must have remarked it.'

'Can't say as I did,' responded his friend with awful irony. 'Spent most of the evening staring at a damned pillar. But Snaithsby!' He shook his head in disgust. 'You might at least have picked on someone who ain't been below ground these three years and more!'

The descent of an unaccompanied young lady dressed neatly, but by no means in the first stare of fashion, from a hackney carriage was watched with an idle and incurious eye by the young man employed by Madame Suresne to usher her illustrious patrons through the exclusive portals of her Bruton Street establishment into the luxurious fitting-rooms beyond. When, however, the young lady, having with great aplomb bent to remove a piece of straw from the hem of her walking dress, began to walk purposefully in his direction, the young man's expression hardened into what he hoped was a look of repelling disdain.

Madame Suresne had been very definite about the kind of clientele worthy of her skills. She had been equally specific about those who should be discouraged, and this inferior person was quite obviously one of the latter.

'I am sorry, miss, but I am h'afraid you have come to the wrong h'establishment,' he announced portentously.

Sylvestra had been in London long enough to recognize this dismissive ploy for what it was, but she had no intention of being fobbed off so easily. The angry impulse of the night before had crystallized into a very firm resolve. Her assault upon Lord Carston's defences would begin tonight, and it seemed a fitting irony that he should have provided her, in the name of Madame

Suresne, with the means of his own downfall.

And so she chose to deliberately misunderstand the young doorman, saying innocently, 'Oh dear! How silly of me, I must have mistaken the address. Perhaps you would be so good as to direct me to Madame Suresne's premises.'

On the rare occasions he had been obliged to put this well-rehearsed phrase into operation the result had always been shamefaced retreat, and so totally unprepared was he for this unexpected response, the doorman could only stammer helplessly and incoherently something to the effect that these were in fact they.

He was rewarded with a bright smile. 'Excellent!' exclaimed Sylvestra cheerfully, at the same time divesting herself of her gloves in a businesslike manner which clearly indicated her resolve not to take the hint. Finding himself a prisoner of that expectant green gaze the young man could only stand aside tamely.

Unfortunately for Sylvestra, Madame Suresne, who had chosen the young man more for his handsome face and excellent calves than for his initiative, had a second line of defence. This took the shape of a lady of indeterminate years dressed in severe black bombazine, who now approached Sylvestra, her sharp features set in lines of strong disapproval. Melting glances and dazzling smiles would certainly cut no ice here.

But Sylvestra was too used to disapproval to allow this to daunt her and she said clearly and confidently, 'Good morning. My name is Sylvestra Harvey. Would you oblige me by informing Madame Suresne of my presence? You may tell her that I am here on the recommendation of the Marquis of Derwent.'

Sylvestra might be lacking in town bronze but she could not fail to absorb some of the do's and don't's that shaped society. No respectable unmarried lady would use a gentleman's recommendation in such a way. If Madame Suresne was the astute businesswoman Sylvestra suspected, the marquis's name would gain her entry; if not, then she would at least have sown the seed of gossip if the collective affronted gasp and openly curious gaze of the various ladies seated in the elegant waiting-room was anything to go by.

'This is a respectable establishment, young lady—'

'Thank you, Miss Winters, I will deal with Miss Harvey personally.'

Madame Suresne was a tall, handsome woman with an indefinable air of good breeding which had been carefully and successfully cultivated for the benefit of her aristocratic customers. Beneath this genteel façade, however, there remained the shrewd business brain of her French merchant background and, as she led Sylvestra into a fitting-room, her mind was working busily.

Madame Suresne had put the same interpretation upon Sylvestra's reference to the Marquis of Derwent as had her assistant and every other occupant of her waiting-room. Gentlemen, particularly those with a reputation such as Lord Evelyn Carston's, only recommended the services of expensive and fashionable modistes to ladies with whom they enjoyed an intimate relationship. In general, Madame Suresne discouraged clients of that nature, for while they were undoubtedly very good customers whilst they remained in favour with their wealthy protectors, she was wary of offending her more respectable patrons. But there is always an exception to every rule and Madame Suresne thought she recognized one in Miss Harvey.

The return of the scandalous Marquis of Derwent to England's shores had done much to enliven an otherwise rather dull season. If this exotic beauty was his latest *chère amie* then she would soon have all the eyes of London upon her. It would do Madame Suresne's business no harm at all if she happened to be wearing that modiste's creations at the time.

'Now, how may I assist you, Mademoiselle Harvey?'

'Well, I know it is rather short notice,' began Sylvestra apologetically, 'but I am to attend a party at Vauxhall this evening and I wish to have a new gown for the occasion. Something . . .' – she blushed a little self-consciously – 'something, well, a little *dashing*.'

Madame Suresne correctly interpreting this to mean a garment designed to attract and hold the attention of a certain lord, who would find no shortage of ladies endeavouring to capture his interest, said she understood perfectly and Sylvestra happily placed herself entirely in the modiste's experienced hands.

'The bronze silk I think. Elise, *s'il vous plaît*!' Madame Suresne signalled to one of her junior assistants, who, rather new to her post and not blessed with more than average intelligence, was foolish enough to stammer, 'But *madame*, surely that is reserved for Lady Swaffham.'

'*Imbecile! Faites ce qu'on vous dit.*'

The French language was a mystery to Elise (Eliza to her family and friends) but those flashing black eyes were enough to send her scampering out of the room in no doubt of *madame*'s meaning.

But Sylvestra was intrigued. '*Madame*, I would not wish you to incur Lady Swaffham's displeasure on my behalf. If the dress is promised to her. . . .'

'Pray ignore that foolish child, *mademoiselle*, Lady Swaffham no longer wants the gown.'

'Oh?' Sylvestra raised her eyebrows in what she hoped was a manner which conveyed she wanted none of Lady Swaffham's cast-offs.

Madame Suresne was quick to reassure her. 'Mademoiselle Harvey, it is not as you suppose. Lady Swaffham ordered the gown some weeks ago, but when she came for the final fitting, she decided she did not care for it after all. Lady Swaffham has, I believe, a weakness for sweetmeats, *vous comprenez?*'

Sylvestra smiled to herself, yes she understood, and she could not deny it gave her a slight feeling of satisfaction. Which is quite ridiculous, she told herself severely. Why, anyone would think she was really in vulgar competition for Lord Carston's interest which was not the case at all! Fortunately, before she was obliged to answer the rather probing questions of her conscience, Elise returned with the gown.

Madame Suresne, with the help of her assistant, lowered the dress almost reverently over Sylvestra's head, and she felt the cool fabric slide silently over her body. Only when Madame had twitched and smoothed and adjusted was she allowed to turn and face the mirror.

The marquis's carriage was due to arrive at Green Street at eight o'clock and five o'clock found the ladies seated in what Mrs Harvey grandly termed the upper drawing-room, but which was in all honesty little more than a cosy private parlour. Mrs Harvey was engaged in her habitual daily perusal of the society columns and Emily was setting tiny precise stitches in a sampler with a neatness and patience Sylvestra could only marvel at. Sylvestra herself had just finished penning a letter of thanks to her cousin Geoffrey who had kindly sent her a gift brought back from his extensive travels abroad. It was an exotic Indian shawl, made of fine silk and with a deep fringe. Mrs Harvey had sniffed and deemed it totally unsuitable for a young lady making her debut, but Sylvestra was delighted with it. The shawl was a riot of sumptuous jewel colours. Peacocks embroidered in rich blues, greens and purples strutted and postured against a background of old gold. It could not have arrived at a better time; it was the perfect accessory for Sylvestra's new and illicit gown.

With that in mind, Sylvestra sealed her letter and said with determined casualness, 'I think I might ring for Duffey and start to dress for this evening; that is unless you have something for me to do, Aunt Julia.'

Mrs Harvey looked up in surprise. Normally her niece had to be chivvied constantly before she prepared for their evening engagements.

'Certainly, Sylvestra. That is an excellent idea. The lemon satin, I think will be most appropriate. Pray do not keep Duffey too long for she is to arrange Emily's hair.'

An hour later, Sylvestra was seated at her dressing-table obediently attired in the lemon satin. In fact 'lemon' did not do justice to its particular shade which was closer to acid green and served to make Sylvestra with her alabaster complexion look positively unhealthy. Judging by the dour expression of her maid, Duffey too had no great opinion of Mrs Harvey's taste and Sylvestra was briefly tempted to enlist her aid. A moment's reflection was enough for her to dismiss that idea; she could hardly expect her maid to take any of the blame. No, Duffey must be able to say with perfect truth that she had dressed Miss Harvey in the prescribed fashion. Still, her gown was not the only aspect of her appearance that could be improved upon.

'Duffey, do you think we might try a different way of dressing my hair?' she ventured, surreptitiously watching the maid's reaction in the mirror.

Duffey, who had just resignedly taken up the heated curling irons, paused. Mrs Harvey's chosen style for her charges was tight bunches of frizzed curls over each ear, a fashion that did not suit Sylvestra's statuesque beauty at all. Duffey would have dearly loved to have turned her considerable skill to a more becoming arrangement, but she also wanted to keep her job. In a straight contest between artistic integrity and expediency, the latter would have certainly prevailed. But the accumulation of petty snubs and minor injustices dealt her by Mrs Harvey tipped the balance in Sylvestra's favour, and the hated irons were discarded.

Having pinned her colours firmly to the mast, Duffey set to work with enthusiasm. Sylvestra's abundant hair was brushed until it gleamed like burnished copper and then in one practised, deft movement the maid twisted the fiery tresses into a heavy knot from which a single full ringlet was allowed to fall and brush one white shoulder. Sylvestra could barely contain her delight. A sophisticated stranger stared back at her from the mirror, a stranger who looked quite capable of competing with the likes of Lady Swaffham. Even Duffey permitted herself a small satisfied smile, not even the debilitating effect of yellow satin could disguise her young mistress's undoubted beauty, and at that moment it is possible that she would have given her support to Sylvestra's deception. In the event she was not asked to, and she left Sylvestra's bedchamber enjoying only the dubious satisfaction of scoring a minor victory in a much larger battle.

Eight

Sylvestra stood before the pier glass in her bedchamber and surveyed her transformed appearance rather anxiously. A slight frown creased her brow and the fingers that smoothed the luxurious fabric of her gown trembled. Anticipation had brought a glow to her cheeks and beneath the silken bodice Sylvestra's heart thudded uncomfortably. When one considered the probable magnitude of Mrs Harvey's displeasure when she discovered her niece's deception, this nervous reaction was not to be wondered at. But it was something more than a dread of her aunt's wrath that made Sylvestra's pulse quicken.

Sylvestra had wasted no time once Duffey had left her in consigning the yellow satin to the furthest recesses of her wardrobe, but the consequence of her impatience to ready herself for the night's proceedings was that having arrayed herself in her dashing new gown she was obliged to kick her heels for the best part of an hour. This gave her ample opportunity to reflect upon the wisdom or otherwise of her plan to 'seduce' the Marquis of Derwent.

This seduction – for so it had begun to figure in her mind – had been the reckless impulse of a moment, provoked by anger and bruised pride. If she had paused to examine it rationally, she would have been forced to concede that the indignation she felt, and indeed the lengths she was planning to go to in order to gain revenge, were perhaps out of proportion to the actual crime committed. But Sylvestra had been in no mood for reason.

Long after the house in Green Street slumbered, Sylvestra had still seethed over Lord Carston's iniquitous behaviour. She had tossed and turned, recollecting over and again each encounter with the marquis, and by the time night had turned into early morning she had discovered a cynical and sinister motive behind his every word and gesture. She had laughed at Emily for thinking the man a monster, but as the hours crawled by and sleep continued to elude her, Sylvestra succeeded in convincing herself that his depravity knew no bounds, and that by bringing this fiend in human form to his knees she would be doing her sex no small service.

Perhaps none quite throw off childish awe of the dark and the mysteries it shrouds, for it is certainly true that under its magical influence mature reason deserts, and notions discarded in an instant in the cold light of day appear not only totally reasonable, but inspired. Unfortunately, Sylvestra had allowed herself no opportunity to give due consideration to her wild scheme. She had been obliged to rise at an early hour in order to visit Madame Suresne without her aunt being any the wiser, and since that time her day had been taken up with the usual round of morning calls, shopping and letter writing. Only now, as she waited with increasing foreboding for Lord Carston's carriage to arrive, did she rather belatedly consider the drawbacks to her audacious plan.

Sylvestra sensed a change in herself, something more radical than the alteration of her physical appearance. She had always been in control of her emotions, always known exactly what she thought. But there was an ambiguity in her feelings for Lord Carston that unsettled her, made her unsure of herself. Sylvestra had been reluctant to come to the capital because of her distaste for the empty, frivolous existence of the fashionable world – or at least that was what she had believed. But it dawned on her that there was another reason; she realized she had been a little afraid,

afraid that all her aunt's unkind words were true, that she was not fit for polite society, that the ton would ostracize and ridicule her. And so she had hidden behind a shield of amused detachment; she had not sought to court society's approval and so she could not be hurt by its rejection. Now she was about to embark upon a new charade, and because she was *deliberately* flouting all the unwritten rules of polite behaviour, the ton's censure could again not touch her.

There was one difference: she was setting out to attract Lord Evelyn Carston, and even though she despised everything about him and her motive was one of revenge, she knew she was vulnerable. She would not easily shrug off his contempt. Something deep inside Sylvestra warned her that she was playing a dangerous game, that she was not just putting her reputation, nor even her virtue at risk, but her peace of mind. She had spent less than an hour all told in Evelyn Carston's company, but in that short time he had planted a seed of doubt in her mind. Doubt about the comfortable, undemanding life she had mapped out for herself, and a vague yearning for something more than the safety and security of marriage to a childhood friend.

What further intimacy with Evelyn Carston would do for her equanimity, Sylvestra scarcely dared hazard. It was as though she was standing close to the edge of a cliff. Part of her longed to take a step forward, to peep over the edge, but part of her hesitated, conscious of how dangerous that step could be. At that precise moment it was her cautious self that held sway, and had it not been for the entrance of Emily, Sylvestra would certainly have rescued the lemon satin from the depths of her wardrobe.

Emily's pretty countenance wore a troubled expression, indeed her whole demeanour was one of severe agitation. Emily had a great deal of sensibility, but Sylvestra knew that even her timid cousin would not be thrown into such a quake simply at the prospect of an evening spent in Lord Carston's degenerate company. Clearly something additional had occurred to overset her and Sylvestra guessed that Mrs Harvey had been busy. Just as Emily had grown accustomed to turning to her cousin for guidance in times of stress, so had it become a habit of Sylvestra's to take the younger girl's cares upon her own shoulders. It never occurred to her, therefore, to do anything other than set aside her own problems, and devote her full attention to soothing her cousin's anxieties.

Emily needed no encouragement to unburden herself, saying in an agitated voice as soon as the door was closed behind her, 'Mama says I must make a greater push to bring myself to the marquis's attention. She says I must contrive to be alone with him this evening, but I have no notion as to how I might go about such a thing! Even if I could – and I know it is my duty to do my best to obey Mama – I cannot help thinking Miss Pinner would frown upon such behaviour. Oh, what should I do?'

Sylvestra was acquainted with Emily's mentor through reputation only, but she was aware that Miss Pinner and any other person of proper feeling, would certainly view Mrs Harvey's crude stratagems with deep disapprobation. If it had not been for her cousin's genuine anguish she could have laughed aloud at her aunt's ridiculous attempts to entrap Lord Carston. But it would serve no purpose other than to increase Emily's distress if Sylvestra were to tell her that Mrs Harvey would be more likely to ruin her daughter's chances by gaining her a reputation for unbecoming boldness than to secure her a brilliant match.

Instead, she said in positive accents designed to strengthen Emily's wavering resolve, 'You should certainly do no such thing! Aunt Julia cannot have properly considered. You may be sure that Lord Carston would instantly see through such a vulgar ploy and it would very like give him a disgust of you, which is the last thing my aunt would want.'

Emily was momentarily cheered by this eminently sensible view. Surely Mama, who set such store by social niceties would feel the force of such an argument? Her optimism was short-lived, however, for it was instantly quashed by the conviction that her resourceful parent was quite capable of contriving this little tête-à-tête without any assistance from her daughter. She said as much to her cousin.

Sylvestra, remembering how Evelyn Carson had in the past adroitly avoided her aunt's snares, thought that was by no means certain. 'And even if Aunt Julia should succeed there is very little likelihood of the marquis proposing,' she reasoned. 'You are in very fine looks, Em, but I cannot believe Lord Carston is the kind of man to let the romance of a moonlit walk with a pretty girl go to his head! Now, if it were Mr Wynchip the case would be different.'

This only made Emily blush and hang her head. She said in a stifled voice, 'Mama realizes that, but she is persuaded that in such a situation it is quite probable that Lord Carston might might . . . overstep the mark, and if he should, she says she will make sure he marries me.'

Sylvestra's eyes widened. She had not imagined Mrs Harvey, for all her single-minded determination, would resort to such ruthless tactics. She was obliged to own that not even the Marquis of Derwent deserved to be blackmailed into matrimony.

Her disgust led her to exclaim unguardedly, 'How detestable! But I fear Aunt Julia will be the one to come off worst. Why, she must have windmills in her head! It is quite obvious that if society's opinion did not make Derwent wed Marianne Devenish, a few stolen kisses in the shrubbery at Vauxhall will not bring him to the altar.'

Sylvestra instantly regretted her incautious words. Emily had turned as white as her crêped muslin gown and her eyes were round with horror as she fearfully imagined her own fate mirroring that of the unfortunate Miss Devenish.

Sylvestra hastened to reassure her. 'You are quite safe, Emily. Lord Carson would not force his attentions on an unwilling female, of that I am sure—' She stopped short. Now why was she sure? After all in the course of the past twenty-four hours she had reached the most damning conclusions regarding the marquis's character and principles. Why should she instinctively feel confident that he would not add rape to his litany of crimes?

Fortunately, before her innate honesty obliged her to explore the reasons behind this contradiction, her anger at Lord Carston reasserted itself and provided her with the answer most acceptable to her present state of mind.

She said with a brittle little laugh, 'Men of Lord Carston's ilk are so puffed up with their own conceit that their vanity demands they should charm their victims into acquiescence.'

But it was not enough to convince Emily, who, caught between dread of incurring her mother's wrath and terror of the marquis, was close to hysteria. With a sinking heart Sylvestra realized that her conscience would not allow her to cry craven. It would be quite chicken-hearted to abandon poor Emily to her fate. There was one solution: only by drawing the marquis's attention away from Emily in the most public and outrageous way could her cousin escape both Mrs Harvey's displeasure and marriage to a man she feared.

With forced brightness Sylvestra cried, 'You are forgetting my own little scheme, Em!' Adding saucily, 'The Marquis of Derwent will have no time to pursue *you*, my dear, for he will be fully occupied with *me*.'

Emily raised her woebegone face to her cousin; her eyes still swam with tears, but a faint spark of hope now kindled in their melancholy depths. 'Oh, Sylvie, I know you will think me dreadfully poor spirited, but I am utterly cast down. I know I should not let you embark on such an odious deception, indeed every feeling revolts, but you are my only hope. . . .' Emily's voice broke on a pathetic sob and she was obliged to hunt feverishly for her handkerchief to stem the tears that spilled over.

'Nonsense, Emily!' said Sylvestra briskly. Faced with her cousin's despair, her own soul-searching seemed trivial by comparison, and she was a fair way to regaining her customary certainty of purpose. 'It will not be odious to me, I assure you. I shall very much enjoy spoiling sport for my aunt!' And deflating the ego of the Marquis of Derwent into the bargain, she added silently to herself.

Sylvestra's air of conviction had its usual beneficial effect on Emily's frayed nerves. She was able to dry her eyes and take notice of something other than her own misery. Inevitably it must be her cousin's altered appearance that should excite her awed attention.

Sylvie, you look . . . magnificent!'

'Magnificent?' queried Sylvestra, with humorous quirk of one eyebrow. 'You sound like Mr Wynchip. The adjectives I hoped to provoke were more along the lines of "shocking!" and "scandalous!", preferably uttered in tones of the strongest censure!'

Sylvestra jumped to her feet and struck a languorous pose. 'Do I not remind you of the merry widow. Pray do not disappoint me! I was sure I was quite *à la Swaffham* this evening!'

'Good heavens, you cannot wish to mimic that creature!' cried Emily.

'But indeed I do! Lady Annabel is my principal role model. Of course,' she added rather regretfully, 'I was obliged to draw the line at scarlet, my colouring does not allow it, but I fancy this will serve the purpose equally well. Come, dearest Cousin, speak plainly. Will I strike the marquis like *un coup de foudre*? At least,' she amended hastily, 'will it be enough to convince the ton that he might well be taken with me?'

Emily did not doubt it. She could not imagine there was a man alive who would not be bowled over by Sylvestra's dazzling beauty. It would be hard to argue with even this partial view. Despite her cousin's comic objection, Emily had chosen her adjective well. Sylvestra truly did look magnificent. Madame Suresne's legendary judgement had not failed her. The gown might have been designed for its present wearer, so well did it compliment Sylvestra's nubile figure and vivid colouring.

The bronze silk fell in graceful folds across Sylvestra's white shoulders plunging daringly low at the neckline and revealing the generous swell of her creamy bosom. The waist was fashionably high and the skirt was straight and narrow, the gossamer fine fabric moulding itself to Sylvestra's form and accentuating the length and shapeliness of her lower limbs. There was nothing gaudy or vulgar about the gown, but it was outrageous in its simplicity. Madame Suresne's unerring taste had permitted no needless trimming or decoration to detract from the elegance of its flowing lines or the rich colour of the vibrant silk, which provided the perfect counterfoil for Sylvestra's alabaster skin and brilliant emerald eyes.

There was a wicked gleam in those eyes as, thoughtfully contemplating her flawless complexion, she said meditatively, 'Of course, if I am to do the thing properly I should paint. But I am persuaded that would not escape my aunt's vigilance, and I would be immediately undone. Fortunately I am blessed with dark lashes, or I would certainly have been tempted to blacken them. However,' she added, twinkling merrily at her awe-struck companion, 'there is something I could not resist.' With a theatrical flourish she lifted her hem slightly to reveal her slender feet, encased in a pair of Grecian sandals, her toenails painted gold.

This was so unexpected as to surprise a shocked giggle from Emily, who was torn between admiration for her cousin's daring and the uncomfortable certainty that Miss Pinner would have been strong in her disapproval of a fashion more synonymous with the ladies of the *demi-monde* than with a delicately nurtured female. But Emily's timid nature inevitably yielded to a stronger mind, and the determination of a much-loved and idolized cousin, coupled with a degree of understandable self-interest, must override the influence of the worthy Miss Pinner, weakened as it was by distance.

Sylvestra, meantime, had succeeded in talking herself out of her earlier misgivings. The prospect of Mrs Harvey's all-out assault upon Lord Carston's bacherlordom did much to harden her resolve, calling as they did for drastic action in return. If she felt a faint flutter of apprehension when noise and movement below-stairs heralded the arrival of the marquis's carriage, she quickly suppressed it. Looking, thought Emily with a turn for the fanciful worthy of Mr Wynchip himself, like a beautiful warrior queen, Sylvestra flung a voluminous black velvet opera cloak over her finery, and went purposefully into battle.

Sylvestra's greatest fear had been that her aunt's sharp eyes would detect her subterfuge before they had even left the house. But Mrs Harvey was in such high croak at actually having the Marquis of Derwent's town carriage awaiting her convenience, that beyond exclaiming critically that there was not the slightest need for a cloak on such a balmy evening, Sylvestra's appearance went unnoticed. A note earlier in the day had brought the news that Lord Carston would drive in his phaeton to Westminster ahead of time in order to engage sculls to carry the party across the water to the pleasure gardens. Mrs Harvey's most pressing concern was therefore that their host should not be kept waiting. 'For nothing irritates a gentleman more than unpunctuality,' she informed her two charges as she bustled them out of the door.

Strangely, once out upon the pavement, her urgency evaporated. She had forgotten her fan; a maid was dispatched to look for it, and so followed ten minutes of futile searching. She was sure it had been on her wrist when she had left her bedchamber, it must be in the drawing-room. No? But of course! She distinctly remembered setting it down upon the satinwood cabinet in the hallway. Not there either? Then she was positive it was on her dressing-table, for when she came to think of it she had no memory of ever picking it up. The maid, flushed and breathless returned a negative. Then it was a mystery . . . unless . . . why yes! It was here in her reticule and had been all along. And so, finally, shaking her head over her own forgetfulness, Mrs Harvey regally ascended into the waiting vehicle, happy in the knowledge that by the following day not one of her nearest neighbours could possibly be ignorant of the fact that she had been handed – by not just one but two footmen in smart livery – into a fashionable town carriage, drawn by a team of perfectly matched bays, and emblazoned with a ducal crest. Set against such a triumph, the loss of Lord Carston's unimpaired good humour through their tardiness was felt to be a minor sacrifice.

The journey to Westminster with a detour to take up the Clives was swiftly accomplished, and Mrs Harvey found herself being handed down by those same smart footmen before she had exhausted half her superlatives in praise of the marquis's elegant equipage, or indeed a fraction of the odious comparisons to be drawn between their present transport and that of the previous evening. She had to be content with remarking to her nephew as they moved forward to greet their host, that it was clear that only the best would do for My Lord Carston. A man of his calibre would not send a hack carriage to collect his guests. But since this provoked only a grave nod of agreement and, 'Very true, Aunt Harvey. He will not be the first reckless nobleman to run through a fortune greater than he has claim to through his addiction to fine living,' it is doubtful whether a journey double in length would have enabled even Julia Harvey to pierce the armour of Mr Clive's self-approbation.

Lord Carston, as usual, was the perfect gentleman. It was entirely probable that he had heard Mr Clive's words, but his smile and words of welcome were all encompassing, and Sylvestra had to grudgingly admit the force of his charm. He was also quite distractingly, irritatingly attractive. Next to Mr Clive with his portly figure and bad tailoring, Evelyn Carston appeared the embodiment of male perfection.

He was a man of fashion without any trace of foppishness. His dark hair was cropped short and curled naturally over his brow, not for him the cunning disorder of the Windswept. His shirt points were of a modest height but crisply starched and his cravat whilst arranged neatly would not have aroused envy in the breast of any aspiring Pink of the Ton. What set him apart from the ordinary was the exquisite cut of his coat. The blue superfine fitted his broad torso like a glove. No broad lapels or buttons the size of saucers were needed to disguise a narrow chest, no wasp waist to compensate for a lack of breadth in the shoulders. That much overworked epithet, Adonis, would not have been out of place regarding Lord Carston, but to Sylvestra's mind even that fell short. The marquis had a masculine presence that no mythical god or classical statuary could command. Even as these thoughts rose unbidden in her mind, Sylvestra banished them, primly reciting in her head that old truism 'Handsome is as handsome does!' Besides she told herself severely, it was he who was supposed to be admiring her.

With this in mind she exclaimed, just as the party had finished exchanging the customary platitudes, 'I think you were right, Aunt Julia, it is far to warm for a cloak, I shall leave mine in the carriage if I may.'

'Really, Sylvestra, you are the most tiresome girl,' declared her aunt irritably. But Evelyn had already signalled to one of the hovering footman and was helping Sylvestra out of her cloak. What he revealed was enough to strike Mrs Harvey momentarily speechless.

Sylvestra turned to thank Lord Carston, at the same time trying to measure his response. His face was inscrutable but there was a strangely intense light in his blue eyes that made Sylvestra's breath catch in her throat.

He said in a low voice, 'I see you took my advice, Miss Harvey.' His tone was bland, registering neither admiration nor disapproval, and Sylvestra found she wanted him to say more. It was on the tip of her tongue to ask him outright whether her new image pleased him, but then it struck her that a *femme fatale* would surely not need to fish for compliments!

She responded instead with a hint of laughter, laying her hand possessively on his arm. 'Yes. I am doubly in your debt, Lord

Carston. Not only did you furnish me with Madame Suresne's address, you also provided me with a much needed *entrée*. "Miss Harvey" would have got me no further than the foyer, "the Marquis of Derwent" however, opens all doors.'

This disclosure, as she had hoped, appeared to startle Lord Carston, and he would have spoken had not Mrs Harvey chosen that moment to regain her power of speech.

'That,' she said awfully, 'is not the lemon satin.'

Since it was not within anyone's power to contradict this statement, there followed an awkward pause. Sylvestra realized rather belatedly that for all her vacillations and doubts about the evening's escapade, she had neglected to consider fully the part her aunt would play in proceedings. That this had been a glaring omission on her part was all too obvious. Judging by Mrs Harvey's wrathful expression, her anger was great, and in this temper she was more than capable of disregarding the embarrassment to all concerned and packing her niece off home, thus making Sylvestra's career as temptress perhaps the shortest in history.

It fell to Lord Carston to save the day. 'Lemon satin!' he exclaimed in tones of strong revulsion. 'I should think not! Excuse me, Miss Harvey, but nothing could be more unsuited to your colouring. I beg you will not think of it.'

It was a masterly stroke. Opposition from such a quarter could not be withstood and Mrs Harvey was reduced to protesting rather weakly, 'That might be so, Lord Carston. But you must agree that it is not at all proper for a girl in her first season to be wearing strong colours.'

Evelyn shrugged helplessly. 'Pray do not expect me to answer such a question. I do not pretend to understand the niceties of female fashion. We men are easily pleased; we will always admire a beautiful woman in a gown that becomes her. Whether it be *proper* is a question that scarcely troubles us, isn't that so, Clive?'

But Mr Clive could not be brought to agree. 'Our principles clearly differ, My Lord. Modesty and decorum are the qualities I admire in a woman. I would certainly forbid my wife to flaunt herself in such an unseemly manner.'

Lord Carston's brows snapped together. 'You go too far, Clive. I would advise you to keep your opinions to yourself.'

Mr Clive flushed in horror. The marquis's tone was unmistakable, and for all his professed contempt of the nobleman, he was not eager to pick a quarrel with him.

'You misunderstand! Nothing could be further from my mind than to cause offence to Miss Harvey!' he blustered.

'Then let us drop the subject,' interposed Sylvestra sweetly. 'What Cousin Frederick wishes his future wife to wear is a matter which can only be of interest to the lady in question, and since she is most certainly not of our number, you will forgive me if I say I find discussion of the issue tedious in the extreme.' She turned a dazzling smile upon Lord Carston. 'Shall we go?'

Lord Evelyn was prompt to take the hint, and Mrs Harvey was obliged to stand by and watch the marquis hand her undeserving niece into one of the waiting sculls, leaving the remainder of the party to divide themselves as they chose between the two craft that were left.

'I see you favour the direct method of sending your unwanted suitors to the right-about, Miss Harvey,' observed Lord Evelyn dryly.

Sylvestra chuckled, her vengeful intentions towards him briefly forgotten in their shared amusement. 'Nothing less will suffice where Mr Clive is concerned, I fear. Even that may not be enough. In my more fanciful moments I imagine myself at the altar, still vehemently refusing his flattering offer, whilst Cousin Frederick confidently assures the parson " 'tis nothing more than a sudden affliction of nerves"!'

Lord Evelyn joined in her laughter, 'But surely, Miss Harvey, you must admire such *amour-propre*? Not for Mr Clive the tragic vacillations of the Prince of Denmark!'

Sylvestra was quick to follow his lead. 'Indeed not! Imagine how he must have frowned upon the unseemly haste of the widowed queen's remarriage. His sense of propriety would not have allowed that to go uncensored!' Despite herself, Sylvestra found herself enjoying Lord Carston's company. Never before had she encountered someone who shared her own lively sense of the ridiculous, and the journey across the Thames, far from seeing the beginnings of an outrageous flirtation which would set the ton by its ears was entirely taken up with this nonsensical transposition of Frederick Clive into the role of Hamlet.

It was a fine clear evening, and in the twilight the pleasure gardens appeared to their best advantage. Beneath the indigo sky the coloured lanterns which lit the numerous walks twinkled cheerfully, adding an air of enchantment to the vista before them. Evelyn led Sylvestra to the centre of the gardens where, in a large clearing, gaily painted and brightly lit booths were arranged in a semicircle facing the Rotunda where there were already numerous couples circling to the strains of the orchestra.

For all he had been dragooned into hosting this particular party and despite a strong inclination to devote his entire attention to Miss Harvey, Evelyn was a practised host and he did his duty by all his guests, helping them to their seats and encouraging them to partake in the lavish supper which awaited them in their box.

It was only then, as Sylvestra was forced to admit, she was freed from the spell of Lord Carston's charm, that the inconsistency of his behaviour struck her. The conversation they had just shared, though light-hearted in the extreme, had revealed Evelyn Carston to be very familiar with Shakespeare's famous tragedy, and yet the previous evening he had begged Sylvestra to enlighten him. At the time she had suspected him of mockery, and now she was sure of it. Her indignation reasserted itself and she cast a look of loathing at the broad back of their host. Lord Evelyn was endeavouring without any marked degree of success to persuade Mr Clive to unbend from his stance of rigid disapproval of the frivolity which Vauxhall's relaxed atmosphere inevitably inspired amongst a group of young people used to the more disciplined environs of the ballroom.

'I hope you will join me in a glass of rack punch, Clive. Vauxhall is rightly famed for it.'

Mr Clive accepted the potent brew with an unctuous smile and an enthusiasm which was apparently feigned since he said the next minute in a muttered aside to Sylvestra, 'Of course, I must accept, but I do not usually partake in strong spirits. Wine, in moderation, is I believe not injurious to the system, but strong spirits have a debilitating effect upon the body and the mind.'

Sylvestra had been eyeing the bowl of punch thoughtfully. 'Pot valiant' was a term she had occasionally heard Captain Maynard employ during his days at Oxford to justify such foolhardy and entirely nonsensical exploits as 'boxing the Watch'. While she did not feel the need for a boost to her physical courage, if alcohol enabled her to overcome some of her inhibitions then it might be a very good thing. It needed only Mr Clive's disapproval to decide her, and refusing the lemonade offered her, she said with a bright smile, 'Are we ladies not allowed to sample Vauxhall's famous punch?'

'Dear me, no! T 'would not be at all the thing!' exclaimed Mrs Harvey with a titter, but she raised no objection when Lord Carston filled her niece's glass. After all, Sylvestra's hurly-burly behaviour could only compare unfavourably with her daughter's irreproachable manners.

Lord Carston appeared to find nothing objectionable in the request, and indeed there was a twinkle in his blue eyes that appeared to Sylvestra to hold far too much understanding. So he thought he knew what she was about. Well, he would not look so knowing for long! She took a defiant gulp and with a supreme effort of will controlled the strong desire to cough violently. Emboldened by her success she took another generous mouthful. Really it was the vilest stuff! But when presently a warm sensation began to creep along her limbs, Sylvestra began to be more appreciative of its merits.

Mrs Harvey had buttonholed the marquis and by dint of a variety of embarrassingly obvious ploys was endeavouring to promote conversation between him and Emily. Mrs Clive was fully occupied with her supper, and Mr Clive, clearly disenchanted by his intended's predilection for hard liquor, had retired disgruntled to the rear of the box. Sylvestra was therefore allowed to drink her wicked beverage in peace, idly watching the colourful scene before her and mentally plotting the downfall of the Marquis of Derwent.

The effect of punch on an already active imagination was prodigious, producing all manner of unlikely but highly satisfactory scenarios in which Lord Carston got his come-uppance. Sylvestra's favourite, and the one she dwelt upon most, was where the marquis, mad for her and suitably chastened, begged on bended knee for forgiveness. At this point Sylvestra would silence his protestations of undying devotion with a single withering glance, and plucking the hem of her gown from his imploring fingers, she would turn on her heel and walk out of his life. She was just debating whether to leave him with her derisive laughter ringing in his ears or to preserve a disdainful silence, when the appearance of nemesis at her side called her mind to the present.

Nine

'Would you care to dance, Miss Harvey? I hesitate to disturb one so obviously engrossed in what appears to be a most satisfying daydream, but it would be a shame for you to miss the rare pleasure of dancing outside the confines of the ballroom, particularly on such a fine evening.'

Icy sarcasm was Sylvestra's instinctive response to the marquis's condescending invitation – the unspeakable arrogance of the man to presume he was her only chance of a dance partner! For an instant, anger blazed from her green eyes and then as she remembered the role she had cast herself in, she smiled in what she hoped was a mysterious and provocative way and eyed him sideways from beneath lowered lashes.

'Oh I am not one of those poor creatures forever building castles in the air while their lives jog along in the same mundane manner. I intend my dreams to come true.'

Lord Carston smiled. 'Words of strong conviction, Miss Harvey. Unfortunately, in my experience those who are the most emphatic in their determination to achieve their ambition are also the most incorrigible pipe-dreamers.'

Inwardly trembling at her own daring, Sylvestra deliberately raised her eyes to meet the marquis's gaze. 'You should not doubt me,' she said, her voice low and intimate. 'I make a habit of getting what I want.' Sylvestra knew by the intense light that burned for a second in those blue eyes that her inference had not escaped him and it took a huge effort of will to hold his gaze squarely. Neither of them spoked but the tension that crackled between them seemed to Sylvestra to fill the silence like the roar of a distant waterfall. She had well and truly set out her stall now! The question was, how far could she go and still retain control of the situation? She feared she would only discover the answer to that when it was too late.

'My dear Lord Carston, you cannot have realized! The next dance is to be a waltz. Sylvestra could not possibly stand up until she has received the blessing of the patronesses of Almack's.'

Mrs Harvey's intervention broke the spell, and the disturbing light in Lord Carston's eyes was replaced with a gleam of wicked amusement as he said with spurious contrition, 'Forgive me, I would not for the world expose Miss Harvey to the censure of those formidable dames.'

Sylvestra did not hesitate to rise to his unspoken challenge. 'A ridiculous edict which I have no intention of observing. You will say I know, Aunt Julia, that I shall not be granted vouchers for Almack's but believe me I view that as no hardship. From what I hear the Assembly Rooms are nothing out of the common way, the company insipid and the refreshments paltry. For *that* I shall certainly not forgo the pleasures of the waltz.'

Mrs Harvey's face had turned an alarming shade of puce during this forthright speech and she fixed her niece with a basilisk stare. 'Really, Sylvestra, you will give the marquis a disgust of us all with your bold manner. If you have not the modesty to obey without question the rules of your elders and betters, then I am sure you do not deserve the honour of admittance to society's most exclusive club, but I hope you are not so selfish as to ruin your cousin's chances with your thoughtless ways.'

'I think we might satisfy both propriety and Miss Harvey's desire to dance,' interposed Lord Evelyn hastily, for Sylvestra's chin had taken on a stubborn tilt which showed she had no intention of backing down. 'I see Lady Jersey over by the Rotunda, it will be the work of a moment to gain her permission.' And before either lady had the opportunity to resume hostilities he had possessed himself of Sylvestra's arm and led her from the box.

'I congratulate you, Miss Harvey, you have succeeded in shocking Mr Clive, infuriating your aunt and intriguing me. I believe you may get exactly what you want.'

Sylvestra glanced quickly up at him, but his face was unreadable and she could not be sure if he was serious or once again merely teasing her. In a moment they were before Lady Jersey, Lord Carston, his usual suave self, making the introductions. Despite her avowed disregard for the opinions of society's leaders. Sylvestra could not help but be interested to meet this lady upon whose yea or nay a damsel's social success depended. She was surprised and pleasantly so. Nothing could have been further from the highly starched matron of her imagination than this chattering, feather-headed butterfly. It seemed laughable watching her flirtatious greeting of Lord Carston that this lady with her decidedly roguish eye could possibly be an arbiter of social decorum.

'Eve, my love! So good to see you in town. There is such a positive dearth of handsome and eligible men this season! How is your dear mother? It is such an age since I saw her. You should have brought dear Helen with you, but of course your poor father is not at all well.' With barely a pause for breath she turned her attention to Sylvestra. 'So you are Sylvester's granddaughter! I should tell you, Miss Harvey, that your grandfather was the most shameless rake in his day; I daresay he broke a dozen hearts before he fell in love with your grandmother.' She gave a nostalgic sigh. 'It is always a little sad I think to see a rake tamed. But, of course, it is lucky for you that it was so for I dare swear otherwise Sylvester would have gambled away every last penny of the family fortune. Well, my dear, reports have not done you justice. Where did you get that ravishing gown? Do I detect the touch of Madame Suresne? Yes, quite a diamond of the first water, wouldn't you say,

Eve?' Lady Jersey quizzed the marquis naughtily over her fan.

'No words I think could do justice to Miss Harvey's beauty.'

Sally Jersey's sharp eyes narrowed speculatively as she took in the gentleman's obvious sincerity and the lady's faint blush. 'Very prettily said, Carston,' she approved. Adding, 'But I warn you, Miss Harvey, do not be taken in by his soft words. I don't doubt all those years roaming the Continent have turned Lord Carston into an unprincipled flirt.'

Sylvestra's heart had jumped uncomfortably in her breast at Lord Carston's words but she refused to be cast into maidenly confusion. Instead she darted him a roguish glance worthy of Lady Jersey herself and said airily, 'Oh you need not fear, My Lady. Lord Carston made the mistake early in our acquaintance of informing me that all heiresses are beautiful, so you may be sure I take his compliments with a pinch of salt.'

Lady Jersey gave a delighted laugh. 'Did he indeed? How very unhandsome of him. Well, I shall give him a chance to redeem himself. Miss Harvey, may I introduce Lord Carston to you as a partner for the waltz? His manners may not be quite to your liking but I promise you he dances divinely.'

Lady Jersey had not exaggerated thought Sylvestra a few moments later. She was finding that it was one thing to carry on a flirtation with Lord Carston from a safe distance and quite another to maintain her charade whilst being held firmly in his arms and whisked about the floor as if she had no more substance than a feather. For the first few minutes of the dance Sylvestra simply surrendered to the novelty of the experience. Her only previous attempt at the waltz had been at the morning dances held by the ladies of Brimpton Mewsey to prepare their daughters for their debuts. Sylvestra's statuesque build had always guaranteed her the male role and it was a surprising and heady change to be swept masterfully through the steps in the arms of a partner whose physical presence made her own seem quite petite by comparison.

Evelyn watched her rapt face in amusement. Miss Sylvestra

Harvey was certainly an original. One moment an ice maiden determined to repel his advances, the next she had melted into a warm, intelligent and witty companion, the next into a flame-haired seductress, and now, with her eyes sparkling in innocent delight, a faint flush staining her smooth cheeks, she was like a young girl at her first dance. Which was the real Sylvestra Harvey? wondered Evelyn, surprised to find how much he really wanted to know.

Sylvestra sensed his eyes upon her and looking up misread the gentle amusement in his blue gaze for mockery. The sparkle faded from her eyes and the colour burned brighter in her cheeks. 'Now what have I done?' exclaimed Evelyn in injured tones, immediately perceiving her change of mood. Sylvestra shook her head mutely. How could she possibly explain her ridiculous sensitivity without giving him completely the wrong idea? She was supposed to be entrapping him; it would not do for him to think he had succeeded in charming her as he had numerous others. In Sylvestra's jaundiced mind, Marianne Devenish was probably just one victim of the marquis's heartless seduction. Doubtless he had left a trail of broken hearts in his wake during his years travelling the Continent. In the end Sylvestra replied rather weakly that she was feeling a trifle warm.

Lord Evelyn brought them to a halt at the edge of the dance floor. Although he was sure there was more to it than that he chose to accept her explanation, but found he did not wish to bring this moment of intimacy to an end.

'Perhaps you would prefer to take a stroll, Miss Harvey?'

'What an enchanting idea, Lord Carston!' Mrs Harvey had been waiting hawklike for the dance to end and was at the marquis's side in a matter of seconds, her reluctant daughter in tow. She was determined that her niece should be given no further opportunity to monopolize the marquis. 'We are quite settled here,' she said, indicating herself and Mrs Clive, who if she felt strongly about anything it was on the disagreeableness of unnecessary exercise.

'But I know you young people will not be happy until you have explored. Now, Emily, you take His Lordship's arm. I am sure I may trust my daughter to your care, Lord Carston. Off you go, do not worry about us, if Frederick will just be kind enough to fetch my shawl from the carriage I will be quite comfortable. No, no My Lord, Frederick will be quite happy to go. You go and enjoy yourselves. Sylvestra may wait for her cousin.'

And in this masterly fashion, Mrs Harvey succeeded in sending off her two charges entirely unchaperoned with the gentlemen she had chosen for them, optimistic of greeting upon their return, one if not two very interesting announcements with a great deal of exclamation and surprise.

The look of desperate appeal which Emily directed at her cousin as she was led away helplessly upon Lord Carston's arm was enough to jolt Sylvestra out of her daydreams and turn her thoughts to the very real problem she now faced. What a ninny she was! The waltz had been the perfect opportunity for her to put her plan into action, and now through sheer missishness it had completed backfired on her. Inwardly berating herself for having allowed her aunt to so easily detach Emily and the marquis from the rest of the party, she waited in seething impatience for Mr Clive to return from his errand. She had known Mrs Harvey would attempt something of this sort and she cursed her own lack of foresight. The return of Mr Clive empty-handed provoked a degree of surprise and puzzlement in her aunt which Sylvestra had no difficulty in labelling spurious. Indeed, she was hard put to keep her tongue between her teeth during the prolonged and entirely unproductive debate which ensued. It was at length decided, after exhaustive consideration of all the possibilities and several impossibilities that the missing shawl had never, in fact, left Mrs Harvey's dressing-room. A circumstance Sylvestra had never doubted for a moment. The marquis and Emily now completely out of sight, Mr Harvey allowed her niece and her escort to set forth on their stroll.

Sylvestra, who had been watching Emily's progress with an anxious eye, immediately directed her hasty steps in the same direction, leaving Mr Clive to keep up as best he might. Frederick Clive could not approve of his aunt's machinations, but he was quite willing to take advantage of them. On balance, the advantages of a considerable increase to his finances and the promise of greater social standing had outweighed the worrying flaws he detected in Miss Harvey's character. These, he had persuaded himself, sprang from nothing more than youthful impetuosity. She was merely dazzled by her first taste of ton life. Away from the temptations and extravagances of a London season, Mr Clive felt sure his own sober influence would have a beneficial effect. And by dint of dwelling upon this aspect of the case he had very quickly convinced himself that it was his duty to marry his cousin so that he might guide her along the paths of correct behaviour.

With missionary zeal, therefore, he set about his courtship. True to his nature, Mr Clive harboured no doubts about his ability to win whichever lady his choice should light upon, but even he was a little daunted at the prospect of wooing a female who was striding along at a most unladylike pace, and who,when he attempted to compliment her upon her beauty, only favoured him with a distracted and slightly impatient frown.

Sylvestra was so absorbed with the need to catch up with Emily and the marquis that she barely heard, let alone paused to consider, the motives behind Mr Clive's unexpected attempts at flattery. She was only aware that his ponderous steps along the leafy walks of Vauxhall were holding her back, and so in desperation she appealed to his sense of propriety.

'Mr Clive, I don't think you can have realized. Our cousin is at this moment entirely alone and unprotected with a man who has the reputation of an unprincipled rake! It is imperative that we find them, for who knows what indignities poor Emily may suffer at his hands!'

In fact, Sylvestra herself was tolerably sure Emily was quite safe from molestation. But since Mrs Harvey was apparently prepared to go to any length to secure this particular matrimonial prize, it was probable she would use this tête-à-tête, however innocent, as a tool to gain her ends. If Mrs Harvey were to claim Lord Carston had behaved dishonourably to her daughter, who, given his past record, would disbelieve her? Sylvestra doubted very much that her aunt would come out of the sordid affair with a marquis for a son-in-law, but the distress it would cause Emily would very likely make her ill.

At any other moment, Frederick Clive would have taken inordinate pleasure in thwarting the Marquis of Derwent's nefarious activities, but at present he had his own concerns, and Sylvestra's melodramatic appeal only exasperated him. It was perversely typical of the girl to be suddenly obsessed with the proprieties when up to that point she had shown on any number of occasions a quite shocking lack of delicacy.

He was betrayed into responding rather brusquely, 'My dear Sylvestra, if my aunt is content with the arrangement then it little becomes you to question her judgement.'

This earned Mr Clive such a look of contempt that even he could not imagine he had succeeded in creating the kind of mood in which his suit might prosper, and so he added hastily, 'But your concern for our cousin does you great credit, my dear. Indeed your kindness of heart is one of the very many qualities I find to admire in you.'

Sylvestra, momentarily diverted by this laughable attempt at gallantry, eyed him incredulously. Were it not for more pressing matters she would have certainly demanded that he list these oh so many qualities; she was tolerably certain he would quickly falter. That he had chosen this inauspicious and highly inconvenient moment to propose she could not doubt, but she was equally determined to stave off a declaration for as long as possible. It had occurred to Sylvestra that if her aunt's sole purpose in bringing her to London had been to see her married to Mr Clive, then once she was obliged to admit failure, Mrs Harvey would very likely wash her hands of her niece and send her home to Brimpton Mewsey. A week ago, Sylvestra would have been more than willing to hasten this outcome, but circumstances had altered, and she could not possibly abandon Emily to her fate.

But while she desperately sought for some means of distracting him, Mr Clive was already plunging into his prepared monologue.

'Sylvestra, you cannot have remained ignorant of my intentions. I came to London with one purpose in mind. It is the duty, I believe, of a man of my years and position in life to look about him for a suitable helpmeet. It is his responsibility to his family and his parishioners. And what could be more suitable than a match which will strengthen already existing bonds of family feeling and affection. It is a match that must provoke universal approval!'

Not quite! interposed Sylvestra silently, but Mr Clive was continuing.

'I came to London, as I have said, with the idea of our union already formed, but you must not think it was a fixed resolve, oh no! Whatever happiness our alliance might bring to our mutual family, I knew it my duty to consider the wider implications. I knew I must choose a wife fitted to the role I offered her. I will freely admit that on occasions I have been beset by doubts. There is a certain recklessness in your character, a tendency towards high spirits that gave me pause. But I am happy to say that I believe these are faults that may be rectified in time. You have, my dear Sylvestra, a quickness of mind which I am sure must allow you to recognize the wisdom of my words. In short, I think if you will allow yourself to be guided by me, you will not prove unworthy of the position I offer.'

Sylvestra listened to this speech, torn between amusement at her cousin's absurdity and indignation at his effrontery. The pompous fool really thought he was bestowing a great honour upon her! Her instinctive reaction was to give Mr Frederick Clive such a raking down that he would be left in no doubt as to how she regarded him as a matrimonial prospect. But tempting as it was to send him away with a flea in his ear, a moment's reflection told her she needed to handle this with a little more subtlety. She could not refuse him outright, for that would send him, she was sure, in high dudgeon to her aunt which would in turn signal her own exit from the capital. No, repugnant as it was to her nature, she must prevaricate. If she could just escape from this ludicrous situation before Mr Clive pressed her for an answer, then she would have bought herself some time.

Thus with a credible impersonation of a young lady thrown into confusion, she exclaimed breathlessly, 'Oh, Mr Clive, this is so unexpected!'

Mr Clive, who to his own way of thinking, had gone to a great deal of trouble to make his admiration and his intentions clear from the moment of their first meeting, felt that to describe his proposal thus was to stretch the bounds of credibility a little too far. However, he was aware that in such circumstances it is not uncommon for the lady to procrastinate in such a way, and as it was something of a relief to see Miss Harvey exhibit some of the signs of feminine helplessness he felt most at home with, he was prepared to be indulgent. He patted her hand reassuringly and said kindly, 'There now, you surely could not have been totally unaware of my regard?'

Sylvestra allowed her hand to tremble in his grasp and, turning her head aside, coyly said in a disjointed whisper, 'Oh no – that is – surely one cannot form an attachment upon so short an acquaintance?'

'Miss Harvey, you fear inconstancy, but be assured your fears are groundless. I hope I have reached an age where I might reasonably be expected to know my own mind. Fickleness of any kind is alien to my nature; once I have fixed my affections they are fixed for ever.'

He was clearly proud of this example of his steadiness of character, but Sylvestra was unimpressed. It was no great feat after all;

anyone might be supposed to view the addition of thirty thousand a year to their income with unswerving delight. Mr Clive continued to press his claims.

'I am glad to say I am not a creature of impulse. It is my belief that if a decision is reached based upon a methodical and rational assessment of the facts available then there should be no reason ever to regret that decision. And now that I have allayed your qualms, perhaps you would be able to give me your answer?'

'Oh but you talk as if – as if you were purchasing a new carriage!' exclaimed Sylvestra involuntarily, repulsed by this dispassionate approach to choosing a life's companion.

Frederick Clive seemed to find the comparison astonishing. 'Dear me no! Naturally I would devote far more time and reflection to the matter of my marriage.'

'I am very glad to hear it!' But Sylvestra's heavy irony was lost upon her companion, who, satisfied that he had overcome any obstacles to their future happiness, waited expectantly for her response.

Sylvestra regarded her cousin with a kind of amused desperation. The complacent smile that hovered upon his lips told its own story. Mr Clive did not envisage a refusal, and she was persuaded that anything other than the most baldly expressed negative would be interpreted as capitulation. If only she need say nothing at all! As if in answer to her prayers the relative silence of that particular area of the gardens was broken by a scream. To be more accurate it was more of a squeal; a not uncommon sound to be heard emanating from the shrubbery of Vauxhall once darkness had fallen, usually signalling nothing more sinister than a very half-hearted protest by one of the dashing young ladies who flocked to the pleasure gardens to the bold advances of some young blade.

But Sylvestra seized upon the sound, exclaiming with a great deal of conviction, 'That is Emily, I know it is. Oh, I knew something of this sort would happen! I must find her immediately!' And with that she turned and fled in the direction of the scream, showing a remarkable turn of foot for a young lady hampered by long narrow skirts.

Chuckling to herself, Sylvestra zig-zagged randomly through the various walks and avenues that crisscrossed the gardens. She could hear Mr Clive calling her name and she presumed he was giving chase. Well, she would lead him a merry dance and see if that did not cool his ardour – if ardour was the right word to describe a proposal of marriage based upon '*a methodical and rational assessment of the all the facts available*'! This thought brought on a fresh fit of giggles and so it was, laughing and breathless, that she turned a corner and ran headlong into the Marquis of Derwent.

Lord Evelyn was taken completely by surprise. One minute he was meandering rather idly along lost in his own thoughts, the next he had acquired an armful of Sylvestra Harvey, looking quite distractingly lovely with her face slightly flushed and her lips parted in surprise. His first impulse was take full advantage of this pleasant quirk of fate by stealing a kiss, but then common sense to a degree reasserted itself, and he set her gently back on her feet. His hands, however, continued to rest lightly on her hips, a circumstance Sylvestra found disconcerting in the extreme.

In fact, her sudden close proximity to Lord Carston had set her heart pounding in an uncomfortable way that could not be wholly ascribed to her recent exertions. She found that even if her brain been working sufficiently to prompt her to say anything, the unaccountable dryness of her mouth would have made speech impossible. It must be the punch, was the only coherent thought she could muster as she gazed mesmerized into those blue eyes. The silence between them seemed to stretch for an eternity, but then the noisy sound of Mr Clive's approach brought Sylvestra sharply to her senses. She looked quickly over her shoulder; if Frederick was find her with the marquis. . . ! But of course! It was perfect!

She turned back to face Lord Carston and before her courage could fail her, said urgently, 'Oh please! Will you kiss me?'

Ten

Lord Evelyn's dark brows snapped together. A moment ago he would have needed no second invitation, but the furtive glance had not gone unnoticed, and he had reached his own conclusions. 'With the greatest of pleasure, my dear.' His voice was harsh and contemptuous and before Sylvestra knew what he was about, he had pulled her roughly off the path and into the dense shrubbery.

'What are you doing?' she exclaimed in panic, but she got no further. One strong arm clamped her firmly to the marquis's chest and a ruthless hand covered her mouth, silencing her protests. Sylvestra writhed and struggled in vain; she was no match for Lord Carston's strength. The sound of Mr Clive calling her name grew gradually fainter until the only noises to break the silence were the buzz of nocturnal insects and the occasional rustle of a small creature in the undergrowth. Sylvestra had ceased to struggle. She now stood rigid in Lord Carston's grasp, her heart thumping uncomfortably against her ribs. Satisfied that Mr Clive was out of hailing distance, Lord Evelyn removed his hand from Sylvestra's mouth, but tightened his grip upon her person.

'Let me go,' hissed Sylvestra through gritted teeth, her eyes flashing emerald fire. 'I will make you sorry for this—' But again she was silenced, not by a hand but by a pair of hard, demanding lips. Again she struggled, again in vain. His kiss was ruthless and insolent, but even so the sensations it sent coursing through

Sylvestra's body left her senses swimming and against her will she found herself responding to his intimate assault. Sensing her surrender, his kiss deepened, and moaning against his lips she clung to him, fingers that had been clenched in white-knuckled rage plunging into his dark hair and drawing his head down to hers. And then, as abruptly as it had begun, it was over, and Sylvestra found herself thrust roughly aside.

Lord Evelyn, his breath ragged, turned away from her, his hands running distractedly through his disordered locks. '*Damn you.*'

To Sylvestra, adrift in a tumultuous sea of conflicting emotion, this bitter recrimination provided her with a focal point. 'Damn *you*! How . . . how dare you treat me so?' she raged, fighting back an irrational desire to burst into tears.

The marquis swung to face her, anger blazing in his eyes. 'How dare I?' he asked, his mouth twisting into a humourless smile. 'By invitation, madam, by invitation.'

'Oh but you were not supposed to—' Sylvestra came to a stumbling halt, biting her lip in vexation.

'Do pray continue. No, let me guess. I was not supposed to kiss you without Mr Clive as witness? You will forgive me, my dear, if I say I find your methods as crude and distasteful as those of your charming aunt. I will admit you had me fooled for a time with your ingenuous ways – I was even willing to believe you dropped my name at Madame Suresne's in all innocence, but I see now it was all part of your plan.'

'My plan?' Sylvestra asked weakly. Surely he could not have guessed the truth.

'Spare me the wide-eyed innocent. It little suits and I find it excessively tedious,' said the marquis with an exaggerated air of *ennui*. He added maliciously, 'Although your plan does display a degree of naivety. Before you try to play off your tricks on some other unsuspecting dupe, a word of friendly advice: a gentleman may certainly recommend a dressmaker to his doxy, but *not* to his future wife.'

'Future wife!' exclaimed Sylvestra incensed. It all became painfully clear. If she had not been so angry it would have been laughable. 'Of all the conceited, arrogant, self-absorbed. . . !' Sylvestra found she had not enough adjectives at her command to do full justice to his insufferable presumption. Something of the incredulity in her tone, however, caused Lord Evelyn to regard her more closely.

'You may abuse me at leisure, Miss Harvey, the fact remains that it is a conclusion that all but the most gullible would reach.' But something of the anger had left his eyes and his expression seemed to invite her to defend herself.

Sylvestra wished she had the self-command to say 'Believe what you will', but she found it intolerable that he should imagine she was trying to entrap him into *marriage*. Equally she could not admit her intention to make him fall in love with her simply to give her the satisfaction of spurning him. She was also loath to mention Emily's involvement. In the end she said helplessly, 'Please believe me, it was not that.'

The marquis's expression hardened. His contemptuous shrug showed clearly that he thought her response feeble, and he said coolly, 'I think we understand each other tolerably well, Miss Harvey. Shall we return to our box?'

Sylvestra knew that if she kept silent then Evelyn Carston would go out of all their lives; no efforts on Mrs Harvey's part would bring him into her net. Emily would be safe and she need not hesitate to emphatically refuse Mr Clive. But although it was the most logical solution to all their problems, Sylvestra found she could not bear Lord Carston to hold such an unflattering opinion of her.

'Oh wait! I will tell you,' she exclaimed, adding rather ungraciously, 'though why I should bother to waste my breath trying to disabuse you of this egotistical notion I don't know!'

Lord Carston looked faintly amused and he murmured, 'Unaccountable is it not?'

Sylvestra judged it best to ignore this provocation and launched straight into the – necessarily partial – explanation of her behaviour. She told him of Mrs Harvey's ambitions, of Emily's fears and of her plan to foil the former and allay the latter by convincing the ton that she and he were on an intimate footing. If it helped to repulse her prospective suitors then all well and good. She was considerably flushed and not a little embarrassed at the end of her tale, but she met his eye throughout and finished defiantly saying, 'So you see, *marriage* was the furthest thing from my mind.'

'So you are telling me,' said Lord Evelyn, his voice incredulous and quivering on the edge of laughter, 'that for your cousin's sake you were willing to risk your own reputation?'

'And to scare away fortune hunters,' she reiterated, for despite the laughter in his voice he made it sound like an act of supreme self-sacrifice, which she was uncomfortably aware it was not.

Lord Carston dismissed this. 'That you are more than capable of doing without going to such extremes. My dear girl, do you not know how utterly you would have been cast off by society?'

'I hardly expected a lecture on the proprieties from you of all people,' said Sylvestra, stung by his patronizing mode of address.

She regretted it immediately when she saw the shadow of pain pass across his face. 'Because I have already gone beyond the pale?' he queried. 'You may take my word for it, it is no pleasant place to be.'

There was a bitterness in his voice that stirred Sylvestra's compassion, and her guilt. Here he was trying to re-establish his credit with society and she had planned to plunge him once more into scandal and infamy. 'I am sorry,' she said impulsively.

He smiled at her wryly. 'Why? It is true.'

'No, I mean, it was thoughtless of me to try and involve you in my stupid plans. I – I suppose you have been given a second chance, and I would have ruined it for you.'

He smiled down at her and she felt an absurd rush of pleasure that she had succeeded in banishing the bitterness from his eyes. 'You are most certainly an original, Sylvestra Harvey. Now come, we had best go back. It would be ironic if, having repented your scandalous schemes, we were to become the talk of London after all.'

Sylvestra nodded mutely, the warmth of his gaze robbed her of speech, and she could only wonder at her vacillating emotions. One minute she was sure she hated him, and the next? Indeed it spoke volumes for the effect Lord Carston's proximity had upon her powers of thought that it was only then as they set off in the direction of the Rotunda that her cousin's absence registered with Sylvestra.

'Good heavens!' she exclaimed, coming to an abrupt halt. 'What have you done with Emily?'

Lord Evelyn regarded her with amusement. 'Naturally, when Miss Emily refused to countenance my lascivious demands, I throttled her in a rage and concealed her lifeless body in the undergrowth,' he responded gravely.

Sylvestra tried to frown at him reprovingly and failed hopelessly. 'I never imagined you would force your . . . your *lascivious demands* upon Emily. But you must have done something to frighten her for she would not have gone off on her own otherwise.'

Lord Carston assumed an expression of injured innocence. 'Nothing, I swear on my honour! I merely made some commonplace remark about the fineness of the evening – I may have mentioned the particular brilliance of the moon – and she looked at me like a startled rabbit, made some incoherent plea for me "not to", and before I could assure her of my willingness to refrain from anything she cared to name, she had taken to her heels.'

'Oh Lord!' gasped Sylvestra in consternation, remembering her facetious remarks of earlier in the day. 'I fear it may be my doing. Only to be fair, I did say you were *very* unlikely to be susceptible to a pretty girl on a romantic evening.'

'What!' His look of bemused astonishment proved too much for Sylvestra and she gave a peal of laughter. 'Oh my poor Emily, I love her dearly but she can be such a widgeon! But surely you went after her?'

'Of course I did. Despite what your hen-witted cousin seems to believe, I am not quite the heartless seducer of innocents. In fact, I flatter myself that I showed a great deal of sensibility, for I refrained from crashing through the shrubbery in hot pursuit, and thus avoided increasing her already insensible terror. I eventually caught up with her to find her in very good hands and, judging that my appearance upon the scene would only reduce Miss Emily to hysterics, I discreetly withdrew.'

'Very good hands?' queried Sylvestra, diverted.

Lord Carston shrugged carelessly. 'I cannot give you his name for I don't know it, in fact I don't believe I have ever set eyes upon him in my life. Handsome young cub, lately returned from the wars I would judge, for he was in a captain's uniform and wore one arm in a sling. Beyond that I can tell you nothing other than he appeared to be exactly the kind of gallant and upstanding young man who could be depended upon to act with perfect propriety when confronted by a damsel in distress.'

'I don't know how you can presume that!' protested Sylvestra, quickening her pace. She would never forgive herself if her own foolish remarks had led her cousin into danger.

But it seemed Lord Carston had judged rightly, for when they at length arrived back at their box it was apparent that the nameless young man had not only restored Emily to the safety of her mother's protection but brought a glow to that young lady's cheeks and a sparkle to her brown eyes that made Sylvestra exceedingly impatient to get her cousin alone and hear the full tale. Of the gentleman himself there was no sign, for, having completed his chivalrous task, he had quickly effaced himself, leaving Mrs Harvey on the one hand to berate her daughter for having got herself lost (for that was the rather lame excuse offered) and thus finding herself obliged to accept the assistance of a complete stranger, and on the other to congratulate her on making the acquaintance of such a personable and prettily behaved young man.

Sylvestra was obliged to contain her curiosity regarding Emily's anonymous saviour until after the Vauxhall party had broken up. If she had been purely concerned with the gentleman's possible wealth or social position then her interest would have been amply satisfied by her aunt's numerous speculations. Such comments as 'Of course, the army is often the career of a younger son, but a captaincy suggests a family of substance', clearly demonstrated the direction of Mrs Harvey's thoughts. In fact it spoke volumes for the charms of the mysterious knight errant that Mrs Harvey had greeted her niece's return upon the marquis's arm with only the mildest of reproaches. Her nerves still jangling from her close encounter with Lord Carston, Sylvestra was too thankful to be spared any probing questions to wonder at her aunt's uncharacteristic forbearance. She was not to know that it signalled a drastic revision of strategy on Mrs Harvey's part.

Mrs Harvey had sent her daughter and her escort off into Vauxhall's shrubbery more in hope than in certain expectation, for it had been slowly dawning on her for some time that there was little chance of the marquis dancing to a tune of her playing unless it was one that suited him. For Lord Evelyn Carston to completely re-establish his credit with the world, it was imperative for him to marry a young lady of excellent background and unquestionable virtue; for as long as he remained single his scandalous past could never be entirely forgiven or forgotten. That was the consensus among society's matrons – particularly those with daughters who satisfied said criteria – and it was with this axiom as her foundation that Julia Harvey had laid her plans.

Regrettably, Evelyn Carston had shown himself either impervious or indifferent to what was expected of him. Since his arrival in London he had made not the least push to fix his interest with any of the countless young ladies of good character thrown in his way. Indeed, the only female whose company the infuriating man had shown the slightest preference for was her niece.

It was not in Mrs Harvey's nature to admit defeat, even in the privacy of her own thoughts, and in that short space of time between Emily's return with her captain and Sylvestra's return with the marquis, she had almost succeeded in convincing herself that the Marquis of Derwent would not make a comfortable son-in-law at all. He had always been scrupulously polite in his dealings with her, but Mrs Harvey demanded rather more from her daughter's future husband. A deference to her wishes, a respect for her opinions, neither of which she could imagine from Evelyn Carston. Worse, Mrs Harvey had a nasty suspicion that the marquis would not hesitate to distance himself from his wife's relations if their company did not please him. Rosy visions of extended stays at Were Court and intimate suppers with the Duke and Duchess of Were had all but faded.

Besides, Evelyn Carston was clearly a hardened rake beyond reform; his predilection for the company of females of Lady Swaffham's ilk demonstrated that. Julia Harvey's sharp eyes had taken in her niece's flushed face and slightly dishevelled appearance and her suspicious mind had reached its own conclusion. Had she not always warned her husband how it would be? Sylvestra Harvey might be the granddaughter of an earl but she was no more a lady than the belowstairs maid! Well, her grand connections and her fortune would count for naught if she went the way of Marianne Devenish! Since she harboured no particular degree of fondness for her niece the only thing to mar Mrs Harvey's malicious satisfaction at having been proved right was the fear that Sylvestra's scandalous behaviour would bring disgrace upon them all. She determined at once to distance herself in the public eye from her niece's actions.

Happily unaware of the miserable fate her aunt predicted for her, Sylvestra slipped into her cousin's bedroom later that night determined to discover every detail about *Le Capitain Inconnu* as she had dubbed him with rather tongue-in-cheek romanticism.

Emily needed no encouragement.

'Oh Sylvie, do you believe in destiny?' she breathed dreamily, 'for I cannot believe our meeting was pure chance! I was so sunk in utter despair, and now. . . .' Emily sighed blissfully and hugged her knees to her chest.

'And now?' prompted Sylvestra, amused and a little startled at this radical transformation in Emily's mood.

Emily turned glowing eyes to her cousin's face. 'I have been so very foolish, Sylvie – *he* made me realize that. Mama cannot make me marry the marquis. All I need is a little resolution. I must simply be firm in my refusal.'

'This is what *he* said?' asked Sylvestra gravely, her green eyes dancing.

'Oh yes, and he is so right! I cannot imagine how I allowed myself to get into such a state.'

Sylvestra let out a peal of laughter. 'Oh Em, you are utterly priceless!' she gasped.

Emily was at a loss. 'But what have I said?'

Sylvestra wiped her streaming eyes. 'My dear, how many times have I said the exact same thing to you as your captain? I see now that I might have saved my breath. Now had I been a handsome young soldier. . . .'

Emily had the grace to blush, but her gaze did not waver and she said with touching dignity, 'Sylvie, I have always valued your advice and known its worth, but I have never had your strength. Now . . . now I think I can find the strength.'

'Whatever has brought you to your senses, Em, I am glad of it. But, forgive me for putting a damper on things, you don't even know this man's name and he does not know yours.'

Emily smiled, her brown eyes shining. 'You may laugh, Sylvie, but I know he will find me. I am sure of it.'

Sylvestra did not laugh, nor did she ask what had lent her cousin this uncharacteristic confidence, for it was written in the delicate flush that stained her cheeks and the stars that shone deep in her eyes. Sylvestra said no more, but kissed her cheek and left her to her dreams.

It was a thoughtful and uncharacteristically pensive Sylvestra who returned to her bedchamber that evening. To her shame, she realized that she was more than a little envious of Emily's new-found love. Sylvestra had too great a fondness for her cousin and too generous a spirit to begrudge Emily her chance of happiness, but it was lowering to discover that her mouse-like cousin whose timidity she had always secretly scorned, had overcome the fears and self doubts to which Sylvestra herself was prey.

Of course, Sylvestra had herself defied Mrs Harvey in her determination to marry a man of her own choosing, but she knew in her heart that that was an entirely different kettle of fish. In her present mood of candid self-analysis, Sylvestra could admit that when it came to saying and doing exactly the opposite of what the other wished, she and her Aunt Julia were as bad as one another. Indeed, she wondered if she would have been quite so fixed in her resolve to wed Captain Maynard had her aunt raised no objection to her choice.

Sylvestra thought back to the time when she had defiantly declared her intentions to Mrs Harvey and realized that in that moment she had invested more meaning and romance into her secret engagement than had ever existed in reality. Sylvestra looked further back into the past to that hot summer day when she had become betrothed to Perry Maynard. It was the week before Sylvestra was to take up residence with her aunt and uncle and only a day before Perry was due to leave to join his regiment and the two friends were spending a last day together. They had planned a ride across the Maynard estate but the heat was too intense to make such an excursion pleasant and by mutual consent they had soon brought their mounts to a halt in the shade of some trees. There they had sat and idled the day away. Perry had been full of his new captaincy and eager to lead his men into the thick of the action and Sylvestra had envied his future life of adventure.

Sylvestra recalled how low she had felt that day. Her father had been dead less than a week, her friend would soon be gone and she herself was being forced to leave her beloved home to live with relatives who might have been strangers for all she knew of them. How had the subject of marriage arisen? Sylvestra could not remember. Perry had said how much he would miss her, how he pitied her having to leave Earlam Park, and somehow it had seemed a short and logical step. Looking back, perhaps she had been quicker to take that step than her friend, but Perry had taken very little persuasion to see what a perfect solution it was. Sylvestra blushed. A perfect solution for whom? Nobody but herself. Poor Perry; she had dragooned him into agreeing to marriage just as in their childhood she had bullied him into countless foolhardy escapades against his better judgement.

But how quickly it had escalated! In a matter of hours a casual agreement between friends had become an official engagement. Lord and Lady Maynard had greeted the news with surprise but raised no objections. If Perry's mother had any doubts about her son's marriage to a girl who had led him into trouble all his life, the worldly advantages of such a match swiftly quashed them and she wasted no time in broadcasting the news amongst her friends and neighbours.

With the benefit of hindsight, Sylvestra could see that she had clung to Perry like a lifeline in a changing world. Their friendship was deep and abiding, but marriage? Sylvestra had always teased Emily's dreams of love, privately believing that her cousin along with every other susceptible female of their generation had succumbed to the present fashion for romance, perpetuated by writers such as Lord Byron and affected by fools like Aubrey Wynchip. But now she was not so sure. Her encounters with a certain lord had filled her with doubts and she now wondered if friendship alone was a sound basis for a marriage.

Once Sylvestra allowed Evelyn Carston to enter her thoughts rational examination of her situation became impossible, for she could think of only one thing – that kiss! However hard she tried, Sylvestra could not stop herself dwelling upon the passionate embrace she had shared with the marquis. Just the memory was enough to quicken her pulse and flood her cheeks with hot colour. And her own response! Any self-respecting female would have done all in her power to resist Lord Carston's rakish advances, instead she had been the easiest of conquests. It was quite ridiculous the way she had gone to pieces. It was not as though she had never been kissed before. But then she had never been kissed quite like that before. She recalled the affectionate peck Perry had bestowed on her before they had parted. Imagine the difference if it had been Lord Carston taking leave of his betrothed!

Sylvestra caught herself up sharply. She was not engaged to Lord Carston and nor would she want to be. Just think of his past! No, you are far better off with Perry, she told herself severely. And if such a prospect was not designed to excite then at least she knew where she was with Captain Maynard which was certainly not the case with Evelyn Carston. And with this judicious thought Sylvestra surrendered to sleep, her dreams, however, refusing to be so rational.

Eleven

It seemed to Sylvestra that she had hardly closed her eyes before she was being awakened by a gentle but persistent knocking on her bedroom door. Bright sunshine slanting through the drapes, however, showed the morning to be already several hours old.

'Come in,' called Sylvestra rather groggily, wondering at the dull ache in her head and with a groan remembering the rack punch. Gingerly she eased herself into a sitting position and looked questioningly at the young maid who hovered uncertainly in the doorway.

'Please, miss. A note for you, miss.' The girl scuttled forward and proffered the sealed sheet of paper with a bobbing curtsy. Sylvestra broke the seal and with an effort forced bleary eyes to focus. The note was short and to the point, and it succeeded in banishing the last remnants of sleep.

Miss Harvey

A drive in the park seems the ideal opportunity for us to continue our interesting conversation of yesterday evening. I will call for you at ten.

Your servant,

Evelyn Carston.

'My servant!' exclaimed Sylvestra with incredulous loathing, jumping impetuously out of bed and immediately regretting it as her head protested strongly to such sudden movement. This only exacerbated her umbrage at Lord Carston's peremptory command and seating herself at her escritoire, she dashed off a note designed to leave the arrogant lord in no doubt of her antipathy for his company.

'You may give this to his lordship's man.'

The young maid, who was considerably in awe of the beautiful Miss Harvey, bobbed another nervous curtsy and said in an anxious whisper, 'Please, miss, Lord Carston's servant did not wait for a reply.'

'Oh.' Sylvestra frowned and hesitated. Memories of her dreams teased her.

'Shall I send one of the footmen?' ventured the maid diffidently.

'Yes . . . that is, no.' Sylvestra paused irresolutely. To her dismay she found that her indignation at Lord Carston's high-handed manner was being inexorably supplanted by the treacherous thought that there was nothing she would like better than to spend a spring morning driving in the company of the Marquis of Derwent.

The note was crushed. 'You may send Duffey to me please, Mary.' The maid flushed pink with pleasure and hastened away to find the dresser. Fancy Miss Harvey remembering her name!

Sylvestra did not wait for Duffey before starting her morning ablutions. The handsome bracket clock on her dressing-table informed her that it was already well after nine – not that she had the slightest intention of making any extraordinary haste for his lordship's benefit. The cold water left in the pitcher from the previous night was just what was needed to refresh her sleepy eyes and cool her aching head, so what was the point of waiting for the maid to bring fresh?

Duffey entered moments later to find Sylvestra dragging a brush ruthlessly through tangled locks. Frowning her disapproval, the maid possessed herself of the silver-backed hairbrush and with less vigour but considerably more skill began to tease the untidy Titian curls into a semblance of order.

'Oh, Duffey, I am expecting a delivery of gowns from Madame Suresne. Have they arrived?' Sylvestra asked anxiously. She had had the forethought to order herself a selection of new ensembles, knowing how unlikely it was that her aunt would allow her a second opportunity to visit the fashionable modiste.

'Yes indeed, miss. I took the liberty of selecting the blue walking dress. Mary is pressing it now.'

'Perfect! That is exactly what I would have chosen myself. You are a mind reader, Duffey!'

The maid unbent sufficiently to bestow a small smile upon her young mistress. In fact, the gowns that had arrived that morning had given Duffey an added respect for Miss Harvey. For all her wild ways she was certainly possessed of more natural good taste than Mrs Julia Harvey.

The walking dress of palest lavender-blue crêped muslin was not as daring as the bronze evening gown, but it was every bit as stylish. Silk ribbon of a deeper hue bound the high waist, trimmed the low square neckline and tied the dashing deep poke bonnet lined with pleated white satin. The exigencies of fashion were uppermost, and so the only concession to the decided chill in the air was a close-fitting redingote of matching velvet and a pair of jean half boots. Studying her appearance with some satisfaction, Sylvestra felt that at least on the outside she was the epitome of the cool young lady of fashion, whatever her inner confusion might be.

Twenty minutes later found Sylvestra seated in the breakfast parlour unenthusiastically nibbling a slice of thinly buttered toast. Of course, her lack of appetite and the fluttering sensation in her stomach could be blamed upon the previous evening's excesses; the overwhelming desire to glance at the clock every few seconds was not so easily explained.

At precisely five minutes to ten, a business-like rap at the front door startled her into setting down her coffee cup a trifle hastily. Thanking heaven that it was the white damask tablecloth rather than her gown that came off worst, Sylvestra rose quickly to her feet and waited impatiently for the butler's ponderous steps to traverse the hallway. The caller clearly shared her impatience, for she had barely time to smooth her gown and don her new bonnet before the door of the breakfast parlour was thrown open – to reveal Mr Frederick Clive.

The level of her disappointment made Sylvestra less than welcoming of her suitor. 'Mr Clive, I am afraid you find me on the point of going out. My aunt and cousin have yet to rise—'

Mr Clive held up his hand. 'It is you I have come to see, Sylvestra, and I shall not detain you long. The reason for my visit I feel sure need not be explained – we did after all discuss the matter in some depth before the evening took on what I can only describe as a *farcical* turn. I come simply for your answer, my dear.'

With a jaundiced eye, Sylvestra regarded Mr Clive's confident demeanour. In her present mood all thoughts of procrastination were banished and she answered him firmly. 'You have come to the point swiftly, Mr Clive, and so I shall do you the courtesy of being equally forthright. My answer is no. I am quite certain we would not suit, and I am sure you would reach the same conclusion were you to give it more thought.'

Rather taken aback by this starkly expressed refusal, Mr Clive was momentarily nonplussed. He did not lose his poise for long.

'I see how it is, my dear.' He smiled at her, his voice taking on an embarrassingly waggish tone. 'I have been too abrupt. I know how it is with you young girls. You yearn for romance. Had I composed an ode to your beauty I warrant you would not be so hard-hearted!'

This gibe at Mr Wynchip's worship of her did nothing to improve Sylvestra's temper. 'Pray, Mr Clive, do not tax your brain with any such endeavour! I promise you it would serve no purpose. My mind is quite made up. I will not be your wife.'

A knock at the front door spurred Sylvestra on to add naughtily,

'Indeed, I doubt very much that I shall ever marry. My fortune allows me to be independent, and why, I ask myself, should I relinquish it to a husband when I am sure I would have much more fun as a single lady.'

Right on cue, the butler announced the Marquis of Derwent, leaving an outraged Mr Clive in no doubt of the kind of fun his wayward cousin was contemplating. His expression became distinctly frosty.

'Then there is no more to be said. I believe I can leave you to your fate with a clear conscience. It is through no fault of mine that you tread this path. I only hope my aunt has greater success in making you conscious of the folly of your ways. I bid you good day, Cousin Sylvestra!' And with abrupt bow and the barest nod in Lord Carston's direction he was gone.

Lord Evelyn regarded Sylvestra with lazy amusement. 'Now what have you been about to put your dullard cousin in such a pother?'

Sylvestra smiled, but distractedly. Mr Clive's parting shot had certainly shown her the folly of her impetuous tongue. It was a certainty that she would be sent back to Brimpton Mewsey when Aunt Julia was apprised of this morning's work.

But she could not say as much to Lord Carston. After all, he believed she could not wait to leave the capital and she could hardly explain to herself let alone to him her sudden contrary reluctance to bring her season to an end.

So she smiled again, mischievously, and said airily, 'I was just informing Mr Clive that I thought marriage would not suit me. I told him I would enjoy life as an unattached lady far more.' She slanted a roguish glance at him through lowered lashes. 'The timing of your entrance was quite perfect, Lord Carston.'

Lord Evelyn gave a shout of laughter. 'Baggage! Are you quite determined to ruin us both?' He paused for a moment, his openly admiring gaze taking in her elegant appearance. 'Though I cannot regret one result of your attempt to blacken my name.'

Sylvestra blushed faintly under his appreciative scrutiny, but wondered at his meaning. Her puzzlement must have shown for he obligingly explained. 'Your patronage – under my aegis, of course – of Madame Suresne.'

Sylvestra's blush deepened as she remembered the unflattering inference the marquis had initially put on her use of his name to gain an entrée into Madame Suresne's rooms, and for a moment her indignation was aroused.

Lord Evelyn correctly interpreting her heightened colour held out his hands in a gesture of appeasement. 'It was meant to be a compliment.'

It was impossible for Sylvestra to resist the laughter dancing in those blue eyes, her own twinkling mischievously back at him as she dropped a saucy curtsy. 'Why, then, thank you kindly, sir! Now, may we go before my aunt decides to rise?'

She did not need to say more. The thought of encountering Mrs Harvey at such an early hour of the morning was enough to spur Lord Evelyn into action. Within a very few moments he was expertly steering his team of long-tailed greys through the city's early morning traffic. It was by no means the modish hour to be seen in Hyde Park, but there was enough of a sprinkling of fashionable promenaders to add colour and interest to the scene. And the sight of the Marquis of Derwent driving the beautiful Miss Harvey was enough to send a ripple of speculation through those members of the ton sufficiently hardy enough to brave the open air before noon. The tale of Miss Harvey's visit to Madame Suresne's had quickly circulated amongst society's ladies, along with any number of meaningful looks and significantly raised eyebrows.

The couple could not remain oblivious long to the stir they were causing. Sylvestra glanced surreptitiously at her companion, but Lord Carston's profile displayed no sign of consciousness and he continued to maintain an easy flow of light conversation. Sylvestra determined to follow suit, but having received the cut direct from no less than three ladies with whom she could claim acquaintance, her responses to Lord Carston's banter became strained and her laughter had a brittle edge.

Lord Evelyn apparently sensed her discomfort, for, as soon as he was able, he turned his phaeton off the main carriageway on to a more secluded avenue, and once they were beyond the gaze of accusing eyes, he slowed his cattle to a halt and signalled his groom to go to their heads.

'Would you care to stroll for a while, Miss Harvey? The first of the spring bulbs make a fine show if you do not object to leaving the path.'

Sylvestra turned to him, her eyes rather over-bright and smiled gratefully. 'I would like that very much, Lord Carston.'

To his surprise, Evelyn found himself more touched by that brave smile than he had ever been by Marianne's easy tears and, as he handed Sylvestra down, it took all his will-power not to gather her into his arms. It was an urge aroused not merely by lust but by a tenderness he had never before experienced. How strange, he thought, that this beautiful, spirited and independent creature could stir not only his senses but his compassion. But, strange or not, it was a feeling that persisted and for the first few moments of their walk he was held silent in wonderment.

Sylvestra, too, was silent as she slowly recovered her composure. After all her brash claims of indifference, how ridiculous to be so affected by the snubs of people who were after all no more than acquaintances. She certainly did not deserve Lord Carston to be so understanding. In fact, had he railed at her for the embarrassment she had caused him, she could not but feel he would have been fully justified. This almost overset her once more, for while her own personal mortification was great, the thought that the marquis was showing such sympathy when he was in all probability wishing her to the devil, plunged her into quite disproportionate gloom.

It would probably be better for all concerned if she did go home to Brimpton Mewsey, Sylvestra thought piteously. Lord Carston would be relieved of her embarrassing presence and she had learnt enough of society to know that her supposed scandalous liaison with the Marquis of Derwent would not live long in the collective memory after her departure. Aunt Julia would certainly shed no tears and it seemed Emily had her own concerns well in hand. Resolved upon the martyr's course – and swiftly suppressing the rebellious thought that it seemed vastly unfair that she should suffer all the unpleasant consequences of an affair with a renowned rake but enjoy none of its rewards – Sylvestra voiced her intentions to her companion in a manner intended to show nothing but unalloyed enthusiasm for the plan.

If Lord Carston felt any relief at her declaration then it did not show. 'What! Run away? I had not thought you so faint-hearted, Miss Harvey.'

This, as it was intended to, made Sylvestra bridle. 'I am not faint-hearted. I have told you before that I have no liking for city life, and now that I have refused Mr Clive's offer of marriage I feel sure my aunt will relent and allow me to return home.'

'I think it very poor of you to abandon me thus,' said Lord Evelyn in injured tones.

Sylvestra regarded him sceptically. 'Abandon you?'

'The beautiful and wealthy Miss Harvey, all set to take the town by storm is obliged to curtail what promises to be a dazzling season and return to rural obscurity in order to escape the unwanted attentions of Lord Evelyn Carston. Imagine what that would do to my credit in society!'

'Oh, but surely no one would think – oh, you are bamming me!' Sylvestra tossed her head angrily and walked on. Infuriating man! How was it that he could manipulate her emotions in such a way?

He caught up with her in a few long strides, a hand on her arm forcing her to stop and face him. 'Yes, I was bamming you. But seriously, if you are thinking of quitting London out of some idiotish notion of saving my reputation then put it out of your head.'

'It's not that at all. I simply—'

Lord Evelyn put a hand beneath Sylvestra's chin, compelling her to meet his gaze, and when she saw the tender, teasing look in his blue eyes her half-hearted protests died unsaid.

He smiled down at her. 'Besides, I shall be envied by the whole of London – well, the male half leastways – when it gets about that I have won the the . . . er,' he paused wickedly – 'the *affections* of the beautiful Miss Harvey.'

Sylvestra blushed, but she was determined not to let his flattery nor his physical proximity distract her. 'Half is right, My Lord. No doubt such . . . such conquests carry a certain cachet within the walls of the gentlemen's clubs, but I can hardly suppose they would be looked upon with the same indulgence by society's matrons.'

'I own I had not thought of that,' admitted Lord Carston, apparently much struck. 'I would be considered a pariah by any mother of delicately nurtured females. I doubt if any lady of proper feeling would have me for a husband.'

This was an aspect that had never presented itself to Sylvestra and it only compounded her wretchedness. The guilt she felt at having potentially blighted the marquis's prospects with the love of his life being second only to a ridiculous and totally unfounded dislike of the unknown lady.

'I am sure society's opinion of you would count for nothing if the lady truly loved you,' she said in a small voice.

'I hope you may be right.' For a moment he was serious, his expression unfathomable. He took her arm and they continued to stroll. 'But, for the moment, if it keeps the matchmakers at bay then I shall consider it a bonus!'

'Then you have no particular lady in mind?' It came out before Sylvestra could stop it, and she was only thankful that the deep brim of her bonnet hid the fluctuating colour in her cheeks.

'Oh, I have a lady very particularly in mind, but as she is an avowed spinster and I am a confirmed bachelor there seems to be no hope for us.'

Sylvestra looked up at him quickly, her heart beating double time. Could he mean? The warmth in his eyes seemed to answer the question in her own.

'Sylvie? Look Georgie, it is Sylvie! Oh, Mama, stop the carriage do! Sylvie! Sylvie!'

It was impossible, however she might wish it, to ignore this untimely intervention and Sylvestra turned to see who hailed her so enthusiastically. She was greeted by the sight of a landaulet carrying a middle-aged matron and two young ladies. As the carriage drew nearer, the identity of the occupants became apparent.

'Lady Maynard! What a surprise! How do you do?'

Lady Maynard acknowledged her son's intended bride with a thin smile. 'I hardly recognized you, Sylvestra; we are not used to seeing you so *à la mode*.'

'No indeed,' interrupted one of the young ladies. 'And with a gentleman too!' This seemed to afford the two girls a great deal of amusement and they dissolved into giggles which the quelling frown of Lady Maynard did little to subdue.

Sylvestra was acutely aware of how it must look; to be discovered walking with a man, unattended by even a maid, in a secluded corner of the park would not go unremarked by someone of Lady Maynard's strict notions. But she had no intention of hanging her head in shame.

'Thank you, Lucy, for reminding me, I have been remiss. Lady Maynard, pray allow me to introduce Lord Evelyn Carston. Lord Carston, Lady Maynard, a friend and neighbour of my late father, and her daughters Miss Maynard and Miss Lucy.'

'I think it vastly unfair that Georgie should be Miss Maynard and I merely Miss Lucy for she is only ten minutes my elder. We are twins you know,' Lucy informed Lord Carston rather unnecessarily since not only had Nature blessed both girls with the same plump rosy features and golden curls, but their mother in her wisdom had chosen to dress them in identical promenade gowns of pink sprigged muslin.

Lord Carston agreed gravely that it was most unjust, prompting another bout of helpless giggles.

'What brings you to London, Lady Maynard?' asked Sylvestra. 'I had thought your intention was to come next year.'

'It is only a fleeting visit. The girls will make their official come out after their seventeenth birthday, but it will do them no harm to see a little of society. Making one's debut can be such a daunting experience for girls fresh out of the schoolroom, don't you agree?'

'Oh, indeed,' concurred Sylvestra, keeping a straight face with difficulty. Since Georgiana and Lucy were busily occupied in ogling the marquis out of countenance, it was safe to say that these particular schoolroom misses stood in no danger of being overawed by the splendours of a London season.

Lady Maynard was continuing. 'Once Perry rejoins his regiment we will return to the country. But what kind of a mother would I be not to come and see her son when he is home injured from the war?'

'Perry is hurt?' asked Sylvestra, genuinely alarmed.

Lady Maynard raised her eyebrows. 'You did not know? I felt sure he would have written to you.'

'No!' Sylvestra hesitated, it was weeks since she had written to her betrothed. 'That is, I am not sure if he has our London address,' she finished rather lamely.

'Well, doubtless you have had many things to distract you since you came to town, my dear.' Lady Maynard succeeded in making this a reproach rather than a justification.

Sylvestra strove to make amends. 'We are in Green Street. My aunt would be delighted to receive you should you care to call, and Perry if his injury allows it.'

Lady Maynard relented a little in the face of Sylvestra's obvious concern for the welfare of her son. 'Perry assures me it is "only a scratch", though to me a ball in the shoulder sounds a good deal more than that.'

'I am glad it is not too serious. Please give him my best regards,' said Sylvestra sincerely, very conscious of her neglect of all the Maynards since she had come to town. She and Lady Maynard had not always seen eye to eye, and she had never had very much in common with the twins, but the whole family had always been kind to her, especially during her father's illness.

The Maynard party soon moved on leaving Sylvestra with the unpleasant sensation of having come back to earth with a jolt. She should, of course, be delighted that she and her fiancé were to be reunited after so many months apart. Why was it then that she felt anything but elated?

Lord Evelyn sensed there was something more to their recent encounter than just a chance meeting with old friends. He should, of course, be grateful for the interruption, for his conversation with Miss Harvey had taken a dangerous turn. He cursed his own stupidity. It had been sheer madness to pursue his acquaintance with the Harveys, but, like a fool, he had pressed on regardless in the mistaken and arrogant belief that he could control the situation. What he felt for Sylvestra Harvey was beyond the control of reason and common sense. Again he cursed his stupidity, but this time it was mistakes made long ago and beyond mending against which he impotently railed.

Their walk had come to an end, and by unspoken agreement Sylvestra and Lord Carston made their way in silence back to the waiting phaeton. Only when they were once more in motion did Sylvestra pluck up the courage to explain her true connection with the Maynard family. What had happened between her and Lord Carston and, more importantly, what would have happened had their conversation been allowed to run its course, Sylvestra was not entirely sure, but her conscience told her that it would be wrong to continue to hide her betrothal from the marquis.

'I think I should tell you, Lord Carston, that Captain Maynard and I are engaged to be married.' She did not wait for a response but hurried on, her eyes firmly fixed upon the road ahead. 'It is a long-standing arrangement, but as you might guess, it does not have my aunt's approval, which is why no official announcement has been made. However, now that I have rejected the gentleman chosen for me by my aunt, I believe there is every hope that she will be persuaded to give the match her blessing.'

There was only the slightest of pauses before Lord Carston replied, his voice devoid of all emotion, 'Captain Maynard is a lucky man. May I be the first to wish you both very happy?'

Sylvestra accepted his felicitations with a slight inclination of her head, not trusting herself to speak. She was on the point of achieving everything she had hoped for, so why did she have an irrational urge to burst into tears?

Lord Carston's cool response to her announcement did nothing to improve Sylvestra's spirits. She found that she had expected him to be disappointed. A ridiculous idea, of course, but having feigned a degree of admiration for her, Sylvestra thought he might at least have continued the pretence with a show of mild chagrin. In fact the marquis was apparently so little interested in her news that having delivered the customary platitudes he had immediately turned the conversation into other channels, namely the upcoming Newmarket races.

Well, thought Sylvestra, ten minutes later as she stalked up the steps of the house in Green Street having taken a very punctilious farewell of her escort, I shall certainly not waste another thought on a man who has more interest in the outcome of a stupid horse race than in my imminent marriage! And discarding her bonnet with unwonted violence, she determined rather contrarily to retire to her room where she might abuse Lord Carston's character at leisure.

In this she was forestalled by her aunt, who, at that moment, came bustling into the hallway and without preamble caught her niece by the elbow and propelled her into the small morning-room.

'Frederick has spoken to me.' Judging by the foreboding manner in which this pronouncement was made, Mr Clive's talent for grandiloquence had not deserted him. Doubtless, thought Sylvestra, Aunt Julia had been treated to a florid description of her niece's scandalous descent into wickedness and depravity. This was seemingly confirmed by Mrs Harvey's next words.

'You are a shameless jade, Sylvestra Harvey! I have given you the opportunity to make a very favourable match and not only have you arrogantly spurned it but you have chosen to repay my generosity by bringing disgrace down upon us all!'

'A very respectable match!' exclaimed Sylvestra, her cheeks flushed with anger. Already out of sorts following her unsatisfactory parting from Lord Carston, Sylvestra's temper snapped. 'I venture to say that it would be a vast deal more favourable for Cousin Frederick than for myself. As to bringing disgrace upon us all, I believe I have reached an age where I might be held responsible for my own conduct, so you may feel free to dissociate yourself completely from my behaviour. Be assured, I shall certainly distance myself from any vulgar attempts to trap members of the aristocracy into matrimony!'

Sylvestra regretted her heated words as soon as they left her lips. She knew it to be extremely ill-bred of her to talk to her aunt in such a way, besides which she had learned long ago the futility of entering into such an acrimonious argument with Mrs Harvey.

She tried to diffuse the situation, saying quite sincerely, 'I'm sorry, Aunt Julia, that was very wrong of me. Can we not agree to differ upon the subject of my marriage? I appreciate your attempts to find me a suitable husband, but really there is not the least need for you to trouble yourself.'

These placatory words did nothing to mollify the enraged Mrs Harvey. Indeed her niece's apology struck her as a double insult, for Sylvestra's recognition of the indecorum of her own words was in itself a criticism of her aunt's unguarded outburst. Mrs Harvey's hands clenched into angry fists, and for a moment Sylvestra believed her aunt might actually strike her. Then Julia Harvey remembered the young man presently sipping tea from her best china in the drawing-room, and she took a deep breath. Why waste her energy on this impertinent hoyden when she was on the point of achieving all her ambitions? Her instinct was, of course, to banish the girl back to Brimpton Mewsey, but a moment's consideration made her acknowledge that she could hardly expect her niece's trustees to fund a season in the capital while Sylvestra rusticated in the Berkshire countryside. Besides, only that morning she had received vouchers for Almack's and accompanying them a very civil note from Lady Jersey that made it quite clear that it was her niece's noble connections that had ensured them this honour. Entrance to Almack's was essential if one was to be fully accepted by the upper echelons of society. Mrs Harvey had never heard of an instance in which they had been rescinded but she was not going to take a chance; if Lady Jersey wished to see the Earl of Beckham's granddaughter that evening then so be it.

To Sylvestra's astonishment, her aunt smiled. 'Perhaps you are right, Niece. No one can say I have not done my best for you. Should you choose to shun all my efforts on your behalf I believe I may face the world with a clear conscience. All I ask is that you refrain from shaming myself or your cousin for the duration of the season. Emily does not have your fortune and therefore cannot be so careless of society's opinion. Now please tidy your appearance and come to the drawing-room, we have a visitor.' She could not keep the note of triumph out of her voice. 'It is Emily's captain, would you believe!'

Even in her present state of mind, Sylvestra could not help but be lifted by this news and interested to meet the gentleman who had so affected her cousin, and she willingly followed her aunt into the drawing-room. The sight that greeted her brought her to an abrupt halt. Perched uncomfortably on a gilt, straight-backed chair, looking the very epitome of every schoolgirl's romantic dream in his dashing hussar's uniform, was Captain Peregrine Maynard.

Sylvestra's first thought as she stood in stunned disbelief upon the threshold was that there must have been some misunderstanding. Her eyes scanned the room in the desperate hope of discovering another young captain with his arm in a sling concealed amongst the clutter of her aunt's bric-a-brac. She knew it to be a forlorn hope. She need only look at Emily's wan face and downcast eyes to know there had been no mistake; Perry Maynard and Emily's *Capitain Inconnu* were one and the same.

Had she been stupidly blind not to suspect, even for a moment? Could it be because Emily's description of a masterful and dashing cavalier was poles apart from her own perception of her childhood friend, or was it that her mind had been so totally preoccupied with a gentleman other than her betrothed? Sylvestra quickly dismissed both possibilities; time enough later to examine the vacillations of her own heart. Besides whilst London was perhaps not seething with handsome young captains, their attraction increased tenfold by an injury sustained in the defence of their country, it was not totally unfeasible that there should be more than just one. No, this was simply one of life's cruel ironies. Of course, thought Sylvestra ruefully, had I known my life was about to take on all the characteristics of a bad farce, I would have been better prepared.

All this ran through Sylvestra's mind in the few seconds it took Captain Maynard to rise to his feet and move forward to greet her. At the same time Mrs Harvey exclaimed, their recent contretemps apparently forgotten, 'Sylvestra, you are just in time to meet Captain Maynard. Was it not clever of him to find us so quickly? He will have it that it is nothing, but I find it most remarkable.'

It was obvious from Mrs Harvey's words and her barely suppressed triumph that she alone had failed to make the connection between the eligible captain and the rackety soldier her niece had vowed to marry. Clearly the immediate priority was to disabuse her aunt of the notion that Captain Maynard had come to Green Street in the hope of finding Emily before Mrs Harvey's heavy-handed hints caused her daughter any further mortification.

'Very clever indeed, Aunt Julia,' Sylvestra interpolated hastily, at the same time shaking the captain's hand warmly. 'Perry, how good it is to see you! I have just this moment left your mama and sisters in the park. It was quite woolly-headed of me not to apprise you of our new address, I hope it was not too difficult for you to find us.'

Out of the corner of her eye Sylvestra saw her aunt's face drop ludicrously. Had it not been for poor Emily's misery, it would have been almost comical. Sylvestra continued to chat to Perry hoping to give her aunt and cousin time to recover from this set-back. In fact, her attempts to carry them all through an awkward situation were singularly unappreciated by her aunt, to whom her niece's attempts at easy discourse with Captain Maynard seemed designed to add insult to injury. Mrs Harvey's only consolation was that Captain Maynard's response to his fiancée's conversational advances was anything but ardent. His replies to her questions were stiff and formal and very soon put Sylvestra out of all patience with him. Emily she had the greatest of sympathy for; obviously her cousin was beyond social niceties. Sylvestra could even feel sorry for her aunt who, for perhaps the first time in her life, had been literally struck dumb by the injustice of it all. But she had thought that she could at least have depended on her childhood companion to come to her assistance, after all they had been in far worse scrapes than this in the past. But Sylvestra searched Perry's face in vain for some flicker of fellow feeling or wry appreciation of the situation in which they found themselves. Apparently his embarrassment was so acute that he could hardly bring himself to meet her gaze. Indeed, she was thankful when he rose to leave at the end of a correct half an hour visit; she would never have thought to find her old friend so sadly changed.

Twelve

'Well, miss, you had best bestir yourself. We are to dine early this evening.' Mrs Harvey's brusque entrance jerked Sylvestra from her reverie. She had passed the afternoon in the library, half-heartedly flicking through the leather-bound tomes left by the owner of the house. At any time, the dry botanical volumes would have held little appeal, but with so many other things to occupy her mind, Sylvestra had soon been sunk in thought.

Mrs Harvey looked at her niece in irritation. 'If it were up to me you would be on your way back to Brimpton Mewsey.' She sniffed. 'Why Lady Jersey should be so insistent . . . but then she has always had a reputation for nonsensical whims. Doubtless she had a *tendre* for your grandfather or some such thing, for I have heard he was a great rake.'

'I will go and get ready,' interposed Sylvestra hastily, heading for the door. Mrs Harvey's discontent was scarcely veiled, and she could see that from recalling old Sylvester's dubious morals it would be but a small step to remarking upon the inheritance of these by his granddaughter.

'I dare say I am wasting my breath asking you to behave with even a modicum of decorum this evening, Sylvestra, but I would ask you to remember that it is customary for girls making their debuts to dress in white at Almack's.'

'Yes, Aunt Julia,' responded Sylvestra meekly. She was certainly in no mood for petty rebellion. Indeed, she would gladly have stayed at home had it not been for her urgent need to see Perry and get this absurd imbroglio sorted out.

It had not taken her long to decide upon her first move. Clearly she must release Captain Maynard from their engagement at the earliest opportunity. The decision not to marry Perry had not been precipitated by the realization of Emily's attachment to him. She recognized now that it had been a slow dawning realization sparked by her arrival in London – and more significantly by her first meeting with the Marquis of Derwent – and culminating in her announcement of the betrothal to Lord Carston this morning. Ridiculous was it not? As the words had passed her lips her heart had cried out something very different. She would not – could not – marry Perry because the only man she could imagine sharing her life with was Lord Evelyn Carston. Quite simply she loved him. And having loved him, she knew she could never commit herself to any other man.

Sylvestra had not surrendered easily to her love. What of his past? How could she possibly love a man who had seduced an innocent girl and then apparently abandoned her and his base-born child to their fate? The evidence was damning, and to her knowledge Evelyn Carston had never said anything in his own defence. But whatever her head might say, her heart could not be swayed; she found it impossible to believe that the man she knew was capable of such blackguardly actions.

But despite her treacherous heart, Sylvestra still had her pride, and she was determined that Lord Carston should not suspect her feelings for him. His attraction to her – if it existed at all – was a most superficial thing. However it might pain her, Sylvestra could not persuade herself that a man violently in love could receive the news of his beloved's engagement to another with the cool indifference the marquis had displayed that morning.

No, it seemed she was destined to be a spinster. Well it could be worse; she was not without fortune. She would retire to the country and breed hunters. And should boredom strike she would cultivate the reputation of an eccentric. The gentlewomen of the parish would whisper about her over their teacups. 'I have heard,' they would say, 'that Miss Harvey rides *astride*. Yes, indeed, quite extraordinary, and that is not all! They say that after dinner she sits with her feet on the dining-table and smokes cigarillos!'

The image had briefly amused her but Sylvestra soon turned her thoughts to more immediate problems. Emily had excused herself as soon as their guests had departed and had spent the remainder of the day closeted in her room. Imagining her pain and humiliation, Sylvestra longed to go to her cousin but instinctively knew that she was the last person Emily wished to see at this time. With a new sensitivity born of her own situation Sylvestra knew that simply telling her cousin of her intention to relinquish Captain Maynard would do little to improve poor Emily's state of mind. No, she must be more subtle than that! Besides, until she had had the chance to speak candidly with Perry she could not be one hundred per cent certain that Emily's feelings were indeed reciprocated. She would never forgive herself if she raised her poor cousin's hopes only to see them dashed again.

But as she climbed the stairs to her bedchamber, Sylvestra was no nearer a solution. Looking back she wondered at her own naivety in thinking a match between herself and Perry could possibly have worked. The pity was that she had taken so long to realize it; this stupid situation should never have arisen and Emily and her captain should have fallen happily into one another's arms. She continued to ponder her dilemma as Duffey prepared her for the evening ahead, agreeing absently to the maid's suggestions for her toilette. Fortunately, the expert dresser knew exactly what was needed for a first visit to London's strictest club, and when Sylvestra descended for dinner not even Mrs Harvey could find anything to quibble at in her niece's appearance which combined youthful charm with graceful elegance. In accordance with her aunt's strictures, Sylvestra wore a gown of white organza over a simple tunic of white satin, the hem delicately embroidered with silver thread and seed pearls. Her rich copper hair was dressed in loose ringlets and adorned with a circlet of tiny white rosebuds.

An hour or so later, Sylvestra was thinking ruefully that had she worn an invisible petticoat and dampened her skirts she could not have provoked more scandalized looks. It seemed that the speculation regarding the nature of her relationship with the Marquis of Derwent had gathered momentum and, judging by the Harveys' reception when they entered Almack's that evening, society had, as was its habit regarding rumour, chosen to believe the worst.

One by one, acquaintances pointedly turned their backs upon the Harveys until they were marooned in a little circle of empty floor. Even Mr Wynchip did not dare approach, casting Sylvestra a weak apologetic smile as his mother bustled him away. Watching Mrs Harvey's chin go up, a battling light in her eyes, Sylvestra felt a moment of camaraderie with her aunt. It was only the briefest of moments because almost immediately Mrs Harvey turned to her and said in a harsh whisper, 'I will never forgive you for this, Sylvestra, never!'

For the first time in Sylvestra's life, Mrs Harvey's words struck home. What she had done *was* unforgivable. She might scorn her aunt's social ambitions, but she did not have the right to ruin them. Sylvestra realized that her behaviour since their arrival in London had been ill-advised and selfish. Well, it might be too late to repair their social standing but she would at least make sure there was no obstacle to Emily's happiness. She had seen Perry enter the room and was relieved to see that he was wasting no time in approaching them.

'Good evening Mrs Harvey, Miss Harvey, Miss Emily,' said Captain Maynard stiffly, bowing to each lady in turn and looking as if he would rather be anywhere else in the world.

'Good evening, Captain Maynard!' gushed Sylvestra, before her aunt could even draw breath, and laying her hand on the captain's arm possessively she smiled sweetly. 'It has been a positive age since I had the chance to talk to you properly, would you care to walk with me?'

Captain Maynard looked anything but enthusiastic, but he took the hint and allowed himself to be led off, leaving Mrs Harvey to fume impotently. Sylvestra waited until they were out of hearing and then sighed theatrically. 'Oh, Perry, I thought we would never be alone! Can we not find somewhere to talk?'

Captain Maynard looked startled, but acquiesced and they seated themselves in the comparative privacy of an alcove. Sylvestra sighed again. 'All those lonely months apart, you cannot know how I have suffered, how I have longed for this moment. . . .' She smiled up at him adoringly.

Captain Maynard flushed scarlet, his face a picture of ludicrous horror. 'Sylvie, I . . . I had no idea, I mean your letters!' He came to a stuttering halt. Then something seemed to strike him and he frowned at her. 'Now don't you try and flummery me, my girl. If half the tales I've been hearing about "the beautiful Miss Harvey" are true then you have certainly not been *lonely* since you came to town!'

'What are you saying, Captain Maynard?' Sylvestra was all injured innocence.

'I hope I have more sense than to listen to gossip, and if it had just been your aunt who had told me then I would have dismissed it as pure malice, for I can see she does not like you above half, but when it comes from my own mother . . . well, I have to believe it.'

'Good Lord, Perry! Come to the point, believe what?' exclaimed Sylvestra impatiently.

'The Marquis of Derwent,' replied Captain Maynard baldly.

Just the mention of his name made Sylvestra's heart leap within her, but beyond a faint blush she did not betray her emotions. 'What of him?' she asked calmly.

'Now don't play the innocent with me, Sylvestra! Remember I have known you a long time. Good God, have you not more sense than to allow your name to be coupled with a man of his reputation?'

Her friend's disapproval stung Sylvestra; she was not used to Perry chastising her, in the past he had always followed her lead. She lowered her lashes to hide the anger in her eyes and said with dreadful coyness, 'Why Perry, I do believe you are jealous!'

'Jealous? Why should I be jealous? I just wish you could have shown a little more judgement. You have made yourself the talk of the town! But then you were always reckless and careless of people's opinion.'

'You were never used to mind my recklessness, Perry.'

'When we were children, Sylvie! Surely even you must see the difference. You are a young woman, I am an officer, and well, I don't like to censure your behaviour, but an officer's wife is expected to comport herself with a certain amount of dignity and decorum.'

'Heavens, Perry, you sound like my aunt! Well, if my behaviour would prove so great an embarrassment to you then you may consider our engagement at an end!'

Captain Maynard opened his mouth to respond in kind but then shut it again abruptly. However great the temptation, it would be most unbecoming in a gentleman, warned his conscience sternly, to accept at face value words spoken in haste and under provocation that in a more rational moment might never have been uttered.

'Miss Harvey, I must apologize unreservedly. It was unforgivable of me to question your conduct in such a way,' he said stiffly.

'Of all the cockle-brained, dunderheaded. . . .' Words failed Sylvestra, and she glared at the startled captain in mute exasperation. She had been privately congratulating herself upon the ease with which she had steered their conversation to this point, but apparently Captain Maynard was determined to be quite infuriatingly dull-witted.

'Peregrine Maynard, you have known me all your life and until this moment you have never had the slightest difficulty in telling me exactly how you are feeling, so why do you not drop this ridiculous façade and say what you are thinking! Namely that you would sooner be boiled in oil than take me as a wife!'

Perry gaped at her helplessly. 'No . . . no really, Sylvie, you have it all wrong,' he protested weakly. 'That is, I would be honoured to marry you, truly you would make me the happiest of men.'

Captain Maynard looked so utterly miserable as he said this that Sylvestra could not contain her amusement any longer. 'Oh, Perry,' she gasped between fits of uncontrollable laughter, 'what in heaven's name has happened to you? You never used to be such a . . . a *stuffed shirt*!'

Perry flushed hotly. He had tried his best and against his own inclination to do the right thing, and had been ridiculed for his efforts.

'If by that you mean I have learned some manners, then I am glad of it! You, on the other hand are quite obviously still the same harum-scarum care-for-naught. When I first saw you I did think you had grown into a young lady, but obviously this elegance is only skin deep – at heart you are still a rag-mannered, little tomboy!'

Far from being insulted, this piece of plain speaking delighted Sylvestra. 'At last! Now may we speak frankly to each other as the old friends we are?'

Perry smiled reluctantly. 'Very well, Sylvie, you have succeeded in reducing me to your level.'

Sylvestra chose to ignore this deliberate provocation. 'Now, I have decided that this engagement of ours must be terminated at once. *Not* because of the barrage of insults to which you have subjected me, *nor* because you have apparently being dallying with my cousin behind my back.' She raised a hand to silence his protests. 'Simply, we should not get married because neither of us has the slightest desire to do so, and I suspect that you never liked the idea so very well from the start.'

Captain Maynard could not allow her last remark to go unchallenged. 'Now, Sylvie, I will admit that as children you may have pestered me into all kinds of pranks against my better judgement, but I will not have it said that I am such a milksop as to allow myself to be bullied into matrimony! At the time I thought it a very good idea, but as one grows older and sees more of the world . . .' – he blushed self-consciously – 'one realizes that there is more to marriage than simply being good friends.'

Sylvestra smiled at him. 'I know, Perry,' she said rather wistfully. 'Now, I suggest you take me back to my aunt and waste no time breaking the good news to Emily!'

A few minutes later, watching Perry and Emily strolling about the room, their heads bent close together, apparently in perfect harmony, Sylvestra could not suppress a stab of envy. Their happiness from now on was so straightforward, their love for each other uncomplicated and true. It seemed she was to be denied the simple contentment and security of a shared love. Despite herself, Sylvestra glanced at the clock. Two minutes to eleven. Not even the Prince Regent himself would be allowed into the club once the clock had struck eleven. She resolutely turned her back to the door; it was quite pathetic waiting and hoping for that familiar figure to stride into the room.

'Miss Harvey, I have been prevailed upon once more to speak for Lord Carston. I beg you will grant him a dance for I fear if you don't he will leave us as speedily as he arrived, and imagine what a stir that would create.' Lady Jersey's face was alight with mischief; Lord Carston's was inscrutable.

'I would be happy to dance with Lord Carston,' responded Sylvestra, marvelling at the calmness of her own voice, when inwardly turmoil raged. The orchestra struck up the waltz and she allowed him to lead her to the dance floor, acutely aware of the speculative glances that followed their progress. Why was he singling her out? She could not imagine there was any reason other than revenge, a wish to fuel the gossips' imagination and thereby give her a taste of her own medicine. But whatever his motive, Sylvestra could not deny the thrill of pleasure it gave her to be once more in the circle of his arms. If this was revenge then it was as sweet for her as it was for him.

'I have learned that Captain Maynard and your cousin's saviour are one and the same. What a charming twist of fate. I hope your fiancé will not object to my commandeering his betrothed for the only waltz of the evening.'

'Not at all, Lord Carston. Captain Maynard's injury unfortunately precludes dancing, but he would not let that stand in the way of my enjoyment,' responded Sylvestra sweetly, perversely reluctant to set the marquis straight on the subject of her engagement.

'That is large-minded of him. If I had been separated from my beloved for so long I would be loath to let her out of my sight for a single second.'

Sylvestra gave a tinkling laugh, determined not to let his taunting probes throw her off balance. 'What a tyrant you must be, My Lord! I sincerely pity the lady upon whom your fancy lights, she will not enjoy a moment's freedom.'

The marquis tightened his hold upon her, the hand at her waist drawing her closer to him. 'Do you, Miss Harvey?' he whispered provocatively in her ear, his warm breath caressing her cheek.

Sylvestra's heart was pounding fit to burst, and she could feel colour flooding into her face. He was playing with her like a cat with a mouse. He knew how she felt about him and he was heartlessly playing on that weakness. She forced herself to respond.

'Certainly, My lord! Surely any woman of intelligence would wish to retain a degree of independence within her marriage!'

'A very rational supposition, Miss Harvey. But love is not a rational emotion, is it Sylvie?'

It was the first time he had used her pet name and it was her undoing. She wrenched herself from his grasp saying in a harsh whisper, 'Why do you not simply come out and say it, My lord? Say that love has nothing to do with my betrothal to Captain Maynard. Well, you are quite right, Lord Carston, and for that reason our engagement is at an end, and I would be grateful if you would spare us all further embarrassment by not referring to it again!' Sylvestra caught her breath, tears were not very far away and she was uncomfortably aware that while the entire room had not come to a standstill a good proportion of the dancers around them were staring at her askance.

Lord Carston was looking at her in complete amazement. He had not for a moment expected her to take his flirtatious teasing to heart. Quickly he took her arm and led her from the dance floor, at the same time murmuring in her ear, 'Miss Harvey, believe me, I had no idea that your engagement was broken, and no intention of causing you distress. Shall I return you to your aunt?'

Sylvestra shook her head mutely. Without her niece's contaminating presence, Mrs Harvey had managed with her usual thick-skinned force, to insinuate herself into a group of chaperons. Emily and Perry were nowhere to be seen.

'No thank you, Lord Carston, I think I will go home, I have the headache.'

'Then I will get you a chair,' declared the marquis firmly. Sylvestra protested weakly, but to no avail, Lord Carston seemed genuinely remorseful and was determined not only to see her into a sedan chair but to accompany her back to Green Street. In fact he was so solicitous that Sylvestra herself began to feel a complete fraud.

'I have not really got the headache,' she said in a small voice, as he handed her into the chair.

This made Lord Evelyn laugh, 'Well, I will forgive you that small deception if you will forgive my clumsy attempts at humorous banter. Truly, I had no wish to hurt you.'

His voice held such a ring of sincerity that Sylvestra found it impossible to remain angry with him. She had come very close to revealing her true feelings to him and she was only thankful that the moment had passed and she was now relatively in control of her tongue and her emotions. She longed to ask him why he had come to Almack's, why he had asked her to dance, but she knew it to be a dangerous topic and so allowed him to turn the subject into more trivial channels. He did this so successfully that by the time they reached Green Street they were well and truly back on a friendly footing and, as Lord Carston helped her from the chair, Sylvestra said impulsively, 'Will you not come in for a moment? I feel the least I can do is offer you some refreshment after taking you so much out of your way.'

Sylvestra was obliged to ring the bell twice before the door was opened to them. Clearly the servants had not expected to see them back at such an early hour. Sylvestra hid a smile as she noted Mosely's loosened necktie and flustered air; she had never before seen the butler looking anything other than coolly pristine. She brushed off his apology with a smile and pretended not to notice the faint aroma of brandy that hung about his person.

'Not at all, Mosely, I daresay you would not have looked to see us for another hour yet. Besides there is only Lord Carston and I.' The last was delivered with a slightly challenging lift of the chin. Sylvestra would not have been surprised had Mosely refused point blank to allow the marquis across the threshold for he was quite as strict in his notions as the sternest of chaperons.

Indeed, the butler had been regarding Lord Evelyn with frosty disapproval, but there was only an instant's hesitation before he signalled to the hovering footman to take the gentleman's cloak and cane. For after all, as he was to say to Mrs Maher, the housekeeper, later that same evening, poor Miss Harvey had little enough chance to catch herself a husband with such a virago for an aunt, and besides, he knew a real gentleman when he saw one, and despite what anyone might say, Lord Carston was certainly that. That said, it would not be so very amazing should the properest gentleman in the land forget himself in the face of Miss Harvey's undoubted charms, and so the door of the small drawing-room stayed firmly ajar throughout. 'You did just as you ought, Mr Mosely,' approved Mrs Maher.

Alone with her guest, Sylvestra found herself suddenly tongue-tied, and she covered her embarrassment by busying herself with the duties of hostess. But all too soon the fire was stoked back into life, the candles lit and a decanter of port set upon a mahogany Pembroke table. The last footman quietly withdrew and the only sounds to disturb the silence were the staccato crackle of the logs in the grate, and the solemn tick tock of the longcase clock standing sentinel in the corner of the room.

'May I help you to a glass of port, Lord Carston?' asked Sylvestra, feeling strangely breathless. She did not wait for an answer but moved swiftly to the table, adding with a nervous little laugh, 'I fancy you will find it quite bearable. If my uncle bestirs himself over one thing it is the quality of his wine and he took it upon himself to supervise the stocking of our cellars here.'

Lord Carston moved to her side and stilled her busy hands with his own. Sylvestra looked up sharply, her heart doing somersaults in her breast. They stood thus for a moment before Lord Carston gently released her and possessed himself of the decanter.

'Then he would not approve of us wasting a single drop.'

Sylvestra looked down at her hands, they were trembling uncontrollably. She blushed and hid them amongst her skirts, laughing self-consciously. 'More to the point, my aunt would not thank me for chipping her best crystal.'

The marquis smiled, and with a steady hand poured two generous measures of port. Sylvestra protested half-heartedly but yielded under Lord Carston's compelling gaze and accepted the drink, seating herself in one of the pair of gilt armchairs that flanked the marble fireplace.

'Pray will you not take a seat, Lord Carston?' She addressed her guest primly, in a vain attempt to regain control of a situation that was fast slipping from her grasp. What madness had prompted her to accept the marquis's offer to escort her home? And why, instead of taking a proper farewell of him upon the doorstep, had she invited him in? Lord knows she had found it hard enough to withstand the man's charm within the rigid precincts of Almack's, how much greater her vulnerability in this intimate setting!

Despite the invitation, Lord Evelyn remained standing, sipping the ruby wine and thoughtfully observing Sylvestra's face. The flickering firelight illuminated the play of emotions across her lovely countenance and he felt a surge of anger against Captain Maynard. How could any man, having held the heart of this magnificent creature, even look at another woman? The fool did not know what he had lost. Anger was swiftly followed by sympathy for the brave girl before him. She had accepted her lover's inconstancy with dignity, he had not heard her utter one word of reproach or blame.

'Will you not talk of it?' he prompted gently.

Unaware that the train of his thoughts was so wildly opposed to her own, Sylvestra blushed fiercely and stammered, 'Talk of. . . ?'

'Captain Maynard.' Lord Carston paused. 'I know it must be painful, but you may find it a release to express your feelings.'

He thought she loved Perry! If he but knew the truth! *That* she had not the courage nor even the words to express, for her love for him was a new discovery, and she must first comprehend its beauties and dangers for herself before she could possibly open her heart to him. But neither could she pretend a love that had never existed, however sweet his gentle sympathy.

Watching her face anxiously, Evelyn thought he had been too quick to probe a fresh wound. 'Forgive me, the last thing I wish to do is cause you further pain, I will leave you.' He set down his glass and made to leave the room.

'No! Please do not go.' Sylvestra started to her feet. 'You have been everything that is kind. But your sympathy is quite misplaced. I do not love Captain Maynard, at least not in the way a wife should love a husband. We will always be the best of friends, but we should never have become engaged, I see that now.'

Evelyn eyed her sceptically. Was this merely another brave front? Sylvestra read his thoughts accurately and shook her head, laughter in her green eyes. 'Pray do not cast me in the role of martyr for nothing could be further from the truth. That accolade must certainly go to Perry, who through some *idiotish* notion of honour was quite willing to sacrifice his own future happiness and that of poor Emily. Really, it put me out of all patience with him!'

The marquis concealed a smile. He was beginning to have more sympathy for Captain Maynard than he would have thought possible just a moment ago.

'In his defence, it is hardly the act of an honourable man to jilt one lady for another, particularly such a near relation,' he reasoned.

'Well, yes, I could understand that if it were anyone but myself. But Perry has known me enough years to know that I would certainly not wish to be with a man who was marrying me only out of a sense of misguided duty!' Sylvestra shook her head and chuckled. 'Good lord, what a mare's nest! I have never come so close to swooning in my life as when I walked into my aunt's drawing-room this morning!' She let out a peal of laughter. 'I wish you could have been there to see it. What a tableau we made! Poor Perry gripping his teacup as though his life depended upon it. My aunt gaping like a fish out of water. And I! Well, I once claimed to have no talent for small talk but in truth it seems I am a regular jaw-me-dead! I assure you 'twas better than any farce you will see all season.'

Evelyn joined in her laughter, but asked, 'And Emily? Does she look back with such amusement?'

Sylvestra shook her head, the laughter leaving her eyes as she recalled her cousin's anguish. 'No, to poor Emily it must have seemed the worst of tragedies.' Sylvestra sighed, shaking her head again at her own foolishness. 'And I could have put everything to rights with a word. Had I but freed Perry from our engagement there and then, how much heartache I would have saved. But instead I simply prattled on, as if talking of the weather would somehow see us through. My God, I have always scorned the superficiality of society, the belief that as long as everything is all right upon the surface then what goes on beneath is not really of any consequence. Appearance is all! My aunt has drummed that philosophy into my head every day since I entered her household; I wonder if she feels any sense of achievement now it has obviously rooted so well.'

'You are too severe upon yourself, Sylvestra. At such moments in our lives we all struggle to do or say the right thing and often fall back upon the commonplace to cover the depths of our feelings. Would your aunt or indeed your cousin have thanked you for magnanimously handing over Captain Maynard as though he were yours to bestow? I think not.'

Sylvestra nodded. 'Yes, I realized that, and I imagine that before I am very much older I will have the devil's own job convincing Emily that I really do not want to marry Perry! Still no doubt it will all turn out for the best. My aunt will probably believe that it is my shocking behaviour that has cost me the chance of making a good marriage, and Emily – if it is possible – will love her darling Perry even more for his noble determination to stand by me.'

'And you? You say you do not love Captain Maynard, but once you must have done or at least thought you did.' Evelyn felt he could not let this point drop. He had to be sure.

Sylvestra smiled rather pensively. 'I did not know what real love was. I thought the friendship Perry and I shared was enough to build a marriage upon. I now know differently. I. . . .' She took a deep breath and looked up at him unable to go on. But words were not needed, her eyes spoke volumes. For a moment they stood as statues and then she was in his arms, his hands plunging into her fiery tresses and drawing her eager face up to meet his kisses.

'Good evening, madam, I trust you had a pleasant evening.' The butler's greeting to his mistress was, as it was intended to be, a clear warning to the couple in the drawing-room and they sprang apart guiltily. With great presence of mind, Lord Carston quickly extinguished the candles and silently drew Sylvestra into the shadows, his eyes gleaming wickedly in the half light as he pulled her close to him. Sylvestra looked up at him, her green gaze a mute protest, but a half-hearted one. She tried desperately to concentrate on the conversation just a few yards away between Mosely and her Aunt Julia, but the marquis's increasingly intimate caresses made rational thought impossible. His touch burned through the thin stuff of her gown as his hands slid over each voluptuous curve of her body and Sylvestra was forced to bite hard on her lower lip to contain the moans of pleasure that rose involuntarily in her throat. The querulous voice of Mrs Harvey issuing last-minute orders to Mosely gradually receded as she mounted the staircase and a few minutes later a discreet knock on the drawing-room door gave the guilty couple the all clear.

Reluctantly Sylvestra pulled back from Lord Carston's embrace. 'You must go!' she whispered.

He cupped her upturned face in his hands, his eyes intense. 'I promise you it will not always be like this, skulking in dark corners. But I need time, there are things I must see to. Will you trust me?'

Sylvestra nodded unquestioningly, his kisses had melted away all her doubts and her heart was entirely in his hands. One last, lingering, tender kiss and he was gone leaving her to creep up the stairs to bed and to dream.

Thirteen

Sylvestra awoke early the next morning but did not, as was her usual habit, rise immediately. This morning she allowed herself the luxury of basking dreamily in memories of the night before, spending a full half-hour in this self-indulgence before she guiltily rang for her maid and began her morning ablutions.

Her good humour did not go unremarked by Duffey, who had been keeping a weather eye on her young mistress's tempestuous relationship with Lord Carston. What she saw this morning was enough to allow her imagination to cautiously explore the possibility of a future in the exalted position of lady's maid to no less a personage than the Marchioness of Derwent.

'I have pressed the velvet habit, miss,' she volunteered. In her present state of mind it would not be at all surprising if Miss Harvey had entirely forgotten her arrangement to go riding in the park this morning.

'Habit? Oh, good Lord yes! Really I am getting more hen-witted by the day!' Sylvestra chuckled to herself. Was this what love did to one? When she had arranged the loan of a mare from the local stables less than a week ago it had seemed the sole pleasure amongst a welter of tedious social engagements. Now she would gladly have spent every evening at Almack's if there was a chance a certain person would be there.

Not that it detracted from her enthusiasm for her morning ride.

Sylvestra had been used to riding every day until she came to London and she had wasted no time upon her arrival in the capital in enquiring from where she might hire a good saddle horse. Having experienced Hyde Park at the fashionable hour, she had soon come to realize that riding in London had little to do with the simple pleasure of exercise and most to do with being seen looking dashing on a showy piece of horseflesh. This was not Sylvestra's idea of enjoyment at all, nor was the prospect of having her every step dogged by a groom. But in her aunt's eyes it was the only way in which the expedition could be undertaken with anything approaching decorum, and Sylvestra felt that there had been enough antagonism between herself and Mrs Harvey without opposing her in this.

Despite this constraint, Sylvestra was determined to enjoy her ride to the full and so she had made her requirements very clear to the livery stable. She was not disappointed. A very nice bay mare awaited her convenience. Light-mouthed and well-mannered she still had enough spirit to tax Sylvestra's skills as they negotiated the early morning traffic. It was only when they reached the calm of Hyde Park's bridleways that Sylvestra could allow her concentration to lapse slightly and her thoughts to drift, inevitably, to sweet memories of the night before.

But her daydreams were not as idyllic as she might have wished. Sylvestra recalled those whispered endearments murmured incoherently between urgent kisses and her pulse quickened. But a broad streak of pragmatism in her nature could not accept Evelyn's words at face value. There remained a niggling doubt; after all, there had been no firm declaration of love and certainly no direct proposal of marriage. What need have I of words, sang back her heart, when his every action, his every glance speaks his love? As they did, no doubt, to Miss Marianne Devenish, countered the cynical voice of harsh reason.

Sylvestra found that however she might wish to draw a veil over the marquis's past, Marianne Devenish haunted her imagination; a pale, tragic figure dressed in rags, and at her side a barefoot child whose mournful eyes reproached Sylvestra's selfish happiness.

Sylvestra realized now that she had been attracted to Evelyn Carston from the start; why else would she have desperately tried to excuse his crimes, chosen to ignore all the damning evidence against him and cling instead to some vague unsubstantiated belief in his innocence? But Sylvestra's usual level-headedness had not entirely deserted her and she could not help but draw parallels between herself and the unfortunate Miss Devenish. Surely no woman would sacrifice so much unless she loved and believed herself loved in return.

Sylvestra almost exclaimed aloud in exasperation. Her mind was running in circles, her mood swinging from joyous optimism to gnawing doubt. The mare seemed to sense Sylvestra's disquiet and jig-jogged nervously beneath her. Sylvestra tightened the reins and pushed her willing mount forward; a good gallop would blow away the cobwebs. The little mare displayed an exhilarating turn of foot and Sylvestra found that the exertion did indeed help to focus her mind, and as she waited for the groom to catch her up on his less enthusiastic mount she resolved upon a decisive course of action. At the earliest opportunity she would ask Lord Carston outright about the fate of his former love. And if his answer was unsatisfactory? Sylvestra frowned impatiently, it would take more than a gallop in the park to solve all her problems.

Her frustrating musings were suddenly interrupted by the sound of rapid hoofbeats coming in her direction. The lingering morning mist obscured the unknown horseman and confused the direction of his approach, but Sylvestra recognized from experience the sound of a horse out of control and prepared herself to give chase.

In the event, no such exertion was required. Out of the greyness erupted a small black pony, ears flattened back, eyes rolling in terror. Clinging grimly to the pony's neck was a young boy. The sudden sight of the mare and rider, however, brought the pony to a juddering halt, sending the boy over its shoulder and tumbling into the grass. Sylvestra quickly dismounted and hurried to the prone figure.

'Are you hurt?' she demanded anxiously, sinking to her knees. The boy sat up.

'What a gudgeon!' he chastised himself in disgust.

Sylvestra's eyes twinkled, there was nothing wrong with this little man other than wounded pride. 'It happens to the best of us,' she said consolingly.

The boy looked unconvinced. Clearly the opinion of a girl on the subject of horsemanship counted for little. Sylvestra hid a smile.

'Of course, a true horseman's first priority should be to check upon his mount.'

The boy regarded her with new respect. In his experience, girls only worried about stupid things like whether they had squashed their hats or muddied their dresses. He struggled to his feet. He was an engaging youngster, probably five or six years of age with a mop of black hair and a pair of startling blue eyes fringed with long dark lashes. Now, rather belatedly, he remembered his manners and offered his hand to Sylvestra saying with a courtly formality hilariously at odds with his extreme youth, dishevelled appearance and a burgeoning black eye, 'I am 'ceedingly obliged to you, madam. If you will 'scuse me I must try and find Nelson.'

'No need for that young sir, I have the little devil here.' Sylvestra's groom, Scoble, appeared out of the mist leading the wayward pony.

The boy's eyes lit up and he scampered across to the unrepentant Nelson and would have remounted had the groom not laid a restraining hand on his shoulder. 'Hold hard, my lad. You'll not be riding him again today.' And he lifted up the saddle flap to expose the girth. The leather strap was all but worn through.

'Good heavens!' exclaimed Sylvestra unguardedly.

'Exactly, miss,' said Scoble meaningfully, his gaze meeting hers over the boy's head. Nothing more was said, it was pointless scaring the youngster, but both of them knew that had the girth given way when the pony had been travelling at speed then its rider might not have escaped with merely a black eye.

Sylvestra frowned, it was a strange contradiction. The boy was clearly from a family of substance, his clothes were of the best cloth and the pony, if Sylvestra was any judge, was pure bred Welsh. The mystery was, what was this sprig of the nobility doing riding in a public park so ill-attended – for there was no sign of an anxious groom. Indeed, no groom worth his salt would have allowed a horse out of its stable wearing such badly maintained tack.

'Are you alone?' she asked the boy.

'Oh no, Mrs Pierce was with me but she is so fat and old she will never catch us up,' he responded cheerfully.

'Your nurse?' hazarded Sylvestra in astonishment.

The boy grimaced. 'Yes. Mama insists she goes everywhere with me.'

'Even when you go riding?' Sylvestra could hardly believe any parent could be so misguided.

The boy eyed her from beneath lowered lashes. 'Not exactly. You see I am not supposed to leave the grounds. But when my – when *someone* gave me Nelson. . . .' His voice trailed off guiltily.

Sylvestra tried hard to look disapproving but failed hopelessly, for she could sympathise completely with his temptation. 'Well, I just hope that your mama will be so happy to have you returned to her unharmed that she will overlook your disobedience. Now, you must tell us your name and where you live if we are to take you home without further delay!'

The boy hesitated. 'Mama did say that on no account was I ever to tell my name to a stranger.'

'Very wise,' approved Sylvestra. 'But you must at least tell us where you live, my dear, or else how are we to get you home?'

The boy considered this for a moment and, as it seemed a reasonable request, he said with the air of one divulging a great secret, 'Grosvenor Square.'

It was no great distance to travel but their progress was necessarily slow. They were a jolly if unfashionable cavalcade with the young boy taken up before Scoble on his docile cob and Sylvestra with her hands full controlling her mare and leading Nelson.

The boy had quickly forgotten his recent tumble and was inclined to view the entire proceedings as a grand adventure. Sylvestra found his innocent chatter a refreshing change and an ideal antidote to the unproductive soul searching that had preceded it. He was a confiding youth with the exception of his determined reticence with regard to his name. He had volunteered the information by way of consolation that one day he would be a 'markiss', but that he would far rather be a groom like Jem. Jem, it seemed was a great gun who had filed his teeth to points and could spit incredible distances. Sylvestra agreed gravely that this was certainly a talent worth aspiring to, but added that she believed there was much to be said for being a marquis.

The boy looked far from convinced. 'When Mama talks of it all she says is that lots of ladies will want to dance with me.' He clearly viewed this as more of a drawback than an advantage, but he did add generously that if Sylvestra wished it he would be quite happy to dance with her. Sylvestra recognized this as a great compliment and replied solemnly that she would look forward to it. They arrived in Grosvenor Square then the best of friends. The boy had been reluctant to give the number of his house, but it took no work of genius to fathom it out, for on only one doorstep was there a parcel of anxious servants on the lookout.

'Oh Jupiter!' said the boy, his face dropping ludicrously.

'Chin up!' said Sylvestra bracingly, with an encouraging smile. She was feeling a little daunted herself by the opulent residence before her and very conscious of her mud-splattered habit and the unruly curls escaping the confines of her hat. But she dismounted with as much aplomb as she could muster and lifted down the young boy from his lofty perch.

'Thank you for your help, Scoble,' she addressed the groom

with a warm smile. 'Do you think you can return Nelson to his stable?'

'That I will, miss. And if you'll pardon me, miss, whoever sent the young lad out with the saddle in that state should be horsewhipped!'

Sylvestra nodded in agreement. 'You may be sure I will raise the matter with his mother, Scoble. I shall walk home so there is no need for you to wait for me.'

'Very good, miss.'

By this time the young boy was already being shepherded into the house by a man and two elderly women, whom Sylvestra took to be the butler, the housekeeper and the missing nurse. None of these worthies apparently had any intention of addressing Sylvestra let alone thanking her for returning the boy to the bosom of his family. Indeed, they only barely acknowledged her presence at all, shooting her embarrassed half glances and, in the case of the nurse, a rather puzzling look of blazing hostility. Sylvestra did not feel the need for profuse expressions of gratitude for she knew she had done nothing more than any decent person would and if it had not been for the circumstances of the badly worn girth she would simply have shrugged her shoulders and made her way home without further ado. But her conscience would not allow her to leave without apprising the boy's parents of the danger he had been in. She might not subscribe to Scoble's draconian measures, but without doubt the groom responsible should be summarily dismissed without a reference.

Sylvestra therefore followed the butler up the steps. 'Excuse me, I should like to see the lady of the house.'

The butler looked embarrassed. 'That will not be possible I am afraid, miss.'

Sylvestra raised her eyebrows questioningly. 'Is your mistress not at home?'

The butler's discomfort increased. 'You must not think us ungrateful, but His Lordship does not like unexpected visitors and

I am under strict instructions—'

A lady's voice from inside the house interrupted the butler. 'Good heavens, Benton, what are you thinking of? As if I would not wish to thank personally the guardian angel who has brought my baby back to me?'

The butler hesitated and then reluctantly stepped aside allowing Sylvestra to enter. Sylvestra had a brief vision of a golden-haired beauty in powder-blue silks before she was engulfed in a lavender-scented embrace.

Sylvestra extricated herself, protesting laughingly that there was really no need for such excessive gratitude. 'Besides I am covered in dirt and you will ruin your lovely gown!'

This had the desired effect and Sylvestra found herself very quickly released. The lady gave a tinkling laugh. 'It would be a dreadful shame to spoil it.' She smoothed the fine silk lovingly. 'Straight from Florence. Of course, I would have preferred Paris, but I suppose that is out of the question at the moment. What a monster that Napoleon is!'

'Er – yes, yes indeed!' responded Sylvestra, repulsed yet fascinated by such blatant self-absorption.

The young boy had been waiting impatiently to recount his adventures to his mother and now piped up with, 'Mama, you should have seen Nelson go! I should think he is the fastest pony in the land!'

'Edward, do not interrupt your elders! And I do not wish to hear how fast that wretched creature can go; why just the thought of it is enough to give me an attack of the vapours! I positively forbid you to ride that . . . that wild animal again!'

'But, Mama, I am not the least bit hurt. And Nelson is *not* a wild animal, he is the best pony in the world!' protested Edward staunchly.

His mother shuddered theatrically. 'Edward, have you no regard for your poor mama's feelings? I declare I don't know where you get such insensitivity from, certainly not me. Now go upstairs with

Mrs Pierce and get out of those horrible dirty clothes.'

'Yes, Mama. Goodbye Miss Harvey.' Looking crestfallen, the boy trailed up the stairs taking all of Sylvestra's sympathy with him.

The lady turned her attention back to Sylvestra. 'Now, I positively insist that you take tea with me. It is an absolute age since I had company.'

'But, My Lady, His Lordship—' protested the butler desperately.

'Benton, his lordship is out, is he not?'

'Well yes, My Lady, but—'

'I will have no buts, Benton. When His Lordship is out I am mistress of this household. Now kindly see to it that tea is served in my boudoir.' She turned to Sylvestra and added in a melodramatic whisper, 'Please do not forsake me, for I truly believe you may be our only hope!'

Intrigued, Sylvestra nodded her assent and presently found herself in pretty withdrawing-room decorated in a delicate shade of pink obviously designed to compliment its owner's ethereal loveliness.

'I must thank you again – Miss Harvey is it? – for what you have done today. You may not realize it but you have almost certainly saved my dearest darling's life. When I heard that Edward had gone out riding the creature that *he* had provided then I prepared myself for the worst. And then when Mrs Pierce returned alone. . .' The wide blue eyes filled with tears and a damp wisp of handkerchief was pressed to trembling rosebud lips.

'Really, I don't believe the pony has any vice in him. He was probably startled by a bird or some such thing.' Sylvestra paused before adding gently, 'I do not wish to alarm you but the girth of the pony's saddle was quite badly worn. Edward would have been in far greater danger had the girth given way.'

'Good God, this proves it! I have suspected . . . but this! This confirms my worst fears.' At Sylvestra's words Edward's mother had paled, her voice rising hysterically.

Sylvestra frowned, trying to make sense of this outburst. 'Are you suggesting that someone meant for Edward to be hurt? Pardon me, but is that not a little far-fetched?'

'Not just hurt. Killed! Murdered by his own flesh and blood!'

'But what possible motive could anyone have for killing a young boy?' asked Sylvestra, privately wondering if the beautiful creature before her was mentally unhinged.

Sylvestra's scepticism must have shown on her face because Edward's mother said, 'You think I am mad. But when you learn who I am, then you will understand.' She paused and leaned towards Sylvestra, her voice now earnest and deliberate. 'You see, my name is Lady Marianne Carston. I am the Marchioness of Derwent.'

If she had wished to stun her listener then Lady Carston was not disappointed. Sylvestra could not move or speak as the implications of her companion's revelation hit her. The room dipped and swayed around her and her stomach turned sickening somersaults. She gripped the arms of her chair and swallowed hard.

'I see from your countenance, Miss Harvey, that the significance of what I have told you does not escape you.'

No, the significance did not escape Sylvestra. Evelyn Carston had done the honourable thing and married Miss Devenish which could only mean that his intentions towards Sylvestra were dishonourable in the extreme.

'But I do not understand. Why has your marriage been kept a secret?' she asked bemusedly.

'Why indeed!' exclaimed Lady Marianne eagerly. 'I have been given excuse after excuse, obliged to spend my life trailing from one unfashionable Continental resort to the next. Believe me, it has been quite insupportable. And now I am back in London and still the truth cannot be told. I am kept a prisoner in my own house. Evelyn says that His Grace is too ill to hear the truth, that it will kill him.' Lady Marianne raised her eyebrows expressively. 'From what I remember of the duke it would take more than the news that he has a daughter-in-law and a grandson he did not know of to carry him off!'

'It does seem a little unlikely,' said Sylvestra weakly. She could barely comprehend what she was hearing.

'Exactly! So you see now why I believe, why I *know* Evelyn intends no one to ever know. And there is only one way he can be certain of that.' Lady Marianne's voice quavered tearfully.

'Good God! Surely you cannot believe he would really harm you or Edward?' exclaimed Sylvestra horrified. Unprincipled rake he might be, but she could not bring herself to believe that Evelyn Carston was capable of coldly plotting the murder of his wife and son.

Lady Marianne smiled bitterly. 'I take it from the certainty of your response that you have met Evelyn. Well, I dare swear he can be quite charming if he has a mind to be. From all the invitations he receives it is clear that the *eligible Marquis of Derwent* has certainly won over society's ladies.'

'But it does not make sense! Why risk discovery by bringing you both into England? Surely it would have been far easier to orchestrate your . . . your disappearance abroad!' reasoned Sylvestra.

Lady Marianne shook her head emphatically. 'No. Believe me I have tried to convince myself that the incidents which have occurred since our arrival are mere coincidence but after today I can no longer ignore the truth. It is my belief that Evelyn has set his sights upon some rich little heiress and he has no intention of allowing Edward and I to thwart his ambitions.'

Ironically, thought Sylvestra, Lady Marianne was not so very far from the truth. Only it was not the heiress's money Lord Carston was interested in and he did not need to go to such lengths to achieve his ends. Marriage to another woman would not have prevented him getting what he wanted. Good God, had she seemed such easy prey to him? And, more to the point, would she have eventually succumbed to his advances? She thought back to the previous evening; who knows what might have happened if her aunt had not returned at that moment. And to her shame she found that despite all she now knew those memories still roused unbidden yearnings deep within her.

'You mentioned other incidents?' Sylvestra could not allow her mind to follow that path and she forced herself to attend to Lady Marianne's fears.

'Less than a week ago I was walking in the grounds near the house when a coping-stone from the balcony above fell and shattered not a yard from where I was standing! I would certainly have been killed had it struck me.' Lady Marianne shuddered at the memory.

'But that could easily have been an unlucky accident,' reasoned Sylvestra.

'That is what Evelyn said. But he is not stupid; of course, he would be sure to make it look like an accident. And then only yesterday, I was taking my afternoon nap when my maid woke me in hysterics. The rug beside the hearth was on fire. I would have been burned in my bed!'

'But a spark from the fire. . . .'

'Don't you see? It is too much of a coincidence. And after what has happened to Edward today! No, Miss Harvey, I am convinced.'

Sylvestra could see that it was pointless trying to reason with Lady Marianne; in her mind the evidence was irrefutable and without firm proof to the contrary her fears would never be soothed. Sylvestra toyed with the idea of confessing the nature of her own relationship with Lord Carston but quickly rejected it. Besides an understandable reluctance to expose her own folly, it would if anything only further fuel Lady Marianne's beliefs.

Instead, she leaned forward and took Lady Marianne's trembling hands in her own, saying as calmly as she could, 'Lady Carston, I truly believe that your fears are misplaced, but if you wish it I shall certainly stand your friend. You need only say the word and I will help you and Edward leave this house.'

Lady Marianne looked helpless. 'Oh dear, I don't know what to do! Evelyn would be so angry. Besides where would we go? I have no family.'

'The Duke and Duchess of Were are your family. We would go to Were Court,' said Sylvestra.

Lady Marianne's eyes grew round. 'Oh, but I don't know if I could face them, not without Evelyn there to support me. I could not simply turn up there unannounced, I would rather die!'

Sylvestra, who was quickly coming to realize that Lady Marianne was an even greater pea-goose than her Cousin Emily, had to bite back a retort to the effect that since death *was*, according to her, the alternative, surely it would be advisable to overcome such social scruples. Instead she contained her exasperation and simply reiterated her promise to stand her friend.

Just as it had always done with Emily, Sylvestra's air of resolution had a reassuring effect on Lady Marianne and even though they had only met a few moments previously the marchioness seemed quite happy to lean entirely upon her new friend for advice and support. Her butterfly brain automatically shied away from the unpleasant or difficult and within minutes of expressing fears for her life she was happily plying Sylvestra for news of the latest modes and the gossip presently circulating the city's fashionable salons.

Sylvestra found such shallowness unfathomable, but she did see it as further proof – if such proof was needed – that Lady Marianne's fears were nothing more than the over-active imaginings of a very silly woman.

Once the subject turned to more frivolous matters, their conversation soon foundered. Sylvestra had not the slightest interest in any of the things Lady Marianne clearly lived for. Whether the fashion this spring was for shallow or deep-poked bonnets was a subject to which Sylvestra could honestly say she had not given a moment's thought. The young marchioness looked askance at her. The tea was quickly drunk, pleasantries exchanged and farewells made. The door of the house in Grosvenor Square was closed behind Sylvestra and she let out a long slow breath.

Lady Vigrow's ball was in full swing. The refreshments were plentiful, the dancing lively and the guests disposed to enjoy themselves to the full. And at the heart of that dazzling colourful scene stood Sylvestra in a dark silent world of her own, nursing a secret that would have brought the whole brilliant carousel to a rude halt.

'Good evening, Miss Harvey. I wonder if I might have the pleasure of this next dance.' Lord Carston bowed before her and offered his hand.

Sylvestra's heart missed a beat. In the hours that had followed her meeting with Lady Marianne Carston it seemed that she had run through the gamut of human emotion, from rage to despair, self-blame to self-pity. In those hours, too, she had tried to prepare herself for this moment, imagining his every word, rehearsing each response. But as he stood there before her that familiar wicked gleam lurking in those blue eyes, Sylvestra learned something new about love; it could not simply be switched off because the object of that love was discovered to be unworthy. His words were punctiliously correct but his eyes spoke to her of the intimacies they could share and it tested Sylvestra's resolution to the limit. It would be so easy, whispered her treacherous heart, to surrender to him. After all, the world believed them to be lovers already. No, countered her head sternly, if he loved you, *truly* loved you, he would not ask such a sacrifice of you, nor would he have deceived you so.

'I am sorry, My Lord, but I am feeling a little tired this evening, and in no mood for dancing.' Her response was cold and she refused to meet his gaze. Her eyes, she knew, would betray her yearning.

But the marquis was not so easily snubbed. 'I am sorry to hear that, Miss Harvey, perhaps you had best sit somewhere quietly.' To the onlooker he appeared all concerned solicitude, but the hand at her elbow was firm, relentlessly propelling her towards the door. It seemed that unless she was to resort to an unseemly struggle in the middle of Lady Vigrow's ballroom, she was obliged to go with him. But that would be her only capitulation, vowed Sylvestra silently, desperately marshalling her defences as Lord Carston guided her inexorably into the privacy of a small ante-room.

Only then did he release her, saying lightly, 'Now what on earth has happened to ruffle your feathers, my dear? Last night—'

'If you were a gentleman – which I know now to my cost you are not – you would not be so insensitive as to refer to an incident which I can only recall with shame,' intervened Sylvestra, hastily turning from him and retreating to the opposite side of the room.

'Shame? Good God, Sylvestra, what is this nonsense? Another one of your charades? I thought we had put those games behind us.' He moved towards her, the warmth in his eyes inviting her to respond. 'I know you are not missish, my love.'

Sylvestra stepped back hurriedly, strategically positioning herself behind a *chaise-longue*. It was imperative that she keep the marquis at arm's length for she doubted that her resolve was strong enough to withstand his caresses.

'No I am not missish, My Lord, but despite what you may think I do have morals. If my occasional disregard for society's conventions has led you to believe I would welcome your . . . *carte blanche* then I am sorry but you are sadly mistaken!'

'*Carte blanche!*' exclaimed Lord Evelyn baffled, 'Great heavens, have I not made myself plain? Sylvestra, I love you, I want you to be my wife. I suppose the sticklers would say I should have approached your guardian first, but even so I hardly think there is any impropriety in an honest proposal of marriage!'

For the briefest of moments Sylvestra's heart leapt; he loved her, he wanted to marry her! Then reality crowded in and her fleeting joy was replaced with cold dread, for there was only one way in which Lord Carston could marry her and that knowledge filled her with horror. She took a deep, shuddering breath and lifted her eyes to meet his, her voice low and unsteady.

'Let us be clear about this, My Lord. You are asking me to marry you?'

Those blue eyes laughed back at her, no hint of guile in that handsome face. 'Yes! Not the most romantic of proposals I will grant you, but better I think than Mr Clive's attempt, and I had hoped a good deal more welcome. Must I get down on one knee? I will do so if that is what it takes to convince you of my sincerity!'

Sylvestra could only shake her head silently, but revulsion was etched clearly on her beautiful face. It was enough to halt Lord Evelyn in his tracks and banish the laughter from his eyes. Could he really have misread her feelings so badly? Memories of the night before filled his mind's eye; no, he had not imagined the ardency with which she had returned his kisses. Something had happened to turn her against him.

'What has changed, Sylvie? Please tell me, give me a chance to defend myself,' urged Evelyn earnestly.

His voice, his whole demeanour, so sincere. Sylvestra stared at him in horrified fascination. Was he mad? 'Today,' she said with great deliberation, 'I met Lady Marianne Carston, the Marchioness of Derwent. Now can you understand why I refuse your *honest* proposal of marriage?'

'You have spoken to Marianne? How in heaven's name did that come about?' Lord Carston broke off abruptly with a harsh little laugh. 'I suppose that is hardly relevant now. So you know our dark secret; believe it or not I would have told you before we were married. I believed – foolishly, I now see – that your love for me was strong enough to allow you to forgive my deception.'

Sylvestra stared at him incredulously. He was mad. He had expected her to condone the murder of his wife and child so that they might be together! How little he had known her – how little she had known him! She thought of young Edward, his dark hair, his blue eyes so like the man before her and she felt sick to her stomach. She wanted to run away, to hide from the awful truth, but then she thought of Marianne and Edward, virtual prisoners behind the genteel façade of the house in Grosvenor Square. She could not desert them.

Sylvestra forced herself to be calm. 'It is as well that the truth was discovered before we both did something we would certainly regret. Now if you will excuse me, I must return to my aunt before I am missed.'

Sylvestra did not wait for a response. She hurried to the door, her trembling fingers fumbling with the handle before she stumbled, half blinded by tears out of the room. She brushed a hand impatiently across her eyes, this was no time for self-pity. Forcing her lips into a bright smile, Sylvestra made her way through the crush of guests to her aunt's side. Mrs Harvey was indulgently watching her daughter in close conversation with Captain Maynard and she did not question Sylvestra's feigned headache nor her desire to go home. In truth it suited Julia Harvey very well to be spared the necessity of chaperoning her niece. Sylvestra's noble connections and handsome fortune had prevented her from being entirely ostracized by polite society, but tongues still wagged and Mrs Harvey was not keen for herself and her daughter to be linked by association in the gossips' minds.

Sylvestra did not wait for a chair, Green Street was only a step away and she felt the need for fresh air after the cloying atmosphere of the crowded ballroom. The short walk gave her an opportunity to collect her thoughts. She must face facts; she could no longer make excuses for Lord Evelyn Carston, his proposal of marriage was as good as an admission of his own villainy. What made it all the more heart-wrenching was that Sylvestra believed he truly did love her in his own way. She hoped desperately that her refusal would put a stop to his murderous plans, but she could not be certain.

This thought made Sylvestra quicken her pace, she must warn Marianne and quickly. Now Lord Carston knew his guilty secret was on the verge of exposure, who knew to what lengths he might go or what madness her rejection would provoke?

'Mosely, I need a footman to carry an urgent letter to Grosvenor Square!' said Sylvestra without preamble, when the butler opened the door.

'Very good, miss. It so happens that a message arrived for you earlier this evening.'

It was a note from Marianne Carston, written in an untidy childish hand and composed in a state of high emotion judging by the profusion of exclamation marks and heavily underscored words.

Dear Miss Harvey
I beg that you will come to my aid! My enemy has grown impatient and no longer even tries to disguise his Evil Purpose! But for a fortunate turn of Fate, he would have succeeded in his Wicked Intent and I would be dead, poisoned by his hand! We must escape before he returns. Please do not fail us. Miss Harvey, for I fear that without your help we are lost!

Marianne Carston, Marchioness of Derwent

Less than an hour ago, Sylvestra would have dismissed Marianne's plea for help as melodramatic nonsense, probably culled from the kind of romantic fiction her Cousin Emily delighted in. Now she could well believe that Lady Carston's fears were not exaggerated.

Sylvestra crushed the sheet of paper between her fingers. 'Mosely, I have changed my mind. I need a hackney carriage not a footman.'

Fourteen

Lord Carston strode up the steps of Derwent House and hammered on the door with his cane, noting with annoyance that the entire house was shrouded in darkness. What the devil was Benton thinking of allowing the candles to gutter in the entrance hall?

'My Lord!' The butler opened the door cautiously and was obviously surprised to find his master on the doorstep.

'Yes, Benton, it is I. A little earlier than you might have expected but not, I believe, justifying such amazement.' Lord Evelyn's response was uncharacteristically sharp. At any other time it might have afforded him slight amusement to wonder to what illicit belowstairs activity his early return had called a halt, but tonight he was in no mood for such trifles.

'No, My Lord . . . that is, forgive me but Her Ladyship implied that you would be travelling directly to Were,' explained the butler diffidently.

'Were? Why in devil's name would I be going to Were at this time of night?' asked Lord Evelyn impatiently.

'Well, My Lord,' stammered Benton helplessly. 'It was the young lady who said it, and what with His Grace taking a turn for the worse—'

'Wait!' commanded Lord Evelyn, his attention now fully caught. 'My father is ill?'

'But, My Lord, surely it was you who sent the young lady to tell Lady Marianne so, and to escort her to Were?'

'Benton, you are talking in riddles. If my father is ill then this is the first I have heard of it and I have certainly not sent any young lady to take Lady Marianne to Were.' The implication of what the servant was telling him suddenly struck Lord Evelyn. 'Good God! Are you telling me Lady Marianne is at this moment on her way to Were?'

Lord Evelyn clenched his fists and raised his eyes heavenward. When Sylvestra Harvey had rejected him he had thought the evening could get no worse; how wrong could he have been. He took a deep breath and addressed the nervous butler with deceptive calm. 'Benton, what have been my instructions from the first day of your employ? Did I not stress to you that on no account, *no account* was the carriage to be brought for Lady Marianne without my express order?'

'Yes, My Lord, but the young lady was so very insistent.' The butler's words trailed off miserably.

'The young lady? Who is this *young lady* who, it seems has greater power in my own house than I do myself?' demanded Lord Evelyn impatiently.

'Well, My Lord, I . . . I did not catch her name.' Poor Benton was become wretchedly aware that he had been sadly misguided in his judgement of the situation.

'And so you are telling me,' the marquis's words were laced with scathing sarcasm, 'that the orders of an unknown female take precedence over my own?'

'Oh, My Lord, that is exactly what I said!' The housekeeper, Mrs Chambers bustled across the hallway self-importantly. 'I said to Mr Benton, depend on it, Mr Benton, if His Lordship wanted My Lady and Master Edward to go to Were then he would accompany them there himself, not send some slip of a girl in his stead.'

'How well you know me, Mrs Chambers,' remarked Lord Evelyn with weary irony.

The housekeeper shot a smug look at her beleaguered colleague and, emboldened by her master's approbation, she continued to voice her opinion on the matter. 'And who is she? That is what I would like to know. Who is to say she is not in league with a band of murdering kidnappers, for all her genteel ways.' She sniffed. 'But then for some people, a pretty face can do no wrong.'

At this snide remark Benton was moved to protest, 'Now Mrs Chambers, I resent that—'

'Stop!' Lord Carston's thunderous tones silenced them both. 'I have no time for this petty bickering. I want to know what has being going on here. In my study, now!'

The two servants scurried ahead of their master into the study where Lord Carston rounded on them demanding peremptorily, 'The young lady. Was she tall and slim with a head of copper curls?'

'Why yes, My Lord,' responded Benton eagerly.

Lord Evelyn nodded his head grimly. 'Miss Sylvestra Harvey.' Apparently not satisfied with spurning his love for her, Miss Harvey was bent on making his life as difficult as possible. 'Tell me, has this lady ever been to this house before?'

'This very morning,' answered Benton. 'She brought Master Edward home from the park.'

'Firstly, how did Master Edward come to be in the park? Secondly, why was he returned home by a complete stranger?'

'It seems Master Edward persuaded his nurse to allow him to ride his pony in the park. I believe the pony bolted and although Master Edward came to no harm, he became separated from Mrs Pierce and the lady brought him home. Lady Marianne was very grateful, indeed the young lady stayed for a full hour.'

So that was how Sylvestra had met Marianne. Of all the damnable twists of fate! He could well imagine the tales with which Marianne had regaled Miss Harvey. If only he had taken the chance earlier to explain the wretched situation to her himself. But no, it wouldn't have made any difference; Miss Harvey had made her feelings very clear.

'So, I have the child's nurse to thank for this damned tangle. I would like to know what she was thinking of taking the boy to the park.'

'I would send for her if I could, My Lord, but she has gone off with Her ladyship,' volunteered Mrs Chambers, who felt she had been silent long enough; adding waspishly, 'It would not surprise me if Mrs Pierce is hand in glove with that bold red-headed piece. I never liked her above half, always sneaking about where she shouldn't. What business, I ask you, has the child's nurse here in Your Lordship's study?'

Lord Evelyn regarded the housekeeper in exasperation. 'But it was you who recommended Mrs Pierce to me. In fact I was under the impression that she was a relative of yours.'

Mrs Chambers shook her head vehemently. 'No, My Lord. I never clapped eyes on the woman before she turned up here.'

'But you did recommend her,' persisted Lord Evelyn.

Mrs Chambers blushed and wrung her hands together nervously. 'Well, My Lord, she did seem a very respectable sort of woman, and what with her having known Lady Marianne since she was a child—'

'Mrs Pierce claimed to know Lady Marianne?' queried Lord Evelyn sharply. From his conversations with Marianne he could have sworn the woman was a complete stranger to her.

'Yes, My Lord,' asserted Mrs Chambers. 'I remember it clearly. She said she was Lady Carston's old nurse. I thought it strange that she should know – well, that Her Ladyship *was* Lady Carston, but then I thought she must know her or how else would she know?' reasoned the housekeeper with rather garbled logic.

Lord Evelyn regarded Mrs Chambers intently. 'So Mrs Pierce referred to Lady Carston and not Miss Devenish?'

'Yes, My Lord.'

Lord Evelyn paced back and forth across the study frowning. He had allowed himself to become sidetracked: his real priority should be to go in pursuit of Marianne and Sylvestra; they could not be allowed to reach Were. But this business with the nurse worried him; something did not add up.

'Excuse me, My Lord,' ventured Benton tentatively, 'but did you say the young lady was Miss Harvey?'

'Yes, Benton, what of it?'

'It is only that Her Ladyship sent a note earlier this evening to a Miss Harvey. Of Green Street, I recall. It seemed to be of some urgency.'

'Have you any idea what prompted Lady Marianne to write this note?'

'Well, of course, Her Ladyship was quite distraught for she had just found her poor little dog.'

Lord Evelyn regarded his butler in bewilderment. He was almost afraid to ask. 'What has happened to Lady Marianne's dog?'

'Dead, My Lord!' pronounced Mrs Chambers dramatically. 'Poisoned. The poor thing must have got to the rat poison in the stables. Her Ladyship was quite beside herself.'

'I can imagine. But I hardly see why Lady Marianne would feel such a burning urge to confide her loss to Miss Harvey.'

'No, My Lord, very odd. But if I may be so bold, Her Ladyship was behaving a trifle strangely. Why, she even threw that lovely box of chocolates you sent her into the fire and there was above half of them left.'

'Chocolates. . . ?' Lord Evelyn stopped short in front of his desk, frowning in bemusement. He was beginning to doubt the sanity of the entire household, including himself. And then suddenly a thought seemed to strike him, for his eyes widened and he said urgently, 'Mrs Chambers, you said a moment ago that Mrs Pierce was in this room. What was she doing?'

'That is what I would like to know. And believe me, My Lord, I did ask her – quite sharply too. She said she had got lost, that she had not quite got her bearings.' The housekeeper's expression clearly demonstrated her opinion of this excuse.

But Lord Carston was already pulling open a drawer of his desk and rifling feverishly through its contents. His worst suspicions were apparently confirmed for whatever he sought was no longer there. 'Hell and damnation!' He slammed his fist down on the leather surface of the desk making his anxious servants jump. 'What a blind fool I have been. Benton, I want my horse brought round to the front of the house immediately and send my valet to my room.'

'Oh, why do we not go any faster?' exclaimed Marianne, for at least the tenth time since they had left Grosvenor Square. She was sitting on the edge of her seat and peering anxiously out of the carriage window, a pointless exercise as it was a cloudy, moonless night and they had long since left the lights of the capital behind.

'We can go no faster in the darkness; it would be too dangerous,' repeated Sylvestra patiently. After all the activity and emotional upheaval of recent hours she was feeling drained, and would have happily leant back against the velvet squabs of Lord Carston's luxurious travelling carriage and allowed the rhythmic swaying of their progress lull her to sleep. Instead, she had been obliged to continually soothe Lady Carston's increasingly irrational fears.

'How can you be so calm, when Evelyn is probably gaining on us with every mile!' complained Marianne pettishly, wringing her hands nervously.

'More likely he has not even left Lady Vigrow's ballroom yet,' reasoned Sylvestra wearily.

Marianne was unconvinced. 'You don't know Evelyn. He has the most uncanny way of seeming almost to know when I am going to flout his wishes.'

Despite the seriousness of their situation, Sylvestra found it hard to contain a smile. She had spent only a few hours in Lady Carston's company, but she could safely say that she had never before in her life met such a transparently self-centred person.

Marianne Carston did not even have the intelligence to disguise her selfishness. She doubted there was anything uncanny in Lord Carston's ability to foresee his wife's actions as Marianne would not have had the sense to hide her fears or indeed her intentions. In fact, it had taken all Sylvestra's ingenuity to prevent Marianne's careless tongue from unduly frightening her son. Now, thankfully, the boy was asleep, his dark head resting on Sylvestra's lap.

'There is no reason why Lord Evelyn should suspect. You did not threaten to go to Were by yourself did you?' she asked.

'Well no . . . that is, not recently. But he will guess; where else would I go?'

Sylvestra could not deny the logic of this, but it would achieve nothing to agree with Marianne other than to further exacerbate her fears.

'Even if he should follow us, we have a good head start, we are certain to reach Were before him. Besides, what can he do to you now? He would surely not be so foolish as to make an attempt on your life before so many witnesses.'

'Witnesses! Jobson and Pierce are Eve's servants, he will buy their silence. I never yet knew a servant who could not be bribed,' exclaimed Marianne scornfully with scant regard for Mrs Pierce's presence.

Sylvestra glanced at the nurse apprehensively, but if she was affronted by her mistress's lack of faith, then she did not show it. 'Well, if that were so, which I doubt, I am not in Lord Evelyn's pay and he certainly cannot bribe me!' responded Sylvestra brusquely.

'Oh, very well, but for heaven's sake let us stop arguing about it! I have the most dreadful headache,' cried Marianne impatiently, flinging herself back into her seat with a exaggerated moan.

Unfortunately, Edward chose this moment to wake up. 'I want to go home.' His small plaintive voice was a world away from the brave and happy little boy Sylvestra had met only this morning and it tugged at her heart strings.

She patted his hand encouragingly. 'Cheer up, Edward! We shall soon be at Were, then you will meet your grandmama and grandpapa. You will like that, won't you?'

'Yes,' said the boy doubtfully. 'But I would rather have waited and come with Uncle Eve. He said I could ride with him in his curricle!'

'*Uncle Eve?*' Sylvestra stared at the boy bewildered. She turned to Lady Carston and demanded urgently, 'Marianne, what does he mean, *Uncle Eve*?'

'What? Oh, Edward positively idolizes Eve, he can do no wrong in his eyes. Ridiculous is it not?' Marianne shrugged carelessly.

Sylvestra shook her head impatiently. 'No, no, I don't mean that. I mean why does Edward call Lord Evelyn uncle?'

Marianne looked at her strangely. 'But Evelyn is his uncle, what else should he call him?'

Sylvestra took a deep breath. Nothing made sense. 'But I thought . . . I thought you were married to Lord Evelyn, that Edward was his son.'

'I, married to Eve?' exclaimed Marianne, in tones of strong revulsion. 'Good heavens whatever gave you that idea?'

Sylvestra gritted her teeth, she was fast losing patience with Lady Marianne Carston or whoever she was. 'You said you were the Marchioness of Derwent.'

'And so I am. I was married to *Vincent* Carston. Eve has never had the least pretension to the title. Really, Miss Harvey, I don't think you can have been properly attending.'

Sylvestra stared at her in speechless amazement, the implications of what she was hearing beginning to dawn on her. '*Vincent* Carston? But how is that possible? I understood that he was married to someone else, Lady Elizabeth—'

'Versoe,' supplied Marianne, sniffing disparagingly. 'I don't see how he could be, seeing as he was already married to me. Vincent loved me to distraction, of course, but he needed Lady Elizabeth's fortune to pay off his gambling debts.' Marianne laughed spitefully. 'Money, that is all Elizabeth Versoe had to offer. I declare I have never seen such an antidote in all my life, positively at her last prayers!'

'No!' Mrs Pierce sat bolt upright her cheeks burning red, her dark eyes strangely fierce.

'Good heavens, Pierce, what on earth is the matter?' Marianne cast Sylvestra a speaking look and mouthed silently behind her hand, 'Quite mad.'

Sylvestra, observing the nurse's tightly clenched fists and quick shallow breathing, was inclined to agree. The woman was certainly a little odd, not at all the kind of person to whom one would wish to entrust a child.

Feeling all eyes upon her, Mrs Pierce struggled to contain her agitation. 'I am sorry, My Lady, I must have dozed off and had a nightmare. I am afraid I am not a good traveller.' She hid her face in her capacious handkerchief and snivelled miserably.

Lady Marianne continued, 'Of course, it was my youth and innocence that was my downfall. When Vincent suggested an elopement and a secret wedding, I thought it so romantic! Well, I have never been so deceived in all my life!'

Sylvestra could scarcely credit what she was hearing let alone comprehend it. 'But if you were married to Vincent Carston, what possible motive has Lord Evelyn for wanting you. . . .' Sylvestra paused, mindful of Edward's curious ears. 'Wanting you out of the way?'

'But it is obvious! Evelyn does not want to lose the title of marquis and all the benefits attached to it. Edward is the true marquis, but no one would ever need to know that if we both disappeared.'

Sylvestra shook her head positively. 'No, you are wrong. Lord Evelyn would never be so materialistic! If he cared so much for the empty pleasures of the ton, why do you suppose he took the blame for his brother's misdemeanours and spent five years ostracized by his family and society?'

Marianne could not answer this, but she had her own telling argument. 'But you cannot deny that he tried to poison me!'

'But that is pure supposition. Just because your pet ate the chocolates does not prove that he was killed by them. It is just as likely that he picked up poison laid down for vermin.' Sylvestra spoke with greater conviction than she felt. The series of accidents that had plagued Lady Carston and her son could surely not be ascribed to coincidence. What she did know now, beyond any doubt, was that Lord Evelyn was not responsible, and if in fact someone was trying to kill them then the sooner they returned to his protection the better. Sylvestra pulled the cord, signalling the driver to stop the carriage.

'What are you doing?' demanded Marianne in consternation. 'We must press on to Were!'

Sylvestra shook her head decisively. 'No, I am sure that is the worst thing we can do. Lord Evelyn is not your enemy, Marianne, and if he is keeping your true circumstances a secret from his parents, then I am sure he has good reason. I really think we should return to Grosvenor Square without delay.'

Marianne stamped her foot angrily. 'Oh! And I thought you were my friend, Sylvestra. I cannot believe you are taking his side after all I have told you.'

But Sylvestra would not be swayed. Why Lord Evelyn had chosen to countenance his brother's subterfuge and taken the blame for Marianne's seduction was still a mystery to Sylvestra, but what she did know was enough to lift the burden of doubt that had plagued her since her first meeting with Evelyn Carston. At long last she was free to follow her heart.

'You may turn the carriage around, we are returning to London,' she said to the coachman with as much authority as she could muster.

'No!' cried Marianne. 'Jobson, I am your mistress and I insist you continue to Were.'

'Yes, My Lady.' The coachman shot Sylvestra a look of helpless apology before remounting his box. His own personal inclination would be to follow the young lady's instructions, indeed the whole expedition had been undertaken against his better judgement, but Lady Carston, as she said, was his mistress.

It was pointless to argue with Marianne, indeed having got her own way, Lady Carston had firmly closed her eyes and was either fast asleep or successfully feigning that state. All Sylvestra could do was to try and comfort herself with the thought that while arriving unannounced at the dead of night was perhaps not the best way to break such momentous news to a man reportedly in poor health, it was after all only right that the Duke of Were should meet his true heir.

Sylvestra sighed, the edge taken off her joy at discovering Evelyn's innocence. The path had been cleared for her to love him unreservedly, but it would be small wonder if he chose to wash his hands of her entirely. Besides harbouring the most abominable suspicions of him, she had caused him nothing but trouble since the moment they had met. It was on this gloomy thought that sleep finally claimed her.

She was woken a matter of moments later by the protesting groan of wood under immense strain followed by a loud crack as, almost instantaneously, the carriage's rear axle gave way. Immediately, the carriage pitched violently to one side, throwing its occupants roughly on to the floor. The carriage continued to move, dragged along on its side by the frightened horses until its weight finally anchored them.

Sylvestra, winded and disorientated but unhurt, found herself at the bottom of the heap, Edward pinned tightly to her chest and Marianne's screams filling her ears. On top of them all was Mrs Pierce. The nurse was shrieking uncontrollably, her limbs rigid with hysteria, and it was clearly pointless to expect her to try and extricate herself. Fortunately, help was at hand. The carriage door, which was now above their heads, was wrenched open and the welcome figure of Jobson appeared.

'Get me out of here, Jobson, at once!' cried Marianne tearfully.

'That I will, My Lady, but first I must move Mrs Pierce. Now come along, Mrs Pierce, calm yourself and give me your hand.' The coachman's placid tone had the desired effect and the nurse was slowly pulled free, allowing the remaining occupants of the carriage to breathe a good deal easier.

'Are you all right, Edward?' asked Sylvestra anxiously, lifting the boy gently to one side. He nodded bravely. Sylvestra turned her attention to Marianne and established that for all her shrieks and moans she had not actually sustained anything more serious than a few scratches and bruises. They were then left to wait for Jobson to return and rescue them. Minutes went by and there was an ominous lack of activity from outside the carriage.

'Good heavens, what is keeping that wretched man!' exclaimed Marianne impatiently. 'Jobson! Jobson, hurry up!' There was no response.

'Perhaps he is busy calming the horses,' suggested Sylvestra, and pulling herself to her feet, she tried to climb out of the open door. She succeeded in getting her head and shoulders through the opening but the angle the carriage was lying at made it impossible to make further progress without assistance. Supporting her weight on her elbows Sylvestra scanned the dark hedgerow. She could make out the shadowy shapes of the horses standing quite calmly on the verge, but there was no sign of Jobson.

'Jobson, are you there?' No reply. With growing unease Sylvestra twisted round to search the road ahead. She felt the hairs stand up on the back of her neck and her mouth go dry. Lying in the road, face down and unmoving, was Jobson. There was no sign of Mrs Pierce. As quietly as she could, Sylvestra dropped back down into the body of the carriage.

'What on earth is keeping the stupid man?' complained Marianne.

Sylvestra put a finger to her lips and whispered urgently, 'Shh. We must be quiet. I think we have been attacked by footpads. Jobson has been knocked out—'

She stopped abruptly; from outside came the sound of someone laboriously scrambling up the side of the carriage towards the open door. Marianne gave a muffled squeal and pressed herself into a corner. Sylvestra, her heart beating wildly, pushed Edward down beneath the seat and moved to hide him from view.

For what seemed an age, the scuffling noise continued and then a silhouette appeared at the opening. At that moment the moon emerged from behind the clouds illuminating the face of Mrs Pierce. Marianne let out a long sigh of relief.

'Mrs Pierce! Good Lord, you scared us half to death! Why didn't you answer us? What has happened to Jobson?'

The nurse did not respond, but simply extended her arm purposefully into the carriage. Held steadily in her wrinkled grasp was a murderous-looking duelling pistol, the moonlight glinting wickedly off its long barrel.

'What are you doing, Pierce? Put that thing down and help us out of here!'

Sylvestra laid a restraining hand on Marianne's arm, her eyes never leaving the nurse's face.

'What do you intend to do with that gun, Mrs Pierce?' she asked, struggling to keep panic out of her voice.

The woman's gaze rested on Sylvestra for a moment, the faded eyes indifferent, contemptuous. 'I have no quarrel with you, miss, but you should have minded your own business. I'm sorry you will have to suffer for the sins of others, but I can't have my poor dead Lizzy's name besmirched.'

'Good Lord, didn't I say the woman was unhinged?' exclaimed Marianne. 'Pierce, I have not the slightest notion what you are talking about but if you do not put that gun down then I can promise you it will go very ill with you when the Duke of Were hears how you have treated his relations.'

'Marianne, I think perhaps we should let Mrs Pierce explain herself,' warned Sylvestra, who, unlike her companion had quickly realized that the nurse posed a very real threat to all their lives. The only thing she could think to do was keep the woman talking.

'Who is Lizzy, Mrs Pierce?' she asked gently.

The nurse's eyes which had focused on Lady Marianne with intense loathing, softened at the sound of that name. 'My Lizzy was a proper young lady. She might not have been a beauty, but a gentler and kinder girl you couldn't hope to find. She deserved better than that wastrel Vincent Carston. I said all along he would bring her nothing but unhappiness, but it was what her parents wanted and she was a dutiful daughter. She was a dutiful wife as well, though she never got any thanks for it. She was so happy when she knew she was with child. "Oh, Pierce," she said. "We shall be happy now, Vincent and I." Poor innocent fool! That's when he told her, the guilt got too much for him. Told her she was not really his wife, that their child would be a bastard. Wept at her feet he did, begged her forgiveness, and she gave it him. She loved him you see. He didn't deserve her. . . .' Mrs Pierce's voice broke, tears rolling unchecked down her cheeks. 'I tried to stop her, pleaded with her, but she was stubborn. Said she couldn't live with the shame, couldn't bring a child into the world without a legitimate father. That was the last time I saw her.'

'What are you saying, that her death was not an accident?' asked Sylvestra, who had listened with such horrified pity to Lady Elizabeth's tragic story, that she had almost forgotten their own peril.

The nurse shook her head. 'No, it was not an accident, I am sure of that. Lizzy did not want the world to know her shame, and Vincent Carston, well, the guilt had eaten away at him for years.' Mrs Pierce turned her gaze on Marianne, saying with bitter triumph, 'You think he loved you, but he chose to die with my Lizzy rather than live with you!'

'But what happened to Lady Elizabeth was no fault of mine! You cannot hold me responsible,' pleaded Marianne, her voice rising hysterically. 'I am as much a victim as she. More so! At least while she was alive she had all the privileges of a marchioness. She did not have to skulk about on the fringes of society. You say you want to save her name, but what of my name?'

'Your name!' Mrs Pierce sneered nastily. 'You already had a reputation as a bold strumpet even before you married in that hole-in-a corner way. Aye, and how many months was it before your lying-in? Not the full nine, I'll warrant!'

'How dare you imply such a thing!' exclaimed Marianne, her fear forgotten in her rage. 'You are just a foolish, mad, old woman and I insist you let us out of here this instant!'

Mrs Pierce's eyes blazed. 'Foolish, am I? Well, my fine lady, 'tis you who is the fool for you shall not live to enjoy your title.'

'Marianne, look out!' Sylvestra read the murderous intent in their captor's face and she thrust Marianne to the floor at the same moment as the nurse fired the pistol. There was a blinding flash and two loud retorts in quick succession.

Breathing hard, Sylvestra pulled herself upright. Mrs Pierce had vanished from sight. There was no time to waste. At any moment the nurse could reappear with her weapon reloaded. She would not miss again.

Summoning all her strength, Sylvestra hauled herself through the open carriage door, her arms trembling with the effort. Along with Marianne's hysterical screams and Edward's terrified sobs, she was dimly aware of a male voice. Please God, Jobson had come round!

A final thrust saw her clear of the doorway and lying precariously along the tilted side of the carriage. In the almost pitch darkness she could see a shadowy figure with its back to her, the menacing shape of a pistol in one hand. Without pausing to think, Sylvestra gathered herself on her haunches and launched herself at the figure. They both hit the ground hard, Sylvestra frantically grasping at the hand that held the pistol. To her dismay, Sylvestra found that her opponent was far too strong for her and, after a brief struggle, she was turned on to her back and pinned mercilessly to the ground. Only then did it register that the person she had thought to be Mrs Pierce was not only tall and well built but dressed in unmistakably masculine attire.

Fifteen

'Be still, you little hellcat! It is me, Evelyn!'

Sylvestra ceased to struggle. 'Eve? Is it really you? Oh, thank God. Quick, Mrs Pierce is trying to kill us all! We must stop her before she has chance to reload her pistol!'

'Mrs Pierce is dead,' said Lord Carston baldly, getting up and pulling Sylvestra unceremoniously to her feet. 'One of the shots you heard was mine. I was just about to check she had not succeeded in hitting any of you. You are obviously uninjured, Miss Harvey, can I assume the same is true of your companions?'

'Yes, yes, we are all unhurt. That is to say Lady Marianne and Edward are fine, but I think Jobson may have had his head split open.'

'I'll be all right, miss.' The coachman appeared out of the darkness, groggily rubbing his head.

'Good man, Jobson. Do you think you are up to helping me get Her Ladyship and the boy free?' Lord Carston turned his back on Sylvestra and strode towards the overturned carriage.

Sylvestra was left standing alone, feeling redundant and strangely forlorn. She knew it was ridiculous to expect him to take her in his arms and kiss her as if nothing had ever been wrong between them, but that did not stop Sylvestra wishing it could be so. The last time they had spoken Evelyn had proposed and she had rejected him; it was hardly surprising then that he should address her so coldly. In Sylvestra's mind, all their differences had evaporated as soon as she had learned the true identity of Edward's father, but she realized that to Lord Carston her rejection must have seemed inexplicable.

'Miss Harvey, do you think you would be able to ride one of the carriage horses?' Lord Carston's voice broke in upon Sylvestra's cheerless thoughts. 'I am afraid we can go no further in the carriage itself. Mrs Pierce may have been completely insane but she was certainly resourceful; the rear axle has quite clearly been sawn part the way through. She was obviously determined that Marianne and Edward would never reach Were.'

'Do you hear that, Miss Harvey? Oh, I wish I had not let you persuade me to make this foolhardy journey. I was against it from the start you know, Eve, but Miss Harvey is so very forceful.' Marianne smiled sweetly at them both. 'Not that I am blaming you, Sylvestra – and nor must you, Evelyn! – for I am sure you thought you were doing the right thing.'

Sylvestra stared at Marianne in disbelief; she could hardly credit what she was hearing. But Marianne simply gazed back at her through guileless blue eyes, the very picture of delicate and vulnerable femininity. Somehow, despite all the indignities to which they had been subjected, Marianne had found the opportunity to pat her golden curls back into place and smooth the skirts of her very fetching blue velvet travelling dress. A protective arm around the child at her side completed the perfect picture, thought Sylvestra cynically. Sylvestra, on the other hand, as she was dismally aware, was in far from her best looks after her undignified scuffle with Lord Carston. Her copper curls were falling in tangled ringlets about her shoulders, the hem of her cloak was liberally coated with mud and she was sure if she had a mirror to hand she would discover a smut on her nose.

Sylvestra took a deep breath and said as calmly as she could, 'Lady Marianne, I was under the impression that you wished to go to Were. In fact, you were quite insistent—'

'It hardly matters now whose idea it was,' cut in Lord Carston impatiently. 'I think we would be better advised trying to find an inn for the night rather than standing out here arguing who is to blame.'

'Oh, I quite agree, Eve!' concurred Marianne quickly. 'Poor Edward is worn to a thread with all this excitement.'

Silently fuming, Sylvestra allowed Jobson to throw her up on to the back of one of the carriage horses and watched with a jaundiced eye as Lady Marianne was tenderly lifted by Evelyn on to his saddle horse. The dazzling smiles Marianne was bestowing on her saviour were a little too much to bear given the circumstances, and Sylvestra looked quickly away, her gaze falling on the macabre form of Mrs Pierce's body.

'What of Mrs Pierce?' she exclaimed. 'We cannot leave her in the middle of the road for anyone to find!'

'Oh, why must you remind us, Sylvestra.' Lady Marianne shuddered eloquently and looked to Lord Carston for support. 'You surely cannot expect us to take her with us, that would be too much to bear!'

'Marianne is right,' stated Lord Carston curtly. 'But I am obliged to you, Miss Harvey, for reminding me.' He strode over to the corpse, which was covered with his own greatcoat, and searched through the dead nurse's pockets. When he returned, he was carrying a single sheet of paper. 'Your marriage certificate, Marianne. Mrs Pierce stole it from my desk. I should imagine she intended to destroy it.' He turned to the coachman. 'If you will help me, Jobson, we will move Mrs Pierce out of plain view. As Miss Harvey says, it would not do for some unfortunate traveller to come across such an obstacle. I shall have enough to explain to the local magistrate as it is.'

That gruesome task completed, the party set off slowly in search of shelter and were fortunate in that a sizeable inn lay only a few hundred yards further along the road. The contents of Lord Carston's purse was sufficient to dispel any doubts the landlord might have about customers arriving by such unconventional means, and they were soon ensconced in a suite of rooms. Sylvestra quickly discovered that as far as Lady Marianne was concerned, she was expected to fulfil the role of lady's-maid-cum-nurse and she was given no opportunity to speak to Lord Carston in private until she had helped Marianne to disrobe and soothed Edward to sleep.

By then the night was considerably advanced and Sylvestra longed for her own bed, but she knew there could be no possibility of sleep until she had talked to Lord Carston. Closing the door of Edward's room behind her, she stood hesitantly on the threshold of the private parlour. Lord Carston was seated before the fire with his back to Sylvestra, engaged in the delicate task of cleaning his duelling pistol. Silently, Sylvestra picked up the lighted candelabrum from the dining–table and moved it to illuminate his work. Automatically, Lord Carston murmured a word of thanks, but then realizing the identity of his companion, his expression hardened and he lowered his eyes once more to his pistol. Sylvestra sat down quietly opposite him and, with her hands folded in her lap, patiently waited for him to finish.

Lord Carston continued resolutely for several minutes but he was clearly distracted by her presence. 'Why do you not retire, Miss Harvey?' he asked impatiently at last. 'You must surely be tired, you have been so very *busy* this evening.'

Much as she would have liked to respond in kind to Lord Carston's biting sarcasm, Sylvestra resolved to remain calm whatever the provocation and so she said steadily, 'Lord Carston, I wish you might give me an opportunity to explain my actions—'

'Believe me, Miss Harvey, no explanation is necessary.' Lord Carston's handsome face was hard and unyielding. 'It is perfectly clear that your pride was so . . . so *affronted* by my deception that you were determined to have your revenge and to hell with the consequences.'

'No!' exclaimed Sylvestra. 'No, you do not understand. It was not in the least like that! Please listen to what I have to say!'

Lord Carston shook his head. 'Your actions speak for themselves and nothing you say can alter their meaning. You bewitched me for a time, Miss Sylvestra Harvey. Your refreshing independence intrigued me and made your surrender all the more captivating, but you will not draw me into your net again with your subtle wiles. I was a fool to believe you were any different from your peers, to fondly imagine that a title or lack of it would mean little to you.'

Sylvestra stared at him in impotent silence. How could she defend herself against such accusations? After all, had that not been her intention, to deliberately and cold-heartedly ensnare him? But for one small flaw she could have exulted, triumphed in her conquest.

'I love you,' she whispered, her eyes bright with unshed tears, her heart and soul in those three words.

For a moment Evelyn did not reply. She looked so beautiful and so vulnerable, her hair burning bright in the fire's glow, her eyes luminous, imploring him, tempting him to succumb. With an impatient exclamation Evelyn started from his chair and turned his back on her.

Sylvestra waited, her heart in her throat. Had she got through to him? But when he turned to face her his blue eyes were hard and cold, contemptuously raking her up and down.

'If you loved *me* then the truth would have been easier to forgive than the ugly rumours that preceded it. Your love, however, was reserved solely for the title you thought I held. Well, that has gone, so you may cease your protestations. I assume they are for form's sake only, unless, of course, you have lowered your sights and decided a younger son will do. No doubt Marianne has informed you that I am not entirely without fortune.'

Lord Carston laughed mirthlessly. 'Cruelly ironic I think you will agree, that my brother Vincent should be such an avid yet luckless gambler whereas I, who, to my father's dismay, have never shown the least inclination for that noble vice, should discover quite by accident an uncanny aptitude for games of chance. Roaming the Continent for five years frequenting the most notorious gaming hells in Europe would not have been my chosen career, but it has furnished me with a very comfortable living. What a pity for your aspirations, Miss Harvey, that you did not discover my circumstances before you showed your true colours. You must be wishing now that you had not been so quick to give up your captain.'

'You have got it all wrong, Lord Carston!' exclaimed Sylvestra desperately. 'I did not reject your proposal because I discovered you were not the marquis! And it was not spiteful revenge that prompted me to help Marianne reach Were!'

Lord Carston flung himself back into his seat, thrusting his long legs out before him and sinking his hands deep into his pockets, the hint of a cynical smile about his lips.

'Then pray set me straight, Miss Harvey, I am all ears! It is some while since I have heard an original fairy-tale. Just why did you lead Marianne and Edward into mortal danger?'

Sylvestra felt her anger rising. He was not giving her a chance and he was quite determined to believe the worst. She took a deep breath and said baldly, 'I thought I was leading them *away* from danger. I thought it was *you* who was trying to kill them!'

Lord Carston sat very still, his face a hard, unreadable mask. The only indication that he had heard what Sylvestra had said was a faint flush beneath his bronzed complexion. Sylvestra longed to say more, to explain how she had come to such an outrageous conclusion, but she could not find the words.

'You thought I would murder my own brother's child and his mother?' Lord Carston's words were so low as to be barely audible. He shook his head uncomprehendingly. 'But why would I. . . ?' And then a thought seemed to strike him and he looked at Sylvestra, revulsion etched sharply in his face. 'You thought I would kill Edward just to keep his title. You thought I was capable of murdering a five-year-old boy so that I might be Marquis of Derwent.'

Sylvestra shook her head dumbly, the tears she had fought to contain, spilling over and pouring unchecked down her white cheeks. 'No,' she whispered. 'No, that was not the reason.'

But Lord Carston was not listening, he was striding towards the door. 'There is nothing more to be said, Miss Harvey. Given your low opinion of me I can quite understand why you might be reject me as a husband. I think we have both had a lucky escape. Now, if you will excuse me, I think I will go to the tap room in search of more convivial company.' With a terse nod he was gone, leaving Sylvestra nothing to do but rage impotently against his intransigence and retire to her bed with her problems no nearer resolution.

Sylvestra endured a disturbed night, drifting fitfully in and out of sleep, her dreams and her waking thoughts alike bedevilled by painful memories of harsh words and haunted by a pair of unforgiving blue eyes. Her mood swung back and forth between frustrated anger at Lord Carston's obdurate refusal to listen to reason and the lowering reflection that after all, one could hardly blame him. Consequently, Sylvestra awoke far from refreshed and far from eager to face Evelyn Carston across the breakfast-table.

Her craven instinct had been to slip away as soon as dawn broke and make her own way back to London, but with no more than a few pence in her purse common sense must prevail and, much as she disliked it, she knew she was entirely dependent upon Lord Carston. Sylvestra busied herself instead with the almost impossible task of restoring her appearance to something approaching respectability. A change of clothes had been the last thing on her mind when Sylvestra had set off on her ill-considered adventure, now with only a crushed and muddied ballgown to her name she wished she had been a little more pragmatic. The eau-de-Nil silk had looked vastly elegant in the brilliant setting of Lady Vigrow's ballroom; in the parlour of a modest inn it looked ridiculous.

A delicate yawn from the opposite side of the room signalled that Lady Marianne had arisen. 'Oh, Miss Harvey, you are up already. I declare you must have the constitution of an ox! I swear I am feeling quite fagged to death.'

The fresh complexion and bright eyes belied this claim; clearly no torments of guilt had troubled Lady Marianne's rest. Her next words seemed to support this. 'Anyhow I am glad you are up, Sylvestra. You may fetch me a cup of chocolate and some lightly buttered bread.' She smiled bewitchingly. 'If you would not mind, that is. I have no wish to see Evelyn before it is absolutely necessary, he is no company at the best of times and now he has been thwarted he will be in a worse temper than usual.'

'But you surely cannot *still* suppose Lord Carston has any sinister intentions towards you?' objected Sylvestra.

'Well, no,' admitted Marianne reluctantly. 'But, after all, it was Eve who engaged Mrs Pierce. You cannot convince me *that* was mere coincidence. He hoped the woman would do his dirty work for him.'

Sylvestra stared at her in amazement. 'Marianne, Lord Carston saved our lives. Without his intervention we would very likely all be dead.'

Lady Marianne pulled her face in distaste. 'Pray do not remind me, Sylvestra. I fear I shall never forget it.' But as she then started to chatter excitedly about her impending establishment as the Marchioness of Derwent, Sylvestra doubted that memories of her close brush with death would trouble her vacuous brain for long. Indeed, when Sylvestra finally entered the parlour it would be hard to say which was greater; her dread of confronting Lord Carston or her relief at escaping Lady Marianne's inconsequential prattle.

Lord Carston was already seated at the table, and beyond a brief frowning glance he did not acknowledge Sylvestra's entrance. Sylvestra conveyed Marianne's request to a serving maid before seating herself opposite Lord Carston. She eyed him surreptitiously over the rim of her coffee cup and her last hopes dwindled and died. A night's reflection had obviously not softened him towards her. His face was set in grim lines and his eyes studiously avoided her gaze. Swallowing her pride and her bitter disappointment, Sylvestra addressed him in a voice devoid of all emotion.

'I am sorry to have to impose upon you, My Lord, but I find myself unable to pay my way. If you could just furnish me with enough to get back to Green Street I shall repay you at the earliest opportunity.'

'You are coming with us to Were,' pronounced Lord Carston bluntly, without even looking up from his plate.

Sylvestra regarded him blankly. 'My Lord, I have no intention of going to Were. I am sure you must have many . . . sensitive matters to discuss as a family. I hardly think you would wish for my presence.'

Lord Carston set down his knife and fork with a clatter and said scathingly, 'It is a pity you did not discover this delicacy of feeling earlier, Miss Harvey. It might have saved us all a vast deal of trouble.'

Sylvestra coloured up, but said with determined calm, 'I have no wish to argue with you, Lord Carston. You have made your feelings perfectly plain and I think it can do neither of us any good to spend any more time than we must in each other's company. It makes sense, therefore, to allow me to return to London.'

Lord Carston shook his head. 'As usual, Miss Harvey, you have acted with scant regard for the consequences of your deeds. Do you suppose for one moment that it has gone unremarked that after being seen together at Lady Vigrow's ball, Lord Evelyn Carston and Miss Sylvestra Harvey have mysteriously vanished? I would lay odds your aunt is already spreading the tale.'

'Oh, as if I care for that!' cried Sylvestra impatiently. 'Besides, when I return alone that will surely quash any rumour.'

Lord Carston raised his eyes to heaven in exasperation. 'Must I spell it out to you, Miss Harvey? As far as the world is concerned you will have spent the night alone in a gentleman's company. Your ostracism will be complete.'

'Even so, I will return to Green Street,' declared Sylvestra stubbornly, though a small corner of her heart was warmed by his apparent concern for her reputation.

His next words shattered that illusion. 'Miss Harvey, to put no finer point upon it, you may take your own path to Hell, but there has been enough scandal attached to the name of Carston already without you adding to it. Now, you will come to Were and, if we are lucky, society may be brought to believe that you arrived there last night and are staying as a guest of my mother.'

'But is that really necessary? Surely there must be some other way . . .' argued Sylvestra desperately. She could imagine nothing worse than arriving at Were, a most unwanted and unwelcome guest.

'Please do not waste your energy thinking on it, Miss Harvey. It is all arranged. I have already sent a message to Were requesting that a carriage be sent to collect us, and my mother is expecting you.'

'Expecting me?' repeated Sylvestra weakly. She dreaded to think how Lord Carston had explained her presence in the party to the duchess.

Lord Carston seemed to read her thoughts because he said dryly, 'Do not worry, Miss Harvey. I have no desire to advertise my own folly. As far as my mother is concerned you are here simply as a travelling companion for Lady Marianne.'

Sylvestra blushed miserably. 'The folly is all mine,' she murmured, more to herself than anything.

Doubt flickered briefly in Lord Evelyn's blue eyes as he regarded Sylvestra's troubled countenance, and it was on the tip of his tongue to ask her to explain her cryptic remark, but then Edward burst into the room and the moment was lost.

'Ah, so you do get up then, you young slug-a-bed!' Evelyn tousled the young boy's hair affectionately. 'Now, get some breakfast and make haste about it. We are leaving for Were shortly.'

Edward needed no further encouragement and was quickly tucking into a mountain of ham and eggs. 'Are you coming too, Miss Harvey?' he asked innocently.

Sylvestra regarded the boy helplessly, aware of his uncle's amused expression. She sighed resignedly, it seemed she had no choice. 'Yes, Edward, I am coming with you.'

The Duke of Were's principal seat was scarcely a half-dozen miles from the inn which had provided Lord Carston and his companions with shelter: but this did not prevent Lady Marianne from declaring the journey interminable. The marchioness exclaimed impatiently and frequently that they would *never* arrive, whilst on the other hand, Sylvestra found herself praying fervently that she might be right.

Nothing happened, however, to check their progress, and within a very few minutes of setting off in the ducal carriage they were bowling up the wide rhododendron-lined drive of Were Court. By this time, Lady Marianne could hardly contain her excitement, even going so far as to lift Edward on to her lap and adjuring him to look about him since one day soon he would be duke and lord of all he surveyed.

This cheerful consignment of the present incumbent to an early grave caused Sylvestra's gaze to fly involuntarily to Lord Carston's face. The sardonic humour that lurked in those blue eyes suggested that through long experience Lord Evelyn had become inured to his sister-in-law's thoughtless remarks. For the briefest of moments their eyes met in silent and shared amusement before Lord Carston seemed to recollect himself and he turned abruptly away. Sylvestra's spirits plummeted. Whatever fonder feelings Lord Carston had felt for her once, they had now quite clearly withered and died. Inwardly she cursed her own weakness; she should have made him listen to her last night. When he had stormed out of the room she should have gone after him and forced him to hear her explanation. She had behaved quite pathetically.

Now it was too late. Anything she said would seem like an excuse, hastily concocted in an attempt to insinuate herself back into his affections once she had discovered he was not such a bad catch after all. Sylvestra stifled a sigh. How could she expect Lord Carston to believe that she had thought Lady Marianne was his wife when she could scarce credit that she had ever imagined it herself?

The carriage came to a smooth halt and Sylvestra resolutely thrust her depressing thoughts to the back of her mind. She would have enough to withstand during this enforced stay with Lord Carston and his family without allowing herself to wallow in self-pity.

Lady Helen, Duchess of Were, was waiting to greet their arrival, a pale and dignified figure in a half-mourning gown of dove-grey sarsenet. By no means eager to be part of this strange family reunion, Sylvestra deliberately hung back as Lord Carston led Marianne and Edward forward to be introduced to his mother. Marianne, her face wreathed in triumphant smiles and chattering nineteen to the dozen, seemed oblivious to the palpably strained atmosphere and obviously did not feel the incongruity of her own behaviour or her very dashing promenade dress of primrose twilled silk in a household plainly still in mourning for her dead husband.

Lady Helen did her best to match her daughter-in-law's mood, but to Sylvestra it was clear that the duchess was far from comfortable. Had Lady Helen grown to love gentle and dutiful Lady Elizabeth in the same way Mrs Pierce had claimed Lord Vincent had? If so, how much more difficult it must be to accept this heartless and heedless butterfly in her place. Of course, young Edward would be her saving grace. Even as Sylvestra watched, some of the strain left the duchess's face as her eyes alighted on her grandson.

'Miss Harvey? Welcome to Were Court. I am sorry my husband

is not well enough to greet you with me. Perhaps you would like to come into the house and refresh yourself?'

The duchess's melodious voice roused Sylvestra from her position of detached onlooker and she realized that while the rest of the party were making their way into the house she was still standing rooted to the spot.

Feeling slightly foolish, Sylvestra moved forward to greet her hostess, dipping a hurried curtsy and saying in a rush, 'Your Grace, it is very good of you to welcome me, when I am sure you must be wishing me to the Devil! Believe me, I would not have trespassed upon your hospitality had not circumstances' – here she could not resist shooting a resentful glance in Lord Carston's direction – 'obliged me to.'

'Oh dear!' exclaimed the duchess, her blue eyes dancing with humour in a way which was disturbingly reminiscent of her younger son. 'I do hope Eve has not dragooned you into coming here. Really, Evelyn, if Miss Harvey does not wish to visit us then it is very cruel of you to force her.'

'No, really,' protested Sylvestra blushing fiercely, 'that is not what I meant to imply at all!'

The duchess patted her hand kindly. 'My dear, I am only teasing you. I understand perfectly. It is very awkward for us all, but we must simply do our best to get through it! Now let me show you to your room.'

It was a charming room, perfectly positioned to catch the afternoon sun and thoughtfully provided with everything a lady could need for her toilette. Laid out on the bed were fine lawn underthings and a green merino round gown. Although she had been too tactful to mention it the duchess had obviously noticed her guest's inappropriate attire and Sylvestra wondered what excuse Lord Carston had offered his mother for her lack of luggage.

Once Lady Helen had ensured Sylvestra had everything she required and arranged for her to be served a light lunch in her room she apologetically excused herself and Sylvestra guessed that the time had come for the Duke of Were to learn the truth about his dead son, Vincent.

Sylvestra sighed and set down her china teacup. She was seated in the deep window seat gazing out unseeingly over the extensive Italian formal gardens and acres of parkland beyond. Everything seemed quiet and peaceful, and yet somewhere in this beautiful house startling revelations were being made and emotions were running high. But Sylvestra's part in this particular adventure had come to an end and she felt strangely in limbo sitting here in Lord Carston's house. When she returned to London, it seemed doubtful that she would ever see him again and if they did meet it would be as virtual strangers. From now on should Miss Sylvestra Harvey and Lord Evelyn Carston happen to attend the same soirée they would merely exchange a cool word of greeting before moving smoothly on.

This depressing thought brought a lump to Sylvestra's throat and, if a knock at the door had not disturbed her dismal imaginings, she would have been sorely tempted to surrender to her misery. Instead, she was obliged to blink away the tears that blurred her vision and turn to receive her visitor. To her consternation it was not as she had imagined, a maid on some small errand, but the duchess herself.

Her dismay must have shown because Lady Helen, after a moment's hesitation, stepped forward and took Sylvestra's hands in her own, exclaiming sympathetically, 'My poor Miss Harvey, what has Eve being saying to give you such a dread of me?'

Sylvestra coloured up and said with difficulty, 'No really, Your Grace, you have been so very kind. . . .' She came to an awkward halt. How could she possibly explain?

Lady Helen smiled. 'Come, let us sit down for a moment. What a lamentable hostess I have been! I have been so preoccupied with my own concerns that I have neglected you quite dreadfully and I suspect your involvement in this sorry affair is not quite so straightforward as my son would like me to believe.' Lady Helen paused hopefully but as Sylvestra did not respond, she abruptly changed tack. 'I am relieved to say that my husband has accepted Marianne and Edward a great deal more easily than I could ever have imagined. He is so delighted to find that Vincent has left a legitimate heir that he seems quite willing to overlook Vincent's appalling behaviour towards both Marianne and Elizabeth.'

The duchess sighed. 'I know this will go no further, Miss Harvey, when I tell you I am quite out of patience with His Grace. Far from offering poor Eve an apology, Gerard is inclined to lay the entire blame at his door!'

'Oh, but that is most unfair!' protested Sylvestra unguardedly. 'I own I have wondered why Lord Evelyn should have assisted in his brother's subterfuge, but really, when all is said the crime was Lord Vincent's.' Sylvestra stopped short. However passionately she might feel about his injustice, it was hardly proper of her to question the duke's behaviour.

But the duchess did not seem at all affronted. 'Do not apologize, Miss Harvey, for I quite agree. What you must understand is that my husband was quite devoted to Vincent, could never see any fault in him. Gerard always thought Vincent was so like himself and, superficially, he was, for they both enjoyed to excess all the pleasures the world has to offer men of rank and fortune.' Lady Helen cast her a speaking look. 'I am sure I need not elaborate, Miss Harvey! But what Gerard failed to see was that Vincent did not share his own instinctive sense of honour and duty. What Gerard presumed to be ingrained in fact needed to be taught.' The duchess sighed sadly. 'I am afraid it took dear Elizabeth's gentle example to make Vincent recognize the error of his ways, but by then, of course, the damage had been done.'

The duchess's eyes were bright with tears, and impulsively Sylvestra stretched forward and took her hand. Lady Helen smiled gratefully and continued, 'It is ironic really. If only Gerard could see that in Evelyn he has a son he could truly be proud of, but I am afraid he never will, it will always be Vincent.'

'What . . . what will Evelyn do now?' asked Sylvestra tentatively.

'Now that he is free from the scandal that has dogged him, there is nothing to stop him rejoining his regiment. He has already voiced his intention of doing exactly that and he expects to join Wellington in Spain before the week is out.' The duchess smiled sorrowfully. 'Of course, I should be happy for him; I know how much it hurt him to resign his commission, but I confess I wish he would stay—'

The duchess stopped abruptly her eyes keenly searching Sylvestra's pale, haunted face. 'Forgive me, my dear, I do not wish to pry, but do you love my son?'

Sylvestra flushed scarlet and turned her face away from Lady Helen's probing gaze. It was answer enough for the perceptive duchess.

'Go to him, my dear. Do not let him leave without telling him how you feel!' she urged.

'I cannot.' It was barely more than a whisper. 'I have said such things . . . he will never forgive me.'

'He will forgive you . . . if he loves you,' responded Lady Helen confidently. 'Look, he is there, go to him.' The duchess pointed through the window to the gardens below. The unmistakable figure of Lord Carston could be seen walking slowly between the well-tended flowerbeds. The dark head was bent and there was a sadness and weariness in his bearing that tugged at Sylvestra's heart, but still she shook her head; she could not bear another rejection.

Lady Helen sighed a little impatiently and said more brusquely, 'Miss Harvey, pride is all very well, but it is a poor companion to a lonely spinster!'

Sylvestra did not respond, but her full lips curved into a slow smile. The duchess was right. This was perhaps her last chance of perfect happiness if he could be made to listen. Starting to her feet she hurried to the door, crying out as she rather belatedly remembered her hostess's presence, 'Oh, pray excuse me, Your Grace!'

Sylvestra's pace did not slacken until she reached the narrow, paved path along which Lord Carston was wandering aimlessly. He had drifted to a standstill before a bed of early summer roses, his gaze resting on the nodding pink blooms. Sylvestra came to a halt about ten feet away from him, her heart pounding uncomfortably, her hands clasped tightly at her waist.

'Lord Carston, I must speak to you.'

Lord Evelyn looked up sharply; he had been so engrossed in his own melancholy thoughts that he had not heard her approach.

Sylvestra took advantage of his surprise, ploughing on determinedly before he had the chance to forestall her. 'Lord Carston, the reason I thought it was you who was trying to murder Marianne and Edward was not because I believed you craved Edward's title, but because I thought you were married to Lady Marianne.' Sylvestra took a deep breath, miserably aware that Lord Carston was regarding her with patent disbelief. 'At first, I thought you wished me to become your . . . your mistress. But then when you insisted that you wanted to marry me, well, I could see only one way that was possible.'

'I must murder my present wife and child,' supplied Lord Carston. He shook his head. 'I am sorry, Miss Harvey, but that is asking me to swallow rather a lot.' He was eyeing her sceptically, but some of the unyielding hostility seemed to have left his eyes.

Sylvestra almost stamped her foot in frustration, but she stifled her impatience, determined not to lose her temper. 'It sounds implausible I know, but Marianne told me she was the Marchioness of Derwent. What was I supposed to think? She did not even mention Vincent until we were halfway to Were! And then, would you believe, she had the audacity to scold *me* for being henwitted!"

Lord Carston's expression was unreadable and there was an agonizing pause before he eventually spoke. When he did, it was in quiet measured tones, with no trace of the former bitterness. 'When I whisked Marianne out of the chapel five years ago, I did not know she was my brother's legal wife, that the child she bore him was in fact his legitimate heir. We were halfway across the channel before Marianne regained sufficient control of her emotions to give me a half coherent explanation of what had gone on. I had thought I was saving my brother from the embarrassment of a persistent mistress, not colluding with him in act of bigamy!' His eyes met hers and all the anger had left his gaze. 'So yes, Miss Harvey, I can believe you.' He gave a shuddering sigh. 'And God help me, Sylvie, I want to believe you more than anything in the world.'

The urgent tenderness in his voice robbed Sylvestra of speech and all she could do was move silently forward into the shelter of his embrace and raise her lips mutely to meet his kiss.

It was some time later before rational conversation was resumed, Lord Carston drawing Sylvestra's hand against his cheek and exclaiming remorsefully, 'Oh, Sylvie, Sylvie, what an arrogant fool I have been! I never offered you the slightest explanation and yet I expected your blind faith. Forgive me my darling, forgive my stupid conceit!'

Sylvestra put a finger to his lips. 'No, Eve, I am to blame. In my heart of hearts I knew you to be an honourable man. I should have followed my instincts and not been so quick to jump to conclusions.'

Lord Evelyn eyes danced. 'Miss Harvey, I hope you are not determined to contradict me on every point, for I had thought we might agree on one thing at least.'

'And what is that, My Lord?' asked Sylvestra, laughing up at him.

'That we shall be married just as soon as it is humanly possible.'

Sylvestra grinned mischievously. 'On one condition, My Lord . . . I am determined that we shall honeymoon in Spain.'

'Spain! You cannot have thought, the country is torn by war—' Evelyn stopped abruptly as he began to understand her meaning. 'Are you serious? It is a hard life, Sylvie, following the drum, harder than you could ever imagine.'

'Lord Carston, you once said that you believed I could do anything I set my mind to, do not tell me it was mere flattery.' Sylvestra eyed him pertly from beneath lowered lashes. 'Besides, it has long been my intention to marry a soldier. Pray do not disappoint me!'

Evelyn pulled Sylvestra against him, his eyes, dark with passion, gleaming wickedly. Then he bent his head, his lips brushing her neck teasingly and sending exquisite tingles down her spine as he murmured provocatively, 'Believe me, my dear, I shall endeavour never to do that!'